Praise for *The Q*

The Quilt Room Secret is a sweet   is a
refreshing tale where a man knows exactly what he wants, and he
goes about the difficult path of earning the love of the girl who won
his heart when he was only a boy. But the path to true love never did
run smoothly. With sweet friends, a well-intentioned farming community, and all the soothing comforts of a rural life, Trini Sutter isn't
sure that it's enough. She's got a list for her life goals, and leaving this
Amish world is item number one! Lisa Jones Baker tugs you into a
cozy world of delectable cooking, lifelong friends, and large, loving
families. It is a sweet and soothing read that will make you hungry for
a simpler life. . .and some delicious Amish baking! Lisa Jones Baker
does not disappoint! She brings you the Amish romance you crave.

–Patricia Johns, *Publishers Weekly* bestselling author

When life strays off the page you've written for your future, look back
to where you started. I really enjoyed Trini and her friends and got
swept away by the Lantz brothers. A fun story full of inspirational
stitches, bouquets of romance, and the perfect alterations to create a
good happy-ever-after.

–Mindy Steele, author of *The Flower Quilter*

THE HEART *of* THE AMISH

The Quilt Room Secret

LISA JONES BAKER

BARBOUR
PUBLISHING

The Quilt Room Secret ©2024 by Lisa Jones Baker

Print ISBN 978-1-63609-775-6
Adobe Digital Edition (.epub) 978-1-63609-776-3

This book is a work of fiction. Names, characters, places, and incidents are either products of the author's imagination or used fictitiously. Any similarity to actual people, organizations, and/or events is purely coincidental.

Cover Design: Kirk DouPonce, DogEared Design

Published by Barbour Publishing, Inc., 1810 Barbour Drive, Uhrichsville, Ohio 44683, www.barbourbooks.com

Our mission is to inspire the world with the life-changing message of the Bible.

ecpa Member of the
Evangelical Christian
Publishers Association

Printed in the United States of America.

Dedication:

To my best friends in the world, John and Marcia Baker, and to Buddy, in heaven, my true love of this lifetime.

CHAPTER ONE

Arthur, Illinois

Trini Sutter didn't fear much. But she wasn't fond of heights. Still, she stood on her aluminum ladder's top step amid her beloved peach tree's green, leafy foliage. Focused on her balance, she held her breath as she extended her clippers to the broken branch. Last night's windstorm had wreaked havoc on her orchard.

Finally, the pruners gripped the limb. Taking great care not to fall, she steadied herself and squeezed the wooden handles together. The moment the sharp blades bit into the wood, a noise startled her from behind. As the limb dropped from the bushy tree, Trini lost her footing, dropped the clippers, and fell.

Branches scraped her face and hands as she plummeted through the foliage. With a quick, automatic reflex, she put her hands in front of her to protect her face as she hit the hard, dry ground. The forceful impact claimed her breath, and when it returned, she released a shaky scream. Excruciating pain bit her left wrist. The pruners had landed with the tips spread in a V, pointed down in the earth.

At the sound of a low voice, she recalled the soft footsteps that had stolen her attention just long enough to cause her to lose her balance. A set of strong arms reached down and lifted her to a sitting position as her heart pounded from the shock of the fall.

She looked up to see a somewhat familiar-looking man with an expression of urgency.

His gentle touch put her at ease. "You. . .you startled me."

"I'm really sorry. But here, let's make sure you're okay. Can you stand?" His soothing voice expressed concern.

Before she could reply, he went on. "I didn't mean to surprise you. Again, I apologize for causing your fall. I'll make sure you're all right."

As she caught her breath, his voice softened. "You're bleeding, Trinity."

Quickly, he pulled a handkerchief from his pocket and dabbed her bottom lip. "I'm sorry."

She winced at the fierce throbbing in her wrist. She'd have to stand without the help of her left arm.

Who is this man? Do I know him? And why on earth is he in my backyard?

She gratefully accepted his assistance to avoid putting weight on her left hand as she rose from the ground. When she looked up at those familiar blue eyes, she almost touched noses with the blond-haired man who'd bent to help her.

Thick brows narrowed in great concern, and his compassionate voice again conveyed deep regret for having made her fall. His sleeves were rolled up to his elbows, and black suspenders accented his navy shirt.

"How's that lip?"

She glanced at the blood on the handkerchief and nodded. "I'll be fine."

Trini was fully aware that independence highlighted her DNA. Except for her *daed*, when he'd been alive, she had never depended on a man for anything—and she didn't plan to start now. Because of that, she wasn't fond of the vulnerable position she'd put herself in. Or rather, that they'd both landed her in. After all, his footsteps had been the distraction that had caused her accident.

"Trinity, let's get you to your house to ice that arm."

She held her left palm up. His face was close to hers, and she could smell his woodsy scent.

Again, she took in his familiar eyes, which seemed to penetrate right through her.

"You don't remember me, do you?" Before she could respond, he said, "Jacob Lantz. I came over to let you know we're neighbors now. Aunt Margaret left her farm to me and my brothers."

The moment she recognized that name, Trini forgot about her pain and everything she'd set out to accomplish that morning. Sweet memories of this man prompted the corners of her lips to curve into a gentle smile.

"Jacob, of course." She lowered the pitch of her voice to a more sympathetic, apologetic tone. "My condolences. You must know how everyone loved her. Me included."

"*Denki.*"

She continued to study him. "I knew I'd seen you before." After a thoughtful pause, she went on. "You're certainly not the little five-year-old boy I pushed on your aunt's swing."

He breathed a sigh of relief.

"You do remember me."

She nodded.

Lost moments escaped her as she absorbed his ruggedly handsome features. In the distance, she barely noticed the two-story houses that dotted the vast landscape of Arthur, Illinois. As a ditch fire's smoke soared upward into the blue sky before gradually evaporating into the horizon, her strength began to return.

I have to get up.

He knew her. And she knew him, even though it had been years since they'd seen each other. She started to ask something but, for a quick second, forgot what it was while drifting back to blissful memories. His once cute boyish features now conveyed a confident yet humble expression. Hazy chalk-white flecks hovered behind his irises. And when he smiled, the curve of his lips softened.

Suddenly, an excruciating, sharp pain in her left wrist claimed her, and agony quickly brought her back to reality. She squeezed her eyes closed a moment to garner strength.

Without warning, he moved, swiftly wrapping his arms around her again. This time, though, his embrace was tighter, as he scooped her up into a standing position. After taking a breath, he dropped his hands to his sides and looked down at her with an endearing expression that was a sweet combination of hopefulness and uncertainty.

His attention shifted. "How are those hands?"

She held them up in front of her, and he gently took her right palm in his large one. He lightly touched different spots around her wrist. "How's that feel?"

She nodded. "Okay. A little tender, but nothing to complain about."

He smiled a little. "*Gut.*"

He warmly pressed her hand in his before guiding it to her side. Then he took her left fingers. His touch was warm and gentle. She couldn't help but wonder how such strong-looking hands could produce such tenderness. As he gently moved each finger one by one, she frowned. "I can barely move them."

Before he could say anything, she went on. "I'm not complaining," she confirmed.

His eyes lit up. As they did, the *blau* color deepened a bit. The shade reminded her of a stormy sky on a summer afternoon and the beautiful quilt she'd recently made for a new grandson of a tourist.

"Why are you smiling at me like that?" she asked.

"Like what?"

"Like you know a secret."

"You really want to know?"

"Of course."

A low chuckle escaped his throat.

"You haven't changed a bit, Trinity."

"I go by Trini now."

He stared deeply into her eyes. To her dismay, her heart skipped a beat. She silently scolded herself for her reaction but reasoned that she was vulnerable right now. After all, a single man touching a single woman was inappropriate. But didn't these unusual circumstances warrant forgiveness? She was definitely in an awkward position. And his attention to her genuinely expressed great concern.

"I mean, those are the same autumn-brown eyes I remember. And your hair is still rusty *braun*. And most of all. . ."

"What?"

A shy smile appeared on his face.

"It's your spirit, Trini. It's still there." After clearing his throat, the volume of his voice became so soft, she could barely hear him. "I always liked that about you."

Her breath caught in her throat with surprised happiness. "My spirit?"

"Your fearlessness. How you took things straight on." An airplane left a white trail in the sky. A loud, demanding whinny came from some distance away.

She turned to the pasture and the horse that had stolen her attention. She joked, "I think Honey might be jealous of you."

He looked down at her with interest. "Honey's your horse?"

"Mm-hmm."

"It's a female?"

"No. But I named him for the beautiful honey-colored hair between his eyes. Trust me—the name fits him well. And somehow he knows that I'm really here to take care of him and not the other way around."

They laughed together.

"I'm sure he appreciates your fearlessness too. I'll never forget when we used to swing. You weren't afraid to go too high. And remember that little garden snake that scared your sisters?"

Trini couldn't stop a laugh from escaping. "*Jah*. I picked it up."

He nodded. "You did."

She'd never thought of herself as fearless. But it pleased her to know that Jacob liked her that way. She warmed inside. He was making her feel so gut about herself that if she warmed any more, she'd catch fire. Happy with his compliment, she let him check the remaining fingers of her left hand.

He looked at her reaction.

"I can't move this thumb at all."

As his fingers migrated to the tender area on her wrist, she tensed and let out a moan, then drew in a deep breath to get a grip on her pain. After a moment, her shoulders relaxed a little. "I rarely see a doctor, but I need to. I think it's broken. It's throbbing something fierce."

He focused on the delicate part of her arm above her wrist. "You're probably right. I'm no doctor, but the break is obvious. The bone is pushing against your skin like it wants out."

He narrowed his brows and continued to compare her arms. When she looked up at him, his tone carried doubt. "Hmm. Your left wrist has started to swell. You think you can make it to the house?"

She couldn't stop her lips from curving in amusement. "It's my arm that's the problem, Jacob. My legs still work, I think. Thank goodness."

He chuckled. "Gut." He hesitated. "Although the thought of carrying you home is appealing."

She knew all too well from her upbringing that her unexplained longing to stay here and talk to him all day was totally wrong. She wasn't sure why.

And she didn't know if he was kidding or if he was serious about carrying her. But she wasn't able to laugh at the prospect of being carried because the stabbing sensation in her left wrist quickly intensified to a whole new level.

"First, let's get you to your house and ice that arm. After that, we'll head to an ER. You know someone who can take us?"

She nodded. While the warm May breeze caressed her forehead, a sense of déjà vu filled her. Trini had never been one to complain. Yet she allowed him to help her.

With light pressure, he pressed his fingers against the small of her back, and they started slowly to her house. Suddenly she realized how disheveled she must look and ran her right hand over her navy dress to smooth it out. As he spoke, his tone was a welcome combination of reassurance and confidence.

"You okay?"

"Jah."

"It looks like that fall got you all scratched up."

"I don't think anything happened that can't be fixed."

In silence, they continued. But the fall—or maybe it was the pain—had stolen some of her energy. Whatever the case, the relatively short distance to her house seemed like a hundred miles.

She tried to focus on the layout of her yard to forget her pain. Trini glimpsed the white flat sheets that gracefully floated up and down with the breeze. The vast stretch of green grass and the quaint, old one-story house she'd bought only a year ago revealed Trini's favorite things. Her generous-sized garden showed the start of tiny green plants in straight rows. Deep red geraniums accented the winding dirt path that leisurely made its way from the garden to the side porch. Simple wire clotheslines extended from two poles next to the side porch. A chicken ran loose in the yard, occasionally pecking the ground.

To some, her method of drying clothes might be considered a

bit prehistoric. But to Trini, the lines helped to contribute a fresh spring scent while nature did its work.

A white propane tank sat next to her porch. The firepit was void of its usual lawn chairs, which had been moved to the barn before the windstorm hit.

"I remember when you lived with your family; it must've been a few miles from here."

She nodded. "Jah. I'm blessed that my local store, and especially the business I garner from the internet site run by an *Englisch* friend, has allowed me to move here. I own The Quilt Room."

"So I've heard. Gut for you."

The day had begun with cleaning up the bends and breaks in her precious peach trees. But the morning had certainly taken a turn south, because right now the only thing on her mind, besides the dull pain in her wrist, was her kind, handsome, soft-spoken neighbor who sparked beautiful childhood memories. As the sun slipped out from under a fluffy cloud, the brightness caused her to momentarily close her eyes.

Trini gave up on diverting her thoughts from her arm and Jacob and instead made herself take a deep breath to focus on reality.

"Whoa there! Careful," Jacob warned. "Go around that hole."

"Oh!"

"The last thing we need is for you to trip too." After a short pause, he added, "By the way, you have an awfully keen sense of hearing."

She contemplated what he meant.

"I mean, you must've heard my footsteps on the grass."

She smiled a little. "Perhaps it's because my ears are trained to listen for customers who enter my shop. That is, when I'm in the back room quilting," she added for clarification.

They continued toward the house. In the far distance, two buggies traveled the country road. Although her home was set quite a distance from a family she went to church with, she could glimpse the five *kinder* playing. The boys went barefoot with their trousers rolled up to their ankles. They appeared to be involved in a game of tag.

"That was some storm last night, jah?"

"Uh-huh. And that's precisely why I was about to trim broken branches. The wind left me with plenty of cleanup."

Enthusiasm edged his voice. "I can help you with that." While they walked, he glanced down at her injured arm, which she clutched at her chest. "If that's broken, you're going to need a hand with chores."

Trini silently agreed. But perhaps her arm would heal quickly. She would soon find out.

She couldn't help noticing Jacob's striking features. In the Amish church, she'd been taught to look at the inside of a person, not the outside. But as a woman, even though she was of the Plain faith, how on earth could she not notice his heavenly smile and strong arms? She still couldn't get over how the years had been good to him.

Several heartbeats went by. "You've changed a lot." After the words had come out, she added, "But of course you have." Her voice sounded soft and unsure as it wavered with emotion. After all, this wasn't what she'd planned for her Saturday. This accident would require her to completely rewrite her day's to-do list, which would result in a total redo of her entire week's list. She let out a disappointed sigh.

For some odd reason, Jacob offered her a much-welcome sense of reassurance. She guessed that his kindness had a lot to do with how unusually vulnerable she was. He reminded her of the outdoors. Like in the fall, how the air smelled when she raked her massive piles of oak leaves. When he looked at her, his deep blue eyes seemed to penetrate her soul. But she was at ease with him. It was a comfortable feeling. Like when she put on her knit slippers on a cold winter's night.

At her side door, she sighed with relief. "We made it."

Inside her kitchen, the fresh smell of recently washed curtains floated lightly through the air. The wood floor shone with polish. He quickly helped her to a chair and got right down to business, wrapping a clump of ice cubes in paper towels.

He smiled sheepishly. "This isn't a professionally made ice pack by any means, but it should do for now."

She held out her arm for him to gently place the simple-looking pack on the injury. She gasped at the sudden cold, but it wasn't long before the ice pack numbed her pain.

Without wasting time, he gently took her other arm in his free hand and carefully placed her palm on top of the pack. "Try to keep the painful area cold while I work on a ride. You said there's someone to drive us to an ER?"

Before she could answer him, his gaze drifted to all four walls where lists were taped in various places. As if not sure which paper to use, his focus finally landed on the white piece in the middle of her kitchen table. When she met his eyes, he lifted a curious brow, and his lips curved in amusement. "I see that you're a list maker. Are these your phone numbers?"

She couldn't help but smile a little. "That's one of my lists, but not the one you need." She pointed at the small corkboard on the wall in front of her.

"It's the yellow paper. And I drew stars by two Englisch neighbors who can usually help me in a pinch. Their numbers are next to their names. Call either one."

He retrieved the list and turned back toward her. "Where's your phone?"

She motioned with her head. "In the barn."

He winked. "Wish me luck." He rushed out, and the screen door sprang shut behind him.

Once he was outside, she relaxed. For some reason, Jacob stirred emotions within her that she hadn't known she had. Definitely, pain was affecting her, as was the tremendous shock from the unexpected fall. But so was the surprise reappearance of Jacob in her life. She hadn't been aware that Margaret Lantz had willed her farm to her nephews.

For a few moments, Trini allowed herself to drift back in time, to fifteen years ago when she and Jacob had bonded at his late aunt's house. Jacob's daed had left his family, and his beloved Aunt Margaret had kept the Lantz brothers while their *mamm* had looked for work in Lancaster County. For the duration of a few weeks, Trini had befriended Jacob during his temporary stay in Arthur. Margaret had been close to Trini's family, and for reasons unbeknownst to Trini, Jacob's aunt had thought she would be a good role model for him. She closed her eyes and vividly envisioned the tire swing that still hung by a thick rope from a strong, high branch in one of Margaret's oaks.

She remembered Jacob pushing her. She could almost feel each shove that he'd given the old tire. She could hear Jacob's soft voice as he'd expressed his sadness and fear that his daed had left them and that he'd planned to get a job to support his family. She smiled. He'd been a mere five years old. He obviously remembered her well, and she'd never forgotten him either.

Perhaps, over the years, I've thought about him more than I care to admit. But this is today. And I have plans for my life.

It was highly unusual for Trini to remember someone from so long ago with any depth. She couldn't name his favorite color or his favorite hymn. In fact, she barely knew anything about him. But she knew his heart. It was an especially kind heart. A heart that had been broken by his father's unexpected departure.

And the soft tenderness in his low voice was so endearing, compassionate. His eyes were the most gorgeous shades of blue she'd ever seen—almost too beautiful to be real.

She moved closer to the table. With great care, she repositioned her throbbing arm on the corner, where she rebalanced Jacob's simple ice pack on top of the tender area.

Trini sat up straighter so her shoulders touched the chair's back. A fly buzzed in front of her, but she didn't dare swat it away. Her ice pack was right where it needed to be, and the cold definitely warded off fierce pain.

She instinctively took in all her lists on the table, the countertop, even the walls, and decided that Jacob was justified to think that she was addicted to relying on penned words. The posts that appeared everywhere might give one the impression that she was disorganized. But the truth was the antithesis of that. She was the most organized person she knew, and her lists kept her that way. She needed them to function.

As pain continued to evaporate, she reflected on Jacob's physical changes since she'd last seen him. She smiled.

He's special. Only it's a different kind of endearing than it used to be. He's definitely not the shy little boy I took under my wing. Ironically, he's now taking me under his wing. Our roles have reversed. For today anyway.

The pain in his young voice echoed in her mind. Jacob had so earnestly and so innocently opened up to Trini about his heartache and his fear. At that time, she'd been unsure how to help. She'd tried her best to reassure him that everything would be okay.

Jacob's honest, open confession had sparked a motherly instinct in her that she hadn't been aware she had. Four years his senior, Trini had tried her best to reassure and protect that little boy, and a strange and wonderful bond had developed between them. To this day, that bond was apparently still strong.

Bright sunshine beamed in from the living room window and shone through the open space between the rooms before landing on the beautiful floral centerpiece in the middle of her kitchen table. For a few moments, her glance lingered on the delicately arranged dried flowers made by Serenity, one of her two dearest friends.

The memory of the wildflower bouquet that Jacob had picked

her behind his aunt's home years ago, right before he'd returned to Lancaster, crept into her thoughts and warmed her heart.

But the upward curve of her mouth quickly sank into a disappointed frown as she considered her future. Over the years, Jacob's plans to stay Amish obviously hadn't changed. At the time, he hadn't hidden his feelings from her. She admired people who, from childhood, didn't doubt their lifetime aspirations.

Unfortunately, she wasn't one of them. And she was sure that if Jacob knew what she truly yearned for and was planning, he would be extremely disappointed in her.

My fondness of him, and his obvious fondness of me—it's special. Still, don't forget that we can never be more than friends. Because I plan to leave the Plain faith.

CHAPTER TWO

That evening, Jacob enjoyed the warm, fresh country air while taking in the vast farmland that now belonged to him and his brothers. He imagined the field of full-grown beans. And corn. They'd rotate crops every year.

Trini had broken her radius and ulna. Amazingly, the area's specialist had a schedule opening to reset the bones. The surgery was done. Rehab and healing would follow. From what he understood, not many within the tight-knit community hadn't heard about her fall and that he'd accompanied her to the hospital. Not owning cell phones hadn't seemed to matter; around here, word traveled fast.

Jacob had taken great care to make sure Trini was comfortable on her couch before he'd left her. So all in all, everything was as good as it could be. He grinned.

Because alone, she hadn't been. The moment their driver had dropped them off at her house, family and friends had begun to check on her and bring food.

Jacob shoved his hands deep into his pockets and whispered a prayer of thanks while he stood in his new backyard. As he took in the garden, sweet memories of his beloved aunt flooded his thoughts until he wiped a salty tear that stung his eyes. That church members had planted vegetables touched his heart.

Jacob recalled the nighttime prayers his aunt had said with him. He remembered Aunt Margaret's words as if they'd been spoken yesterday, especially her emphasis that Jacob ask forgiveness for his daed and to pray that he'd return home. The request had been something he would have expected from his aunt.

She had always stressed that Jesus was all about forgiveness. At the same time, she'd reminded Jacob that there was still hope that his role model would come back. Jacob frowned. Unfortunately, the long-awaited return had never materialized.

Another memory flooded Jacob's thoughts until he bit his bottom lip with emotion.

When Aunt Margaret had visited them in Lancaster County, she'd surprised him with something she'd thought up just for him. She'd had the most vivid imagination from which all sorts of creative ideas had blossomed. She'd related a story while walking him to the house for dinner.

It was about a boy who fished in the nearby creek. The boy had gone home with enough walleye and crappie to feed his entire family. At the remembrance, Jacob couldn't stop a chuckle from escaping. From a very young age, he'd loved to fish. His daed had often taken him and his older brother fishing. Looking back, Jacob guessed that the story's purpose had been to reassure him that he could still fish, even without a father. And that fish would still bite. That in many ways, Jacob's life would be the same as it had been.

While Jacob thought of her, kindness and love filled his chest until his heart ached for her. His daed's only sister had never married. Yet her life had been as full, or even more so, as someone who'd married and birthed ten kinder.

She'd told him that a life rich with God's blessings meant doing for family, others, and even people you didn't know. That His purpose wasn't the same for everyone. And throughout life's bumps and hills, a person would eventually discover the Creator's purpose for them.

Jacob could envision the light in his aunt's expressive eyes as she'd served him and his brothers, Gabriel and Stephen, their favorite meal—chicken and dumplings—as well as the most delicious meat loaf Jacob had ever tasted.

The tomatoes, onions, and green pepper had come from her own garden. And she'd always assured them that her recipe contained a secret ingredient. Jacob grinned. He and his brothers had finally determined that the secret ingredient was extra ketchup.

She'd been one of the few Amish in this area of the country who'd actually made her own butter. And her delicious yeast bread had watered the mouths of everyone around. Jacob had watched in awe as she'd kneaded large balls of dough. The delicious aroma of the yeast mixture could even be smelled outside the house.

Her mashed potatoes were blended with tons of creamy butter. He clearly recalled the basement's potato bin and scooping its sand into his hands.

A voice startled him. He turned. "Gabe." After a slight pause, Jacob added, "Looks like the windstorm left us a lot of cleanup."

"We'll get 'er done. Hey, how'd your day go?" His older brother gave him a pat on the shoulder.

Jacob thought a moment. Then he shrugged. "Bad and gut."

Gabe gave a low laugh. "Care to explain?"

Jacob smiled a little. "Remember Trinity Sutter?"

They began to walk while they conversed with no destination in mind.

With a wry grin that showed half amusement and half curiosity, Gabe's eyes twinkled mischievously as if he knew a secret. Before Jacob could go on, he was fully aware that Gabe had intended his initial question to come off as casual. As if he'd been mildly interested.

Jacob knew him well and was sure that Gabe, underneath his pretense to be *casually* interested, craved every detail of Jacob's afternoon with Trini.

Gabe nodded. "Jah." He pointed. "Our neighbor?"

Jacob told him about Trini's broken wrist and what had led to her fall. He ended with a description of the trip to the ER and explained how their neighbor now wore a removable cast to reset two broken bones.

Gabe shook his head. Several heartbeats later, he lowered the pitch of his voice, and his eyes widened. "Not to be nosy or anything, but I seem to remember that you. . .once upon a time. . .carried quite a crush for Miss Trinity."

Jacob hesitated. Not because he wasn't sure what to say but because he was fully aware that his older brother was being downright nosy. Gabe was a great brother, but Jacob had known him too long to be unaware that Gabriel loved hearing everything.

And this time, Jacob was at a slight disadvantage for two simple reasons. First, if Jacob talked, he might accidentally spill his feelings for Trini. Second, Jacob had never been good at offering short, simple answers. Gabe had a knack for dragging things out of him.

Jacob knew all too well how things worked when he talked to Gabe. At first Gabe's questions merely required short answers. But more questions followed. And soon Gabe knew every detail and every second detail that had occurred. Every specific.

Jacob caught his brother's expression that demanded an immediate answer, so Jacob quickly came up with something that would hopefully put this conversation to rest while planning to keep his feelings for Trini to himself.

"She's tough. But she'll recover. You know that she owns The Quilt Room?"

"Uh-huh."

Having offered what he felt needed to be said, Jacob deliberately changed the subject. "Before you came out here, I. . .I was thinking about Aunt Margaret." He paused and extended his hands to the farmland close to the house. "Just look at her gift to us."

Gabe offered a quick nod and responded. "I know." He shrugged. "I can't believe she's gone. This place sure stirs a lot of memories." He cleared his throat before continuing in an emotional tone. "I wonder, how were we so lucky to have her?"

Jacob shrugged before glancing up at the darkening sky. "It's a gift from above." He pointed upward. "We lost Daed, but in many ways, *Gott* made up for it by giving us her. I remember when he left us; she came to Pennsylvania to help Mamm get things under control." He shook his head. "She was a godsend."

"Yup. No doubt about it."

Slow steps continued them along the border of the lot and the farmland.

Gabriel pressed his lips together in a firm line. A long, tense silence ensued while Jacob considered their daed and his painful absence from their lives. As he did, the much-familiar sadness he knew all too well rushed into his heart. But Jacob silently ordered that unwelcome emotion out. Years of practice had served him well. *There's no reason to mourn over someone who deliberately left me.*

Jacob sensed the comfort in Gabe's voice as he spoke in what came out as barely more than a whisper.

"I know what you're thinking. And I understand."

Jacob remained silent. While the warm breeze caressed his cheeks, he stayed deep in thought. He shoved his hands into the roomy pockets of his work slacks. While he looked out over the numerous acres of fertile farmland, he considered his brothers and his tight relationship with them.

"Never forget what our aunt taught us."

Jacob looked at Gabe before the response came to him. "Something gut always comes out of something bad."

A long silence followed while two-story homes loomed in the distance all around them. Their casual stroll continued. Jacob did remember the important things his aunt had taught him. He didn't disagree with something good coming out of something bad, but the reality was that had never been enough to ease his pain.

Jacob cleared his throat. "You mind if I ask you something personal?"

"Go ahead."

"Gabe, what do you think the gut was?"

After a slight hesitation, Gabriel swatted away a mosquito that buzzed around his face. "You mean about Daed leaving us?"

"Jah."

When they reached the well, they stepped onto the concrete slab and watched the muted orange sun dip in the western sky. Gabe softened the tone of his voice to a more serious, thoughtful pitch. "For what it's worth, here's what I believe. There was absolutely nothing gut about Daed leaving us. Nothing. It caused heartache and work for everyone."

Jacob agreed. With great affection, he touched the bucket, silently recalling how he'd once closed his eyes and asked Gott for Trinity's love. Of course, he'd never tell his brother. Or anyone. "I used to love helping Aunt Margaret bring up water."

Gabe smiled a little. "Remember when we used to look for that tiny lizard that hung out here?"

Jacob nodded before they stepped off the concrete slab and continued their stroll. Several heartbeats later, Gabe's voice expressed regret. "Jacob, the way he left us was awful. . .beyond awful. But in the end?" He shook his head and looked down. "Something good definitely came from something bad. I think that his absence, and the huge responsibilities we inherited because of it, made us three the strong men we are."

A few seconds later, he jumped back in with more enthusiasm. "Never forget what Aunt Margaret told us—that strength is a great trait to have, but oftentimes a high price is paid for it."

Jacob absorbed the wise comment and offered a nod of agreement.

"In this case, like always, she was spot-on."

A short silence lapsed while Jacob considered his brother's opinion. Then he narrowed his brows. "But we would've been strong anyway, don't you think? I mean, we inherited tough DNA from Mamm and from our grandparents. And of course, Aunt Margaret."

Gabe breathed in. Their arms brushed against each other's while they sauntered. In the distance, a black buggy traveled one of the country blacktops.

"I've given a lot of thought to this, Jake, and there's no way to know just how strong we would've been if Daed had stayed. But realize the deep connection between us. I think it's reasonable to believe that it's stronger because of what happened. And the way we keep our word—I don't know about you, but commitment means more to me than it ever would have if we hadn't experienced such a devastating loss. I can tell you that in all my life, I will never go back on a promise. To anyone."

"I know, Gabe."

For several heartbeats, they stood in silence. Finally, the two brothers turned back and made their way toward the house. A squirrel scurried in front of them, and they stopped a moment before going on.

"Something gut did come out of something bad," Jacob concluded.

Gabriel offered a slow nod. "You think that's why Aunt Margaret favored us?" Before Jacob could answer, Gabe went on in a voice that was half regret and half positivity. "I do. I've always thought that her terrible guilt over what her brother did left her devastated. When she visited, she'd always try to overcompensate for the love that we missed out on." He flexed his fingers. "I mean, she never said that, but she didn't have to."

At the same time, they both touched an oak branch as they continued. Jacob sensed that his brother needed to talk about their father's departure from their church and from their family. In his heart, Jacob yearned to discuss it too. It had been so long since anyone in the family had mentioned their daed.

Jacob lowered his gaze to the jade-green grass. "I've always been too ashamed to mention it."

Gabe nodded. "Me too."

After a thoughtful pause, Jacob added, "Do you miss him?"

Gabe considered the question. He shrugged. "I'm not really sure."

"What do you mean?"

Jacob stopped and turned toward the soybeans that dotted the large plot of land. Without thinking, he kicked a dirt clump into the field. He stepped around a large limb broken by last night's windstorm and let out a deep breath.

"I try not to miss him because he left us. If we'd meant something to him, he would have stayed. It's a tough pill to swallow."

"Yeah. It is. I wish he hadn't done that. Not only for our sakes, but for Mamm's. I'll never forget when I caught her crying one night in her room. And when I went to bed. . ." Jacob expelled a jagged sigh while they continued their walk along the grass-dirt line that separated their yard from rich soil. "There was such emptiness." Jacob didn't like to admit that he'd ever been afraid, but his words came out before he caught them. "I was so scared, Gabe."

Gabe wrapped an affectionate arm around his brother's shoulders, and they went on in companionable silence.

The only sound came from a tractor that could be seen from where they stood. Jacob wished that his resentment for his daed could disappear just like the sun. "Gabe, we have to forgive him. Sometimes, I think I have. But I'm not sure, even though I'm fully aware that harboring bad feelings doesn't benefit us in any way."

Gabe breathed in and looked down at Jacob. "You know what helps me?"

"What?"

"What our bishop said a long time ago. That Daed's actions are on him. Not on us. In our own hearts, we know that we did nothing wrong. But still, forgiveness is a blessing. We must forgive." Several steps later, he went on in a more serious tone. "We survived. And because of what happened, gut definitely came from bad." After a sigh, he patted Jacob's shoulders and changed his tone to a more positive pitch. "Right?"

Before Jacob could comment, Gabe went on. "I believe with full confidence that his absence deepened our relationship with each other and with Mamm. And with Aunt Margaret. When I look back on all she did for us, I know she's our angel in heaven, don't you?"

Jacob smiled. "She was definitely our angel on earth. She helped us paint our house, remember that?"

The seriousness in Gabe's voice lightened. "Jah. After Daed left, she moved in with us and stayed a long time." He chuckled. "I thought she'd become a permanent member of our household. Boy, could she cook."

The last statement prompted Jacob to relax.

"That's one of many things I miss about her. Her chicken and dumplings must've been sent from heaven."

Jacob let out a low, appreciative laugh. "You know what I miss most about her, though?"

"What?"

"The security of having her with us. She was such a steady presence in our lives." He lifted his shoulders in a small shrug. "She was there whenever we needed her."

"Yeah. In many ways, she was our female daed."

Jacob nodded. "And she was so supportive of Mamm."

"She was just like a real sister to her." A short silence lapsed while they glimpsed the sun's final bow on the horizon. A kaleidoscope of colors filled the western sky, as if Gott had dumped different colors of paint together to create the most beautiful hues imaginable. The vision nearly stole Jacob's breath.

The view in front of them was something money couldn't buy. Something a human being couldn't begin to create.

"Gabe?" They continued toward the house.

"Uh-huh."

"Did you forgive Daed?"

Silence was Gabe's initial response. Several moments later, he offered a slight nod. "I suppose so." He stopped a moment to look down at his brown leather boots. When he looked up, he tapped the toe of his right boot against the dry earth. "Like Aunt Margaret told us, 'learn from every problem.' "

Without warning, Gabriel's voice took on a different tone. In fact, his pitch bordered on curiosity. "So, how's your friend Trinity?"

Jacob tensed because he sensed what was coming. Of course, this was how Gabe operated. He'd dropped the subject of Trini, but now he picked it up again in a way that Jacob knew was intended to sate the enormity of Gabe's curiosity.

"Everyone's talking about you taking her to the doc."

"She goes by Trini now."

"Okay. How's Trini?"

Jacob forced his composure and attempted to keep his voice void of anything that would spark more questions. He had expected talk after he'd spent a large part of the day with Trini in the hospital. Although he hadn't been in Arthur long, he'd already learned that word traveled quickly.

Silence continued, but Jacob knew instinctively that his brother was trying his utmost to downplay his curiosity. Jacob also was aware that his older brother was as protective of Jacob and Stephen as a lioness guarding her cubs. So Gabe's inquisitiveness didn't really bother Jacob because his brother had Jacob's best interests in mind. He glanced over to take in his brother's serious expression.

Jacob couldn't stop a grin from spreading across his face. Gabe was a couple of inches taller than him. His broad shoulders and strong build reflected years of work on their neighbor's Lancaster farm.

The combination of Gabe's jet-black hair and burly physique often worked in his favor. To Jacob's knowledge, no one had ever started an argument with Gabe.

And Jacob knew that physically, no one dared to challenge Gabe, who could easily manage a heavy bale of hay in each arm. But for being so manly, there was a side of Gabe that had always amused Jacob—his curiosity about others' business. Chitchat about the scoop was something that Jacob considered more of a feminine trait. The need to know rumors was just something that obviously interested Gabe. Something that seemed out of place in his DNA.

When a red fox appeared briefly before disappearing into the field, Gabe's low voice pulled Jacob from his musing. "I remember when you two were kids."

He's not going to give this up.

"You and Trinity—I mean Trini."

Jacob pretended to count the years on his fingers, even though he knew that it had been fifteen years since he and Trini had met. The summer they'd exchanged turns pushing each other on the swing that hung from one of the high oak branches in his aunt's yard.

When Jacob didn't respond, Gabe did it for him. "Uh-huh. Jah. And if I recall correctly, you liked her quite a bit."

"I never told you that!"

"You didn't have to. When we got back to Pennsylvania, you were still talking about her."

In Jacob's humble opinion, Gabe had crossed the precarious border that separated *curious* from *nosy*. Jacob's deep feelings for Trini for nearly two decades had been his secret, something he had hidden deep inside his heart. Yet he was instinctively aware of where this conversation was headed. Worse, the subject was unlikely to end without a response.

His feelings for her had been special and unique. *They still are.* Gabe looked at Jacob. Still, Jacob didn't rush to reply. Thoughtfully, he searched for a simple explanation that would satisfy Gabe so that he'd once and for all drop the subject.

"Trini Sutter." He clenched his palms before stretching his fingers. "Let me think. . . ." Jacob extended his hands in front of him and bound them into a fist. When he dropped his arms to his sides, he lifted the pitch of his voice to one that was of eventual recollection. "It was so long ago."

The warm breeze caressed his face, and while he mentally drifted blissfully back to that summer, his heart warmed. "I was only five. The three of us—you, Stephen, and me—spent part of the summer here on the farm with Aunt Margaret before she went home with us. She was good friends with Mary Sutter and her eleven kids. Trini was the youngest."

Gabe let out a low laugh. "I remember. The Sutters produced a large brood, didn't they? If I recall correctly, ten girls and one boy."

When Jacob didn't reply, Gabe continued. "And again, if I recall correctly, you spent most of your time with Miss Trinity."

Jacob nodded. When he responded, he could hear emotion in his soft voice. "At that time, Daed had just left us, and Trinity. . ." He paused. "She didn't live next door then. I remember her getting out of her family buggy while her mamm tied their horse. I guess you could say that she took me under her wing. She was a born nurturer. It was as if Gott gave her to me that summer. We talked and played. And I opened up to her about my fear of being without a daed."

"What did she say?"

Jacob's voice caught in his throat. "That she'd keep me in her prayers. And that Daed would regret leaving us. But she assured me that I'd be okay."

Salty tears stung Jacob's eyes, and he blinked. "She told me she was sorry, and that if I lived here with my aunt, she'd make sure to take care of me." He gestured to Aunt Margaret's old two-story home.

Gabe's jaw dropped. Several heartbeats later, he spoke in a tone that hinted at appreciation and surprise. "That was kind of astute for a little girl, Jacob. I'm surprised she said that."

"Why?"

"Well. . ." Gabe fidgeted with his hands. "She seemed like such a tough little girl. So independent, especially compared to her sisters. But what she said to you—it's very sweet." Gabe chuckled and shook his head. "I'll never forget watching her pick up that little garden snake that made her sisters scream. She told them not to worry." He paused. "Looking back, jah—she definitely had a protective streak."

A laugh escaped Jacob's throat. Then Gabe laughed with him. "I had so much fun with her. She was like the older sister I'd always wanted." He lowered his voice, trying to keep his emotion at bay.

Gabe edged his voice with what seemed to be a sweet combination of sympathy and understanding. "It sounds like Gott placed her in your life, at that certain time, to help you heal."

"That visit was just what the doctor would have ordered." As Stephen waved to them from the front porch, Jacob nodded with a half smile. "You think that's why Mamm sent us to Aunt Margaret's—to put us in a healthier environment?"

"I do. And here"—he extended his arms widely—"how could we have been anything but happy?"

"Jah. I think that's why I bonded so strongly with Trini. It was at the time in my life when I needed joy. And she somehow managed to brighten my darkest days."

The soft chirping sounds of crickets serenaded them as the spring breeze cooled slightly.

"How about now?"

Jacob considered the question and played naive. "What do you mean?"

Gabe lifted a brow. When he glanced at Jacob, the curve of his smile reflected half amusement and half curiosity.

Jacob was fully aware that Gabe knew him too well. That Jacob could only pretend so long that he had no feelings for Trini. He tried unsuccessfully not to smile while he considered his neighbor. Finally, he opened up. "There's just something about her, Gabe. I just never ventured back here. You know; with work and helping Mamm, it didn't happen." His voice softened. "But deep down inside, I always wondered what it would be like to see her again."

"I understand."

"You do?"

Gabe nodded.

A wave of brotherly love filled Jacob's heart while they faced each other in reassuring silence.

"She certainly comes from a good family. The Sutter clan is well respected."

"I asked her to marry me, Gabe."

Gabe stopped and his jaw dropped. "Today?"

"No." A laugh bubbled out of Jacob. "When I was five."

"I knew that you liked her, but..." His next words came out in a surprised hush. "You must have *really* had a crush on her to do that!"

At the house, Trini continued to fill Jacob's thoughts. She had something within her that no other woman he'd ever met possessed. She was extremely independent compared to other single Amish women he knew, yet that very day, she'd allowed him to take care of her. Their original roles had reversed. And he'd enjoyed every minute of it.

Gabe let out a deep sigh. "You know, Jake. You always knew what you wanted. Even when you were little."

"What makes you say that?"

"Many things. For instance, when you were seven or so, you drew a picture of the home you planned to build when you got older."

"I remember. And you know what?"

"What?"

"I still intend to build it. Just like the picture." He chuckled. "Only now my vision is much more detailed than the elementary sketch I drew when I was a kid. And I've added more bedrooms."

Gabe looked amused. "You want a big family?"

"Absolutely. It's one of my dreams. It's what all of us Amish men want, right?"

When Gabe didn't respond, Jacob nudged him. "Don't you want a wife and a house full of sons and daughters?"

"No."

Jacob took in a breath of shock. "You're kidding."

"I'm serious. No wife for me, Jake. And no kids." When they looked at each other, Gabe's serious expression turned into a wry smile.

"What?"

"Relationships mean drama. There was enough of that after Daed left." Gabe gave a strong shake of his head. "I like my life as is. Folks back home tried to interest me in a couple of women at our church, but. . ." He gave another shake of his head. "No." He extended his palms in front of him and smiled with satisfaction. "I like living alone. That way I do things on my own schedule."

Jacob considered what his brother had just conveyed and offered a nod of acceptance. "I respect your decision, Gabe. We all have different needs. Different aspirations. But you know what's also important to me?"

"What?"

"Making sure Mamm's okay. Eventually, when we are settled in, I'd like to bring her here."

"I was thinking that too." Uncertainty edged his tone. "Although, her knickknack shop is doing well. In fact, that deal she just made with one of the tour companies might be the best thing that ever happened to her. The bus will stop by her store every day and give the tourists fifteen minutes at her place."

Jacob grinned. "She told me that business is better than ever. But if she takes me up on my offer, I'll care for her the rest of her life. With the money we'll make from the crops, she wouldn't have to work. I'd like to make up for the way things went down with Daed."

At the top of the concrete steps, Stephen greeted them and opened the door to allow Jacob and Gabe in. But as Jacob stepped inside, Gabe put a brotherly hand on his shoulder to stop him.

The screen door sprang closed. Stephen quickly stepped into the kitchen. "I'm about to throw three rib eyes on the grill."

"Sounds good." Gabe and Jacob spoke at the same time.

Then, with curiosity, Gabe said, "I'm wondering, Jacob—about that proposal you made to Trini."

Jacob looked his brother in the eyes and asked, "And what do you wonder?"

"Well. . ." Gabe lifted his palms before dropping them to his sides. He lifted his chin and squared his shoulders as he gazed into Jacob's eyes. "What was nine-year-old Trini's answer?" The warm breeze floated inside through the screen. He could hear Stephen drop something in the kitchen.

"That she'd think about it when we were older." After the words came out, Jacob realized something and added, "She knew how to satisfy me and at the same time not hurt my feelings."

Gabe nodded. "I'll admit"—his tone became more serious— "she certainly was an astute little girl."

"Jah."

Jacob started to step into the kitchen, and again Gabe laid a firm hand on his shoulder. "You're both older now."

Jacob nodded.

"So is she thinking about it?"

A bead of sweat made its way down Jacob's spine. Warmth

burned his cheeks because Gabe was asking exactly what Jacob was wondering.

He lifted his palms in an uncertain gesture before stepping over to the kitchen countertop and opening a bottle of water. "I don't know. It's possible that she has completely forgotten about the entire conversation. It happened so long ago."

Jacob contemplated Gabe's question. In a way, it felt good talking about his heartfelt confession to Trini that he loved her and his genuine proposal. Trini had been the only girl he'd ever proposed marriage to. And as far as her response that she'd consider it when they were older?

Right now, he had a strong excuse to spend time with Trini. And although he hadn't intentionally caused her fall, the opportunity to help her certainly wasn't an inconvenience to him.

"Jacob, you didn't answer my question."

"Patience, Gabe. Here's what I'm thinking: I don't know if she even remembers my proposal, but when the time is right, I intend to find out." After a slight hesitation, Jacob's heart warmed, and his words came out in a soft yet certain admission. "And this time? *Marrying her is no longer a youthful dream. It's my intent.*"

Gabe looked at him to continue.

"If she accepts, I will be the happiest man in the world."

CHAPTER THREE

"Gut Monday morning. How's that arm?"

Jacob faced Trini at her front door. While she greeted him and motioned him inside, he took in her demeanor. Saturday, he'd been privy to her vulnerable side. Today, she seemed all business as she waved him to a chair at the kitchen table and invited him to sit down.

"Nothing to complain about."

As he breathed in the mouthwatering scent of yeast rolls, she offered him one. He held up his hand and shook his head. "No, but thanks. It's a workday for you, and I'm guessing that handling your horse with a broken arm might prove to be a bit difficult." He paused before taking on a more optimistic tone. "I came by to give you a lift." When she hesitated, he could tell by the uncertainty of her expression that she wanted an excuse to deny his help.

All night, he'd thought about Trini. And although he wasn't happy about her broken arm, he didn't deny that it offered him a legitimate reason to be with her. He'd taken full responsibility for her fall, so he intended to help her. Broken bones didn't heal overnight, and he looked forward to spending time with her and getting reacquainted.

Frustration accompanied her soft voice when she finally responded. "You're right. How thoughtful of you, Jacob. Hitching the horse to the buggy would certainly present a challenge. A ride to work would be a blessing. Thank you, Jacob."

He watched as she scribbled something on a pad of paper next to her sink. When she put down her pencil, she smiled at him. "So do you think you'll like Arthur?"

He nodded. "Jah. How could I not? But when I was young, I never realized the differences between the Lancaster County *Ordnung* and here. Little things, you know?"

She looked at him to continue. "Like. . ."

"Mamm's curtains are green; here in Arthur, they're blue. And Lancaster buggies are gray, while they're black here. Trust me. My brothers and I know we're blessed, and we'll easily adjust. In the meantime, it's a relief to all three of us that Mamm's small tourist business is doing well."

He studied her for a moment. While they stood in absolute silence, he thought he glimpsed a light flush of pink in her cheeks. He cleared his throat. "You wanna know something?"

"What?"

He looked down at the wood floor before meeting her eyes with a shy smile. "It's like I told you, you haven't changed."

When she narrowed her brows in uncertainty, he went on to clarify. "I mean. . ."

He lifted his palms in the air and eyed her from head to toe. "Of course, physically you're different, but as far as your personality?" After a short hesitation, he grinned. "You're the same ol' Trinity Sutter I always liked." He lowered the pitch of his voice for emphasis. "And that's a compliment."

"How am I the same?" He could hear the Velcro separate as she tightened one of the straps on her removable cast while she spoke. The light, even beat of her wall clock sounded over the window above her kitchen sink.

He rocked on his toes before shoving his hands into the

deep pockets of his work trousers. "You were always independent for an Amish girl." A few beats later, he added, "It appears that hasn't changed."

When she didn't respond, he wanted to make sure she knew that it wasn't something bad. "I always admired that about you."

His clarification seemed to satisfy her, and she smiled appreciatively. All the while, he wondered if she remembered that very important question he'd asked her years ago on their last day together before he'd gone back east. And equally important, her response. But, of course, right now wasn't the moment to ask. There would be an appropriate time, he was sure.

While she busied herself at the countertop, he glimpsed a baking pan of scrumptious-looking cinnamon rolls. *That's where that aroma is coming from.* He licked his lips.

She caught his focus on the pastries and smiled. As if reading his mind, she opened a drawer, pulled out a serving tool, and proceeded to scoop up a roll with her good arm, place it on a paper plate, and walk to the table with it.

She motioned to the pastry. "Have a seat and enjoy. My friend Serenity made them."

"Have you tasted them?"

"Not yet. But there's no need to sample before I tell you they're delicious. Serenity's one of the best pastry makers in the area. In fact, she's almost as good at baking as she is at arranging flowers. She owns the Pink Petal."

He glanced over at her while taking a seat. "No kidding."

Trini offered a quick nod. "How do you take your coffee?"

When he looked at her, she was smiling amusedly. "You can't eat that yummy roll without coffee."

"You talked me into it. Black. And thanks."

With newfound energy, he watched her approach with one mug, place it next to his roll, and proceed back to the countertop to grab her own treat and coffee and claim the chair across from him.

He took advantage of the opportunity to study her. When she looked down, he could see her thick, rust-colored hair. One lone strand had carelessly escaped her *kapp*. She moved with ease and agility, even while sporting a broken arm.

As she looked down, he could see her determined expression. Her thick lashes hid her brown eyes until she looked at him with a grin.

"You seem to be doing pretty well with that cast."

"I think I am. This afternoon I start therapy. Someone will come to my house."

He tried to hide his disappointment. He'd planned to accompany her to her appointments. At the same time, he smiled in satisfaction that she would have convenient in-home help.

He relaxed. "You were right about your friend and her roll-making talent." He forked a second bite and held it to his mouth. "This is one of the best pastries I've ever tasted. And that's a big statement."

She swallowed. "Let me guess. You're referring to your aunt's culinary skills."

He nodded.

Trini softened her voice to a sympathetic pitch. "You must really miss her."

Jacob cleared his throat and nodded. "Mamm always said that she was one of the great blessings in my life."

The light green halos surrounding the brown in Trini's eyes lightened. "Jacob, what a sweet thing to say."

"But it's true. My mother always emphasized what an important role Aunt Margaret played in our lives."

Trini sipped her coffee before returning her cream-colored mug to its coaster. "She was a smart woman. But what you said—it works both ways."

He looked at her to explain.

"You and your brothers also played an important role in her life." Trini sat up straight in her chair and darted him a confident glance. "I even heard her say that."

Jacob's heart warmed. "She did?"

Trini nodded and finished her roll.

"Trini, you've just made my day."

Her eyes widened in surprise. Her brows narrowed with uncertainty. "Why? You surely knew how important you were to her."

He nodded. "I guess. But it's nice to hear it." After a lengthy pause, he explained. "I think that deep down inside, even though I knew I was loved by her. . .and by Mamm, part of me"—he pointed to his chest—"it felt like I wasn't quite good enough to deserve love."

Her jaw dropped.

"I mean, for a long time, Daed's leaving really affected me. Amazingly, my brothers and I eventually worked through it together. Plenty of folks in our church helped Mamm set up a shop and restart her life."

She paused. "I can't even begin to imagine how difficult things were. But you've always known that wasn't your fault. Not at all."

He tried not to sound defensive. "I realize that. But I guess I needed extra love, especially the first few years after he left." Jacob lowered the pitch of his voice to a tone that came out as an odd combination of half-shy and half-self-assured. "Emotionally, it kicked the life out of us. We went through shock, fear, sadness—everything you never want to experience. But what we suffered made me more attuned to people's feelings, especially my own. And when Mamm and Aunt Margaret made me feel loved, it meant the world to me."

Trini sat perfectly still with her lips slightly parted.

"It's true. A long time ago, Aunt Margaret told me to hold those who made me feel special close to my heart. That life isn't easy, and that a person's ability to make another feel gut is something that doesn't come along every day."

"Your aunt was such a blessing to you, Jacob."

He held her with his eyes, and when he spoke, his words came out as barely more than a whisper while his gaze penetrated her heart and her soul. His eyes sparkled with moisture.

"And, Trini, so were you."

Something was different. Thirty minutes later, Trini bounced lightly up and down on what used to be Margaret's navy buggy cushion while Jacob's buggy left her long drive. She wasn't sure what to think. Something had happened inside her during her serious conversation with Jacob. An issue that had absolutely nothing to do with her broken arm. Jacob casually chitchatted about how he loved to farm and couldn't wait to bring his mamm to Arthur.

Margaret's standardbred Survivor, which now belonged to Jacob, made an uneven *clomp-clomp* on the uneven blacktop road leading to town. Trini took in the vast countryside. She silently admitted that having someone take care of her wasn't a bad thing. But she wasn't used to it, either.

While they traveled to The Quilt Room, Trini's mind wasn't on the two-story country homes that dotted the farmland. Nor was it on the soybeans that stuck up out of the fields like little green thumbs or the large number of quilt projects that needed to be sewn and how she would complete them with a broken arm. She was sure she could still quilt, but her efforts would be at a much slower pace and would require tremendous patience on her part and on the part of the customers who eagerly awaited their projects.

Her heart stirred with new, unfamiliar emotions because this morning's conversation at her kitchen table had revealed something significant about Jacob that she'd never acknowledged. *I'm special to him. Really special.* She pressed her lips together thoughtfully and drifted back in time to when she'd been only nine, and Jacob, a mere five years of age. He had deeply bonded with her. And she had bonded with him. How could she not have loved that little boy who'd so earnestly poured out his sad heart to her?

At that time, she'd tried to calm and reassure him. But their young relationship was significant not only because she'd helped him but because of what he'd done for her. Of course, he didn't know that. Still, Trini had loved that he'd listened to her and taken her words to heart. Having someone pay special attention to her and take her seriously had made Trini very aware of what she had rarely experienced, being the youngest of eleven.

He turned to her. "Nice day, huh?"

"Lovely."

But her focus wasn't on the weather. No, she wasn't really paying close attention to anything except her enlightening table conversation with this good, honest man. A man who'd obviously been tremendously impacted by their time together as youngsters.

As they veered to the side of the road, they both waved at the driver of an oncoming SUV. After the vehicle was past them, they continued back to the center of the blacktop.

The sound of a lawn mower echoed from a distance, and Trini breathed in the scent of newly mowed grass. *It smells so gut.*

She was still trying to absorb how Jacob felt about her. At least how she perceived he felt about her. As she attempted to take in his youthful adoration for her, a warm sensation welled in her chest.

His kind words have awakened something inside me that's beautiful. No one has ever really looked up to me in this way. On the contrary, Trini was very much accustomed to her older siblings and her mother telling her how to do things.

She loved and appreciated that they were so protective of her. But it had been that very protectiveness that had played a role in the independent spirit she now embraced. Perhaps it was because the need within her to prove her ability to do things on her own was so strong that she found it difficult to allow someone to take care of her.

Not sure what to think, she frowned. What she was certain of was that these thoughts would need much more consideration if she continued to spend time with Jacob.

Letting out a satisfied breath about the decision she'd made, Trini glimpsed the main street in town. While the buggy turned a corner, she continued to consider the man next to her. His wise aunt had once told her that sometimes one would seek difficult-to-find answers. And on those challenging occasions, the preferred way to gain the best direction was to make a list of the pros. Then list the cons. Penning her thoughts would help her to see things more clearly. Trini sat up straighter and raised her chin with newfound optimism. Things were okay. Her arm was still broken, but as far as the unexplained emotions that whirled inside her, she knew what to do to better understand them.

At present, her relationship with Jacob was a loose end. And uncertainty was her nemesis. Trini constantly struggled to be in control of every situation in her life. Of course, now wasn't the appropriate time to pull out a notepad and write, but at home after therapy, she would carefully organize the facts to resolve her uncertainty. As long as she could figure out things by making lists and using her God-given logic, everything would be okay. She relaxed her shoulders and crossed her legs at the ankles.

The buggy took the road's gentle bumps, while warm air caressed Trini's face. She turned to Jacob, and he glanced at her. Fresh air had added color to his cheeks. She noticed how very relaxed and happy he appeared.

"Here we are," he said as he pulled up in front of The Quilt Room.

"Thanks for the ride."

He darted her a grin. "The pleasure's all mine. And don't worry. I'll be by later to get you home, safe and sound."

Jacob helped her out of the buggy and down the steps.

She waved goodbye and tried to focus her efforts on business. Inside The Quilt Room, Trini watched Jacob's buggy turn out onto the main road heading south. What appeared to be a calm Monday morning greatly conflicted with her chaotic emotions.

With her good arm, she flipped the CLOSED sign on the door to OPEN and began readying the cash register before opening the blinds. She lit a cinnamon-scented candle near the back room before turning on the ceiling fan and noting its light whirring sound. The air lifted some looser papers from her work area, and she quickly retrieved them and covered them with a paperweight. The store had solar power, and the fan added a nice touch of simplicity.

After she organized a display of sewing items to better appeal to the eye, she pulled over the nearest pen and notepad and started thinking of how to make lists of why her emotions were moving restlessly inside her.

She looked around at the impressive display of quilts that hung from the ceiling and on the walls. There were so many; the extras decorated cabinets that housed thread and fabric. Anxious to figure things out, she tapped the point of the pen against the lined paper and tried to untangle her thoughts.

I don't know Jacob's favorite color. Or what he thinks about first thing in the morning. But nearly two decades ago, he put his trust and his faith in me, and today his bond with me is as strong as it was when I pushed him on the swing at his aunt's farm.

Her last day with Jacob at his aunt's farm flitted through her mind until every little and big detail landed in place. She parted her lips in awe of the sweet memory. Jacob had picked her a bouquet of wildflowers and had handed them to her with a red heart he'd drawn just for her. On the swing, as she'd accepted his flowers and his heart, she'd noticed the words neatly printed beneath the heart.

"Will you marry me?" She'd been touched by how innocently and genuinely and honestly he'd asked her. Tears stung her eyes until she finally blinked. *Surely he doesn't feel the same way about me now. It's been years. Yet I sense that he does. Or perhaps my pain is enhancing my already-vivid imagination. I know Jacob's heart is good and kind. And without a doubt, he will make a wonderful husband for some lucky Amish woman. I'm not sure what his plans are for us, but whatever they are, I must be careful not to lead him on. Because I can't be his wife. My move has been set.*

She closed her eyes and breathed in. When she opened her lids, she couldn't stop a frown from forming. *My soon exit from the Plain faith has taken months to put into place. Telling Jacob is not an option. He is a kindred spirit, and I like him. But he can't interfere with my plan. I must be very careful to guard my secret. . .and my heart.*

CHAPTER FOUR

Wednesday afternoon, Trini sensed a newfound excitement in the small confines of the back room of her quilt shop. Thankfully, things were beginning to normalize—although she was fully aware of the compromises she had to make while her bones healed.

For now, though, she focused only on the positive, and most especially on what secrets this afternoon's quilt time would reveal. While the fresh scent of lemon furniture polish floated through the room that shelved all sorts of fabrics and threads, Trini's mind was on this special day of the week when she and her two besties, Abigail and Serenity, got together to share their deepest, darkest secrets. Of course, they quilted while they talked. Trini couldn't justify wasting time, so she considered the quilt room talk as a sort of therapy.

She reasoned that despite the smile their conversations usually brought to her face, talking about things that no one else within their tight-knit Amish community would understand was beneficial for the soul. Getting other viewpoints was gut for her.

Serenity and Abigail disagreed on what fabric color would be best for the quilt's backing. The frame on which their current project rested took up a good portion of the room, so the three placed themselves next to different corners. As usual, Abigail was determined to choose the hue for their newest project. And Serenity, as usual, insisted on postponing the decision until the top was finished.

Although Trini kept her thoughts about Jacob to herself, the time they'd spent together since her fall filled her head. Even this afternoon, while her friends bickered about how this particular project's theme should look at its completion, Trini could still hear Jacob's soft, sincere voice, as if he were physically here. His mesmerizing blue eyes were imprinted in her memory. Even if she tried to forget, she doubted she ever would or could.

Despite having no plans to confess her secret or the mutual attraction she and Jacob seemed to have for each other that remained from their closeness many years ago, something inside told her there was still much to talk about today.

The three friends had just started quilting when Trini closed her eyes and let out a painful moan.

Serenity stepped quietly to her side and gently touched her shoulder. "Trini, you don't need to do this."

Abby joined in. "Have you actually tried using scissors with your cast?"

Determined, Trini looked up before proceeding to cut around her plastic form. "Jah. Fortunately, I'm right-handed, so I can still use scissors."

Serenity watched her a moment before adding her two cents' worth. "But you need both hands to sew. . .with or without the machine."

Trini admitted defeat. "Okay. Point taken. From the moment I fell, I knew without a doubt that my work wasn't going to be easy. I can barely move the fingers on my left hand, but. . ." Her eyes twinkled. "I also am sure that much can be done when determination is a key factor." She smiled at Abby before turning to Serenity. "I'll just have to be patient."

"Gut thing you've got us, my friend." The nervous, excited edge of Abby's voice had disappeared.

"And if I'm correctly reading this list"—Serenity motioned to the piece of paper that was taped on one of the shelves that housed extra sewing tape—"you're going to have to call your customers and change your deadlines for their projects."

Trini's fingers shook as she contemplated altering her list. If she didn't stick to the established deadlines on it, why on earth did she even bother with a list?

Abigail glanced at Trini's cast and agreed.

Trini lifted her shoulders in a shrug. "Nonsense. Two broken bones aren't going to keep me from what I do."

Serenity added vitamin powder to a glass of iced water and gave it a quick stir before taking a drink. "Trini, I know how you like to cross things off, but, honey, sometimes things happen when we need to just sit back and let out a sigh. And by the way, you surely know not to take on any new orders—at least, not until you're healed."

Even though Trini would never verbally admit it, she wished she shared Serenity's easygoing personality. The blond woman with light, hazy blue eyes never ceased to impress Trini. At the same time, there was a mystique about Serenity.

Even though the Amish focused on inner beauty rather than physical looks, Trini couldn't deny that Serenity's natural, clean beauty had been the target of a healthy dose of male interest over the years. But for one reason or another, Serenity had never been courted by anyone.

Abigail's rosy cheeks deepened a shade as she expressed her opinion. "And realize that despite what happened, things still need to get done." Abigail laughed. As Trini took in her obvious sincerity, her heart warmed.

Trini loved this woman with her whole heart, but she wished she could do something to curb her dark-haired friend's obvious overexcitement and enthusiasm at nearly every subject she broached.

Serenity paused her needle in the air while darting Trini an expression of understanding. "I understand the importance of being organized. But, honey"—she lowered her voice to a concerned pitch—"lists can always be rewritten."

Trini sat up straighter, positioned her casted arm on her nearby worktable, and after several tries, carefully threaded her needle. She glanced at her friends and spoke with half desperation and half determination. "I know you two always laugh at my lists, but I can't do without them. For me not to have a list would be like you"—she looked at Abby—"trying to hem someone's dress without measuring." And turning to Serenity, "Or you planning flowers for a wedding without knowing the bride's favorite color."

Trini's scissors clicked as she cut around her plastic pattern piece. As she struggled to hold the pattern in place with her casted hand, the fabric dropped to the floor. She didn't bother to look at her friends for their reaction. *I will do this.*

Trini considered her friends' thoughts. They made good points, and at times her stubbornness was her shortcoming. But despite the reasonableness of what they said, Trini knew in her heart that her lists were here to stay.

"Trini, we're not asking you to part with your lists, dear." Abigail's voice was firm and unyielding while she began stitching around a corner piece. "All we're trying to say is that without them, life would go on."

Serenity's soothing voice quietly filled the room. "Trini, darling, did anyone ever tell you that you're an overachiever?" Before Trini could respond, Serenity went on. "I love you just the way you are. But sometimes I wonder if you would be happier without writing everything down."

Trini's jaw dropped. "What?"

"All I'm saying is, it's just nice to sit back and smell the roses." She breathed in. "And enjoy life."

Abigail chimed in. "Or at least, think about smelling the roses.

Our blond friend here has a point, you know."

Trini frowned. Her mind was still stuck on the mention of forfeiting her lists. *What are they thinking?*

Abigail cleared her throat. Her eyes followed Trini as she moved to adjust the blinds so that the sunlight landed on the quilt.

When Trini reclaimed her chair, she glanced up to see Abigail staring at her with a mischievous expression. "What?"

Abigail looked away a moment before refocusing on Trini. Serenity sat in silence, diligently guiding her needle in and out of the teal-colored fabric. Trini knew that the only way to find out what was going on under that thick, dark hair was to ask. "Don't keep me in suspense, Abby. You look just like a cat watching a bird in a cage. What's on your mind?"

Serenity looked up and smiled. "Abby, do tell us what you're thinking, honey."

Abby licked the end of a thread before sliding it through the eye of the needle. She proceeded to tie a knot at the other end before pausing to glance at the two. The expression on her face was a bit sheepish. "I'm a little ashamed to say what's on my mind." She paused then added, "It crossed my mind how that cast could benefit you."

Trini and Serenity glanced at each other before focusing on Abby. Suddenly Abby's voice filled with newfound excitement. "I can't believe neither of you has already brought this up, but hello!" She let out what was obviously a pent-up sigh. "Why aren't we talking about the Lantz brothers?" Frustration edged her tone as she tapped the toe of her sturdy black shoe against the wood floor. "Trini, the entire town knows that Jacob Lantz is practically courting you!"

Inside, Trini laughed, but in order not to offend her friend by showing that Abby's impatience didn't surprise her, she pretended a sudden interest in the blinds that now allowed a bright beam of sunshine into Trini's storage area, where it highlighted the project they worked on.

There was something so comforting and peaceful about this place where she and her two best friends came together every Wednesday afternoon to quilt and, even more importantly, to talk in confidence. Over the years, deep secrets had been revealed and discussed. Secrets that were never supposed to leave here. And never had.

She blinked and forced herself to stay quiet. She'd known Abby for a long time, and one of Trini's unspoken rules was to let her friend offer her opinions first. After that, she usually calmed down.

Trini took in the hopeful sparkle in Abby's eyes as Abby eagerly explained herself. "You know, Serenity, many years ago, our dear late Margaret confided in me that I'd be a perfect wife for Gabriel."

The admission prompted Trini to stop and look at the dark-haired owner of Abby's Alterations, located south of The Quilt Room. The Pink Petal, Serenity's floral shop, was north.

As much as Trini didn't want to talk about the Lantz brothers—Jacob in particular—Abby's admission piqued her curiosity so much that she asked, "What on earth are you talking about, Abby?"

The only sound was the snipping of scissors. Abby's gaze drifted from Serenity to Trini. When she had their full attention, she smiled in satisfaction and looked back down at her work while she explained. "It's just as I said. Many times while chatting with Margaret, the topic of her nephews came up. And more than once, she made it very clear to me that I would make the perfect wife for Gabriel."

After that admission, Abby's cheeks glowed. Trini knew at that moment that Gabriel Lantz had been spoken for, whether he was aware of it or not.

Serenity let out a sigh while she slowly cut around a plastic form. "Honey, we all know you will make a wonderful wife and mother for some lucky man, but. . ."

The corners of Abby's lips sank a bit as she put a hand on her hip and looked Serenity in the eyes. "But what?"

Trini waited, anxious to hear Serenity's reply. It was common knowledge within their church that Abby was sensitive when her goals were challenged, and obviously her mind was set on marrying Gabe. Abby's heart was kind, and her intentions were good, but when she went after something, she reminded Trini of a bulldog going for a bone.

Serenity pulled in a breath and softened her voice to a more sympathetic pitch. "Abby, have you ever met Gabe?"

Abby shook her head before meeting Serenity's gaze. "No." She appeared to focus on hand sewing a corner that the old sewing machine wouldn't reach. When Abigail spoke again, her tone was tinged with both irritation and determination. "But I will." She lifted her chin. "I'm sure that over the years Margaret must've told Gabriel about me." Her face froze in a determined smile.

Trini decided it was time to try to ease her friend's obvious frustration. "Abby, I don't know Gabe. I only met him when we were kids. But Serenity and I, well, we're both sure that Margaret knew her nephews. And if she told you that you and Gabe were a perfect match, then it must be meant to be."

Abby pursed her lips.

Then Trini added, using a softer, less challenging tone, "But that doesn't mean you won't need to convince him."

Serenity looked at Trini, then Abby, before nodding. "She's got a point." It was common knowledge that Abby was a bit assertive for the usual laid-back Amish men in their community.

"But I've already planned my family," Abby protested. "Ten baby bibs are waiting to be worn." She sighed and sat up straighter. "And I'm already thirty years old."

Trini realized that she wasn't the only woman here with a dilemma. And to Trini's horror, it appeared that the obvious obstacles Abby faced might surpass her own. She wondered if Gabriel

Lantz had any idea that a woman he'd never met already had bibs sewn for the ten children she planned to bear with him. Trini didn't know whether to cry or laugh.

For years, Abby had been determined to marry and produce children. But until now, Abby's plan had been all talk and no action. Now Trini wondered how her dark-haired friend planned to go about explaining to Gabriel Lantz that she planned to wed him—and that time was of the essence.

"Abby, I want only the very best for you." Serenity's tone took on a pitch that bore a tremendous amount of doubt. Trini did a double take of her blond friend to make sure that the pessimistic tone actually resonated from her lips.

A short, tense silence followed while Abby and Serenity stared at each other. Abby's expression seemed to indicate she didn't appreciate Serenity's concern. Finally, Abby lifted her palms in a helpless gesture. "But. . ." She began tapping the toe of her sturdy black shoe against the shiny wood floor. "What were you planning to add to that?"

Serenity swallowed. She looked down at her work and softened her voice in defeat. Trini was sure that Serenity wasn't up for a long explanation. "That's it, Abby. I want what's best for you, and. . ." She smiled demurely. "And I'll do whatever I can to help you become Mrs. Gabriel Lantz."

Abby grinned widely, and she clapped her hands in excitement. The action was followed by laughter from all three women. Suddenly the laughter stopped, and the two friends focused on Trini. Abby extended her hand to Trini. "Well? What do you say, my quilt friend?"

Trini considered the situation beyond crazy, but as she took in the jubilant expression on Abby's face, her heart melted with love.

Trini relaxed and offered a small shrug. "When on earth was Margaret Lantz ever wrong?"

More laughter erupted between the three until the entrance

bell sounded. Immediately, the room quieted, and Abigail's and Serenity's eyes doubled in size as they looked at each other. Abigail whispered, "I hope no one heard our conversation."

Trini quickly stepped into the sales area. A woman was closing the door behind her. Trini ran her palms over the front of her apron to smooth the wrinkles. She changed her demeanor to what she referred to as customer mode. "Can I help you?"

"Sorry. Wrong shop."

Trini offered her a smile. "No worries."

Again, the bell sounded as the door clicked shut.

When Trini reentered the back area, two sets of wide eyes regarded her in silence. Trini waved a dismissive hand and spoke in a low, soft tone. She wasn't sure why—no one was here except her two best friends.

She reclaimed her seat and continued her work. "We've really got to be more careful." She adjusted for a more comfortable position in her chair.

Still swept up in the excitement of their conversation and of the mental image of Abby explaining to the eldest Lantz brother that they were getting married, Trini smiled a little at the other two. "We'd better get back to work." She finished sewing her corner piece and reached for the scissors to clip the thread.

The smell of cinnamon filled the room as candles continued to burn. The feel of the cotton material reminded Trini of her new sheets. "Just out of curiosity, Abby, how are you going to convey this plan to Gabriel?"

Now a sense of urgency filled Abby's voice, which had suddenly lost some of its confidence. "That's where the two of you enter the picture."

Serenity's jaw dropped. Trini held her breath, awaiting Abby's explanation.

Abby glanced at her. "I have several ideas, but to be honest, I think something like Trini's situation would work well." Both mischief and guilt emanated from her eyes.

Trini stopped what she was doing while she absorbed Abby's unexpected take on the predicament with Jacob. It began to sink in just how very serious Abby was about marrying Gabriel. "My situation?" she asked. "What exactly do you mean?"

Abby smiled a little before standing up and walking over to the window, where she quickly pivoted to face both women, hands on her hips.

"You both know how much I treasure your friendship, and by no means would I ever want to impose on either of you in any way, but. . ." She lifted her hands in a helpless gesture. "I suppose there's no way the two of you could arrange for Gabriel to startle me and cause me to fall?"

"Abby!" Two voices expressed disapproval.

Serenity laid her work on top of the quilt frame and stood, pointing her finger at Abby. "Shame on you, Abigail! That's enough. Only you would find a way to look at Trini's fall as a blessing. There's no way our Trini would ever do something so irrational! Just look at how miserable that fall has made her! The accident has turned her life upside down. It's even causing her to rewrite her lists!" A laugh escaped her throat. "And that's no blessing!"

For long moments, Trini studied Abby, whose face was contorted in sheer desperation. All Trini could feel for her seamstress friend was sympathy. Remembering the lack of parental attention growing up that had taken a toll on Abby, Trini found a sympathetic tone to try to convince Abby that she was absolutely out of her mind.

Trini hadn't yet decided on the right words when Abby sank back into her chair and formed a pout with her full lips. "Is it really necessary to chastise me, Serenity? All I want is true love."

"With a quick snap of your fingers, honey! And nearly a dozen children to go with it!" Trini added with a laugh.

"It's what we all want!" Abby's voice was firm.

Trini and Serenity both stayed mum on the subject. Deep inside her heart, Trini yearned for the rare kind of true love that her mamm and wonderful daed had for each other when her father had been alive. Abby was right.

But what Trini's two dear friends weren't privy to was her secret plan to move to Rhode Island and live with her Englisch brother and his wife. Trini hadn't yet joined the Amish church and very much longed to become Englisch.

Trini pressed her lips together with a combination of guilt and excitement. She and her brother had already taken numerous steps to emancipate her from the church she'd attended her entire life. But a few loose ends remained. Her brother had even purchased a basic cell phone for her and had charged it. It would come any day.

Even so, Abby's statement stuck with her. *It's what we all want.* Trini gave the innocently proclaimed statement serious thought.

Is that really what I want? I've been thinking so much about becoming Englisch, I don't know if I am well suited to be a wife and a mother. And I notice that Serenity didn't comment either. As long as I've known her, she's never expressed an interest in men. I can't help but wonder if there's something she hasn't told us. But my secret belongs to me. And if Serenity also has a secret, it belongs to her. It's none of my business. She has certainly garnered plenty of male interest over the years, but she's never even courted. Maybe she too plans to leave the Plain faith.

CHAPTER FIVE

That evening, Jacob stopped working to enjoy the kaleidoscope of colors on the horizon as the sun set. "Wow," he whispered in awe as the sky flooded with Gott's art. The breathtaking picture mesmerized him.

As he returned to sharpening the plow blades, Stephen's low, steady voice pulled him back to reality. "Need a hand?"

"Hey, Stephen. Sure. How's it going?"

"No complaints."

Stephen stood and watched Jacob for a few moments. Jacob considered his younger brother and smiled a little. Stephen was very much like him in many ways. For instance, Stephen yearned for a wife and a family. They both loved riding horses and enjoyed church events, especially where lots of food was served.

The two men were quite different as well. Jacob's passion was thinking about and designing the home he hoped to someday build. Stephen's passion was making sure everyone was well fed. He had a generous heart and enjoyed growing extra vegetables for those in need. He also loved to fish. Of course, so did Jacob. But Stephen always had the instinct to pick the spots with the big fish. And he was quite interested in nature, including trees and wildlife. He had an uncanny knack for bonding with wild animals and held an usual but great respect for how they lived.

Jacob checked the plow blade before looking up at his sibling. "We have more tools that need sharpened." He paused to dart Stephen a half smile. "That is, if you're looking for something to do."

Stephen disappeared for a moment. When he came back out by the barn, he pulled a tool from a dark green box. "I don't know how Aunt Margaret kept up this farm all by herself. So far, the chores take all of us." He swatted away a fly. "Not that I'm complaining, of course. Definitely, I'm not."

Jacob didn't look up from his task. The evening breeze floated gracefully against his face, prompting him to silently give thanks for nature's blessing.

Stephen continued in a thoughtful tone. "I never dreamed we'd lose Aunt Margaret. She was always the epitome of good health." He gave a sad shake of his head. "How quickly life changes."

"It certainly does."

"Jacob, did you ever think we'd move out of state and start over?" After a slight hesitation, Stephen lowered the pitch of his voice, expressing his loss. "I never imagined a day that we'd be without Aunt Margaret." He sighed as the sun took another small dip in the sky.

While the loud whinny of a horse floated from the pasture to where they worked, Stephen ran a cloth over the blade he'd just sharpened, dropped the rag next to his foot, and proceeded to pull another blade from the box. His eyes didn't leave his work as he started sharpening the blade. "I was just remembering a time Aunt Margaret let me eat ice cream in our buggy."

"No kidding?"

Stephen grinned and nodded.

"One of the reasons I loved her so much is because she let us try things we normally didn't get to." He chuckled. "And you remember how I always loved those sorrel mushrooms?"

Jacob nodded.

"Once, when they were in season, she told me she had plenty and gave me an extra helping."

Jacob licked his lips. "They're a delicacy. And the season for finding them is quite short."

Stephen nodded. "Uh-huh. Anyway, I found out later that she'd given me every mushroom she'd found. Every single one. Didn't save any for herself."

When Jacob glanced up, he noted moisture in his brother's eyes. Jacob blinked at the salty sting in his own eyes. It was still difficult to talk about his beloved aunt without tears. "And that's exactly why she'll always hold a special place in our hearts. Mamm once said that Gott puts angels here on earth as backup mothers."

Stephen smiled a little. "And Aunt Margaret was our backup mamm."

Looking down, Jacob nodded. "And our backup daed, too."

Jacob silently ordered himself not to become emotional. Although he'd been a child, Jacob would never forget how Daed had told him and his brothers that real men didn't cry. Of course, Jacob didn't respect much of what his male elder had said, because when he'd left them, he'd lost all legitimacy. Even so, some things he'd told them stuck. And men not crying was one of them.

An open notepad on the ground close to Jacob's boots suddenly caught Stephen's attention.

"You sketch?"

The question took Jacob by surprise. Then he remembered his house plans. For a moment, he considered an explanation that wouldn't encourage too much conversation. The house he'd thought of building for Trini and himself had been on his mind over the years when he'd lived in Pennsylvania. And he'd never mentioned it to anyone since it had been merely a dream. Over the years, he'd known that Trini had never courted or married from phone conversations and occasional visits from his aunt.

"Never mind."

Jacob looked up at the earnest expression on Stephen's face. Stephen's rugged looks sometimes conveyed a false impression of the brother who was most sensitive. Jah, he was tough. And strong. But Stephen was on the quiet side, and Jacob was fully aware that his younger brother had perhaps been hit the hardest by their daed's unexpected departure.

As a five-year-old, Jacob had tried his best to explain their loss to his four-year-old brother. Jacob's heart had broken as he'd conveyed to his kid brother that sometimes they were forced to take on situations that would make them stronger men.

The explanation had appeared to help Stephen a little, but for some time, his younger brother had not fully understood what had actually happened and that their role model might not ever come home.

Sadly, Jacob had been correct. Because as much as the three boys and their devastated mamm had hoped that their family leader would come home and things would return to normal, reality had eventually kicked in. Eli Lantz had never resumed his God-given duty as father. And he never would.

Now, as Jacob took in Stephen's soft side, his heart melted, and he decided to spill his big secret. Because right now his younger brother needed to know that he was worth confiding in.

"Someday in the near future, I plan to build a home for my future wife and children." Jacob continued in a low, thoughtful tone, "It's something I've never discussed with anyone, Stephen. Except for you."

Stephen's brown eyes widened, and Jacob realized that opening up to Stephen might actually help both of them.

"I keep changing the plans." Jacob chuckled. "Because I don't know how many kinder I'm going to have."

Stephen's grip loosened on his blade, and it nearly got away from him. He shifted his hips for a more comfortable position. "I had no idea, Jake." After clearing his throat, he went on. "I mean, I always knew you were a planner. But I had no clue that you were designing a home." His smile widened. "That's inspiring."

Jacob darted him a wry smile. "If I'm going to have a brood of kids, I'd better be on top of things."

Stephen's eyes widened, and his jaw dropped. "Aren't you going to get married first?"

Jacob laughed. "Of course."

"Who's the lucky woman?"

Jacob hesitated. "Hopefully, our neighbor." He tilted his head in the direction of Trini's home.

Stephen's cheeks turned a light shade of pink. "Does she know?"

Jacob pulled in a deep breath and expelled it. "Not yet." A short silence ensued while Jacob considered how to explain without mustering drama. "For years I've thought about her." He related the story of how they'd met, right here at Margaret's home.

Stephen shook his head. "I barely remember that visit. At the time, I didn't get why we were here." He let out a low whistle. "I guess ignorance can be a gut thing."

The temperature dropped a bit. So did the location of the sun.

"Quittin' time," Jacob muttered while wiping dust off the blades. With great care not to cut himself, Stephen carried the piece he'd sharpened inside the barn. He followed Jacob to the place where they carefully laid the blades close to the wall.

Jacob glimpsed Trini's firepit from one of the side windows. As he took in the edge of her peach tree grove, reality hit him, and he pressed his lips together in deep thought.

Stephen came up behind him and offered him a gentle pat on his shoulder. "I had no idea that all this time you were harboring feelings for Aunt Margaret's neighbor."

Jacob turned, and the two stepped outside and headed toward

the front porch. He turned to Stephen and narrowed his brows. "What's wrong?"

"Why do you ask that?"

"I know your voice like a book. And I believe I just detected a hint of pessimism."

A mosquito landed on Jacob's hand, and he swatted it. They made their way past the large oak and the famous tire swing that hung from a strong, tall branch. Every time Jacob walked past the swing, his thoughts filled with Trini.

Stephen walked a couple of steps ahead of him. As Jacob reached down to pull a smartweed from the ground, he thought of marrying Trini and all that he yearned to provide for her. He smiled at the idea of helping her up the buggy steps and going to church with her. And his plans to build their home warmed his heart.

When Stephen didn't respond, Jacob stepped up next to his brother and, with amusement in his voice, asked, "What's going on underneath that wavy head of hair?"

Stephen chuckled and glanced down at his work boots. Jacob sensed that something was awry because Stephen didn't like confrontation, and whenever he didn't want to discuss something, he avoided Jacob's gaze.

"Jacob, I have always admired that you're decisive and that you've always known what you've wanted." Stephen let out a low whistle and grinned as he stepped onto the dirt path to the house and kicked a rock out of the way. "Even when you were a kid, you did grown-up things."

"Did I?"

"Jah. Like when you helped me say my prayers at bedtime. And when you constantly made sure I ate enough green vegetables for dinner."

The last admission prompted a laugh. Jacob stretched his arms in front of him and turned to smile at Stephen. "You always enjoyed food that was gut for you."

Stephen nodded.

A comfortable silence hovered between the two before Stephen finally broke it. "But on a serious note, Jake, I owe you. And even if I tried repaying you the rest of my life, I'm sure I couldn't."

Jacob wrapped an affectionate arm around his brother as they approached the concrete steps leading to the house. As they stepped on the porch, the boards let out a creak. The old swing that hung from the roof groaned as the breeze nudged it.

Jacob followed Stephen inside to the kitchen. He smiled at his younger brother's six-foot-one height. Without a doubt, Mamm had offered more attention to her youngest. And as a child, Stephen had been small. Jacob and Gabriel had protected their baby brother, who'd struggled with asthma. Stephen had been ill a lot of the time, and as a result, he'd garnered special treatment.

Because of his weakness, he'd spent more time inside than his brothers and had helped their mamm to shelve her homemade items in her Lancaster shop. Looking back, in a way Stephen had benefited from his health setbacks. His yearlong stint indoors had offered him numerous opportunities to deal with the Englisch who'd stepped off the tour buses to purchase Amish goods. Jacob firmly believed the generous exposure to the vast array of people who'd visited their shop had helped develop Stephen's excellent communication skills.

The moment the youngest Lantz had reached puberty, miraculously he'd shed the debilitating illness that had prevented him from being outdoors. And he'd shot up in height.

At that time, he'd begun to help Jacob and Gabriel in the field. Now, as an adult, Stephen had broad shoulders and a strong, firm body that made him quite the antithesis of the small, sickly boy he'd once been.

Jacob contemplated Stephen's future. Jacob yearned for his little brother to find a woman who would appreciate his warm, sensitive side. In Lancaster, Jacob hadn't missed the impressive amount of female interest in his younger brother. Church functions had offered Stephen more than enough opportunity to court, yet despite the interest in him, he had never pursued anyone.

Now that they were in Illinois, perhaps there would be a new opportunity for Stephen to make a fresh start. Would he find someone to love and to marry?

———————— ⚓ ————————

The following afternoon, Abigail slowly counted to ten in silence. But the excitement of meeting Gabriel Lantz fought her resolve to stay calm. Her hands shook as Serenity's horse, Angel, approached the turnoff to the long dirt lane in front of the Lantz home.

As Abby and Serenity bounced a little on their seats, Abby took note of her friend's motherly glance at her. "What's with the checkup look?"

For some reason, Abby's honest observation made Serenity laugh. "I know you're nervous about meeting Gabriel. And that, my friend, is exactly why I scented my bench cushion with drops of lavender oil."

Abby frowned. "What on earth does lavender oil have to do with me meeting Gabriel?"

As the horse slowed, Serenity darted Abby a wink. "It helps you to relax."

The next laugh came from Abby. "Then you'd better send jugs of that stuff home with me."

Angel stopped and sounded a long, drawn-out whinny. For long moments, they sat very still before Serenity leaned toward Abby and whispered, "We're here. And you're going to be just fine."

With great affection, Serenity took Abby's cold hands in her warm ones. She squeezed her fingers before releasing them. "For what it's worth, I said a special prayer for Gabe to instantly love you."

The admission pulled at Abby's heartstrings. Her voice cracked with emotion. "Denki, Serenity. You don't know how much that means to me."

Abby stayed in her seat while she watched Serenity slide open her door and step down to the ground. *Keep breathing the lavender.* She and Serenity were opposites, but right now Abby sensed an unspoken bond with her blond friend.

Abby thought about her special gift for the three brothers while Serenity tied her horse to a fence pole. *Gabriel Lantz. I can't wait to meet you!* Abby took in a deep breath and slowly let it out. *Don't appear too eager.*

Before Serenity returned, Abby turned and reached for the large basket of Serenity's treats behind them. Serenity extended her arms, and Abby carefully handed her the welcome gift. Then Abby turned and reached for her own large box to give to Serenity.

Abby carefully stepped down, pulling up the hem of her long navy dress. Once both feet hit the ground, she quickly closed the door before running her palms over the front of her apron to smooth any wrinkles that had resulted from sitting.

The standardbred let out another loud whinny before stirring dust. Serenity laughed. "The brothers certainly won't be surprised at our company. Thank you, Angel, for making our arrival formal."

Abby's hands shook as she acknowledged that this would be her first impression on Gabriel. She'd silently coached herself to speak slowly and to try not to appear overly excited. Yet she couldn't rid the obvious excitement that she was about to meet her future husband.

She carried her large box while Serenity toted her desserts. They stepped to the front porch. "We'll finally meet them."

Serenity stopped to get a better hold on her basket. Abby did the same with her box.

Careful to watch her step, Abby held her hand on the blue bow that decorated her package. With the other hand on the white cardboard, Abby squeezed her eyes closed a moment to garner strength from Gott. After she opened her lids, she drew in a deep, uncertain breath that was sparked by a potent combination of fear and longing. *Dear Lord, only You know my insecurities. Please help me to present myself in my best light. I so want Gabriel to like me. Over the years, I've heard all about him. I'm practically ready to become his wife. His beloved aunt loved me just as I am. She nourished me with extra security that I needed. But now she's gone, and she's not here to reassure me.*

Serenity pulled Abby from her reverie. "The place looks great. Looks like they've done a lot of work since Margaret's passing." To Abby's dismay, her friend's calm, sweet tone lacked enthusiasm. Abby bit her lip in frustration. *I'd love to challenge this woman to convey anything but calmness. At the same time, maybe she is nervous, and maybe she's good at concealing her feelings. Whatever the case, I have every right to jump at this opportunity to meet Gabriel. We're going to be married!*

On their left was Margaret's garden spot. From the looks of it, the small vegetables looked healthy. She imagined the green zucchini leaves that would soon be so large, it would be impossible to pick the produce underneath them without pulling each leaf to the side.

Abby continued her silent prayer. *I know that even though she willed me to marry Gabriel, it's up to me to win his heart. Please gift me with the right words. Amen.*

Their sturdy black shoes made light sounds on the porch boards. On both sides, long oak branches floated gracefully with the light breeze that made the early May afternoon so comfortable. In the far distance, behind the property, a black buggy made its way down the country road. An SUV passed it.

Abby breathed the sweet scents that emanated from Serenity's basket and smiled a little. "Without a doubt, they'll love your sweets."

"I hope so!" Serenity seemed to sense Abby's anxiety, and she whispered, "Be calm, Abby. Life's too short." After a slight pause, she went on in typical Serenity logic, as Abby called it. "Besides, stress isn't good for the body. Or the soul."

Despite Serenity's view of life not exactly mirroring Abby's, she agreed. Abby stopped. The old tire swing had been there as long as Abby could remember. She spoke with emotion. "This is my first time here since Margaret's death."

That Margaret was no longer alive to welcome them was a bit more difficult than Abby had originally anticipated. When her hands began to shake again, she nearly dropped her box. She lightly bounced it in her hands for a better grip. A sense of awe nearly stole her breath while she mentally envisioned Margaret next to her on the swing while Abby chitchatted about her sewing business.

"Serenity?"

"Uh-huh?"

"Did you know that Margaret helped me start my shop?"

"Hmm. Now that you mention it, jah. Didn't she come up with the catchy name, Abby's Alterations?"

Abby offered a quick nod. "And I'll never forget the expression on her face when she voiced it. She was so excited."

"I remember when you worked on a wall quilt. Didn't Margaret cross-stitch a buggy in the lower corner?"

The question prompted a happy smile to light up Abigail's face. "She did. And it's remarkable. Without it, the piece would have been beautiful. But her addition added a personal touch that made it extraordinary."

"I'd forgotten how much Margaret did for you from the get-go. Now I remember how she garnered customers for you, and boy, did she have the contacts!"

The two shared a sentimental laugh.

"Is there anyone she didn't know?"

Abby shook her head. "She had plenty of friends, Amish and Englisch, that's for sure. And the first day I opened my doors, tons of projects landed on my desk. She wrote my first review and had an Englisch friend post it."

"And you used that Jones lady to create your Google page."

Abby nodded. "Our Ordnung isn't fond of technology, so thank goodness we can hire out. Because in this day and age, social media is a must for small businesses like ours."

Abigail drew in a breath and smiled a little at Serenity. "Here goes." She knocked. The two waited. No answer.

While Abigail's heart pounded to a fast nervous beat, she turned to Serenity. "I don't see anyone in the field."

When there wasn't an immediate answer, Serenity looked around. "We could leave these inside the door. But then we'd lose our opportunity to introduce ourselves and welcome them to town."

The handle clicked, and the door opened.

Anxiety prompted Abby to speak first. "Hello! I'm Abigail Schrock, and this is my friend, Serenity Miller."

A broad-shouldered man offered his right hand to each woman in turn and gave a slight smile. "Stephen Lantz. To what do I owe this visit?"

With a wide grin, Abby handed him her box. "I brought something special for you and your brothers to welcome you to town. I hope you like it."

Stephen motioned. "Please."

Abigail and Serenity stepped inside.

While Stephen took Abby's box and laid it on top of the small table, she tried to hide her disappointment that Gabriel hadn't answered the door.

"How kind of you." He focused on Abby for a moment before shifting to Serenity, where he lingered awhile longer.

Serenity smiled graciously and handed him her basket of sponge cakes. "I own the Pink Petal," she said with her soft voice. "Your wonderful aunt taught me how to make sponge cakes. I hope you and your brothers enjoy them."

Stephen's face broke into a handsome grin. He pulled back a piece of plastic to smell the beautifully arranged desserts. When Serenity explained that the porcelain plate had been gifted by Margaret, she told him to keep it as a remembrance of the woman who had willed the brothers her home.

Stephen's eyes lit up, and the two gazed at each other. Abby glanced at him before shifting her attention to her quiet, polite friend. Perplexed, Abby thought she detected an expression in Serenity's light blue eyes that she'd never seen. She'd never observed Stephen, but from what she could tell, he appeared to be spellbound by Serenity. Either that, or he just couldn't find words to thank her.

Abby wondered where Gabriel was. Her heart raced with excitement and nervousness while she looked around. *Surely I will meet him today. He must be outside.*

She could hear the uneven clomp-clomping of a horse's hooves that appeared to come from the back lane. She closed her eyes a moment in great anticipation that Gabriel Lantz would soon step inside. She started to join the conversation but quickly decided not to as she took in the back-and-forth between Stephen and Serenity.

For something to do, Abigail stepped quietly to the oak chair to run her hand affectionately over the cushion she had sewn for Margaret. Abby's daed had made this beautiful rocker for Margaret's birthday years ago.

But Abby's attention wasn't solely on the soft tan cushion. Her peripheral vision was on her friend and the very masculine-looking Lantz brother whose biceps appeared to push at the thin fabric of his blue cotton shirt with rolled up sleeves.

While her friend and Stephen chatted, Abby took in the all-too-familiar surroundings and swallowed an emotional knot. *Margaret's no longer here physically, but this will always be her house.* Abby's memories of her role model would linger forever.

She glanced at the wall leading into the main living area where a gorgeous horse-and-buggy cross-stitch hung. She smiled as warm thoughts filled her mind.

To the naked eye, the work within the dark oak frame might look like a typical cross-stitch. But Margaret had created the beautiful wall piece when her horse, Noah, named for Margaret's favorite biblical character, had passed from a virus that had claimed a number of livestock in their Amish community. She had captured the standardbred's strong spirit, large brown eyes, and thick, black lashes well in this piece of art.

Suddenly Abby noticed that the conversation had stopped, and she turned to Stephen, who eyed her with curiosity. She immediately recalled her purpose and motioned to her box. "Please. Open it." As he undid the sides, she added, "It's not edible, but I think the three of you will treasure it." Her heart picked up speed as she waited with pent-up anticipation.

After placing the used tape on what appeared to be a pile of unopened mail, he removed the lid with both hands. He laid the top on the floor next to the table and slowly reached inside.

With great care, he removed and unfolded a quilt and held it up to admire. He moved the mail to a chair and spread the piece so that it was flat on the table. As he took in the details, he ran his hand over the fabric.

When he looked up at Abigail, the expression in his eyes showed great appreciation. "This is beautiful. Denki, Abigail."

She smiled at him. "You can call me Abby." Several heartbeats later, she remembered the words she'd carefully prepared. "I thought you'd like it because it's actually quite special."

With an inquisitive expression, he met her eyes.

Abby's voice caught in her throat. "You see, before she passed, your aunt pieced together the beautiful squares that make up the picture of her garden."

With great care, he took the fabric and held it by the top and seemed to absorb every detail. Abby's heart warmed at his obvious love of his aunt's work. When he parted his lips in awe, she went on. "All I did was sew on the backing." She softened her voice with great emotion. "This is Margaret's last work."

Stephen didn't respond as he took in the wall quilt. "When did she make this?"

"Eight or nine months ago." Abigail confirmed the number of months on her hands. She turned to Serenity before her gaze migrated to Stephen's face.

Several heartbeats later, he carefully placed the piece back on the tabletop and nodded in appreciation to Abigail. "My brothers and I will cherish this. Abby, thank you for this most special gift. And Serenity"—he smiled at her as the back door clicked—"denki for the delicious-looking treats."

He chuckled beneath his breath. "I'm sure this platter won't last till dinner." He hesitated and narrowed his brows. "Do you mind if I sample?"

Serenity nodded. "Please."

He closed his eyes as he bit into a sponge cake. After chewing and swallowing, his attention was on Serenity. "Absolutely delicious!"

Abigail's heart pounded as footsteps became more audible. *It might be Gabriel!*

An intimidating-looking figure joined them. Stephen immediately introduced the two women to Jacob. Abigail tried to hide her disappointment. *Patience. I can't meet him if he's not home. Looks like I'll have to wait.*

At the same time, she took in whom she knew to be the middle of the three brothers. "Nice to meet you, Jacob."

Serenity chimed in. "Same here."

Stephen quickly briefed his brother on the welcome gifts from the women, and Jacob thanked them. He touched the quilt, and

Stephen explained its background.

A somber yet appreciative look filled Jacob's eyes. Afterward, Serenity said in her calm, sweet voice, "Again, Jacob and Stephen, welcome to Arthur. And if you need any help with anything, you can find me at the Pink Petal."

Abby jumped in. "If you need alterations, I'm the shop two doors down."

After saying goodbye, Abigail walked slightly behind Serenity. Outside, they stepped toward the buggy. Abby widened her arms as she looked up at the sun. "Gorgeous day!"

Serenity agreed.

Inside, Serenity sat next to her on the sturdy, cushioned bench. The carriage jerked a bit as Angel pulled the buggy toward the county road.

Again, Abby breathed in the relaxing lavender scent and smiled a little, reminding herself that there would be more opportunities to meet Gabriel.

"Stephen's something else, isn't he?"

Serenity's unexpected comment made Abby's jaw drop in surprise. As long as she'd known Serenity, her friend had never so much as hinted at an interest in a male.

Abigail realized that Serenity awaited a response. She offered a quick nod. "Jah. He seems to be a fine man. So does Jacob."

Serenity's voice softened as Angel's hooves clomp-clomped down the country blacktop. "I'm sorry you didn't get to meet Gabriel, Abby." As the buggy jogged up and down over a small pothole, Serenity added, "But there's always another time." Several seconds later, she turned to Abby and winked with a hint of encouragement. "You know the saying—everything happens for a reason? Well, Gott must have reserved a more opportune time for you to meet Gabriel. That's got to be why he wasn't there."

Abby stared at the straight rows of soybeans in a field beside the road to hide her grimace. She decided to mourn her loss when she got home. There was no reason to try to discuss her disappointment with Serenity, because her friend was too positive to offer realistic input. And if she worked through her disappointment in private, Abby could utilize her pent-up anguish to plot a new way to meet the oldest Lantz brother. Later she would seek Trini's take on things. She was usually more sympathetic about Abby's endeavors.

Serenity broke Abby's train of thought. "Jacob doesn't seem like Trini's type, does he?"

Abby narrowed her brows. "Why do you say that?"

Serenity tucked a stray hair back underneath her kapp. Abby watched while her friend adjusted her backside into a more comfortable position before running her palms over her navy dress.

"I don't know the least bit about him. Only what I've heard from Trini and from the grapevine. But"—she pressed her finger to her lips and looked off in the distance—"I've always believed that first impressions are often right on." She let out a small laugh. "In the few minutes I met him, I saw an easygoing man."

The statement prompted Abby to grin. "Are you insinuating, my dear, that our Trini isn't easygoing?"

The two laughed.

After a long pause, Serenity shook her head. "I wish I could get Trini to throw away her lists." She lowered her voice to a more serious pitch. "Abby, have you seen her kitchen lately?"

The question sparked a bigger smile from both friends. Finally, Abby found her reasonable voice and responded. "You can barely see her walls—lists are everywhere. And you want to know what I think?"

"What?"

"That they've become an obsession. To be honest, I have no idea how she keeps track of where each one is and what's written on it."

"You think she actually knows?"

"Oh jah! Once when I was at her house, I asked her for the list of churchwomen who had volunteered to take food to the Troyer family."

"And?"

Abby let out a sigh. "Our list maker proceeded straight to the side door and stepped on her tiptoes to untape it from one of the walls. And her grocery list?" She shrugged. "By the kitchen window. And you won't believe what I'm about to tell you."

Serenity's eyes grew large as she leaned closer. "What?"

Abby paused for effect. She pressed her lips together while ascertaining how to best convey what she'd seen. "She even keeps a to-do list of tasks to complete before she starts work. That means everything from making breakfast to giving Honey a sugar cube before that horse thinks about pulling her buggy."

In a lower tone, she continued. "Trini even keeps a back-up list in her buggy in case she's running late to work."

Serenity opened her mouth to speak, but no words came out. She slowed her horse as they turned into Abby's drive and said goodbye.

While Abby waved to Serenity, she contemplated the afternoon and was left with three things. Number one: she missed Margaret more than she'd ever dreamed possible. Being inside her home had stirred up a myriad of memories, and Abigail needed to sort through them. Number two: something was developing between Stephen and Serenity. And number three: she was more determined than ever to meet Gabriel Lantz.

CHAPTER SIX

That evening, the moment Trini answered a knock at the door, Mamm and four of Trini's sisters—Ruth, Mildred, Sarah, and Emma—bounded into her home. Trini forced a pleasant smile as they joined her.

Once inside, they bunched at the door. Tall Ruth appeared to be genuinely interested in Trini's progress. Her voice was naturally gruff as she planted her palms on her hips and looked down at Trini. "We haven't heard from you all day. We've been worried sick. Why didn't you call and leave us a message?"

Trini looked down at the floor piled with stencils and material to address the obvious concern. "I'm sorry. But my arm makes my job a bit more difficult. It's taking me longer to get things done. Because of that, I worked through the day."

Mildred's low voice echoed concern. "Is your arm better?"

Trini nodded. "A little. They said that therapy would be hard at first. From what I understand, bones are very slow to heal." She smiled optimistically. "But I think therapy will help."

Hopeful expressions on all five faces followed the statement. Sensing that her family needed extra reassurance, she said, "I'm just fine. But oh. . ." She released a long sigh. "I won't shed a tear when this cast comes off. Still, for right now"—she motioned to her wrist—"it protects my break."

"But it's not even a real cast," Sarah protested. "If it was an old-fashioned one, we'd be able to sign our names on it."

Trini lifted her arm for display. "It is real. And it's removable. So I'll be grateful."

Glass clinking against glass made Trini turn toward the sink. Mamm raised her voice to be heard. "Gut thing we stopped by to catch you up on your dishes."

Next to her, Emma's exaggerated tone caught everyone's attention, and they all turned to her as she peeled foil off a casserole. "You need nutrition, Trini. You've got to keep up your strength so your arm heals. How about a helping of pork roast and cabbage?"

Before Trini could respond, Mildred chimed in from Mamm's other side. "And homemade yeast rolls. Made this batch this afternoon. They've always been your favorite."

Trini thanked them for their concern and their efforts. Their visit had nixed her plan to work all evening, but she appreciated the well-intended efforts of her family and didn't want to seem unappreciative. So she quickly gathered her pattern pieces from the floor and moved the piles to an end table in the living room.

As she did so, Trini considered her family. Ruth, the most forward of the clan, enjoyed taking charge. Once she set her mind to something, there was no stopping her from making it happen.

Brown-haired Emma was the sweetest of the bunch. Still, when she decided to act, her sweetness could quickly morph into aggressiveness.

Sarah was usually the last to express her opinion. But when it was her turn, she made sure to carefully define what she wanted and how she intended it. She was intellectual. And she craved learning new words. In her spare time, she did crosswords.

Mildred lived her life to spawn offspring. At thirty years of age, she'd already produced four boys and three girls. Having babies made her happy, and she made it clear to everyone that she was just getting started.

Mamm lowered the pitch of her concerned, motherly voice to a tone that Trini was sure was intended for her ears only. "Trini, I've been hearing an awful lot about you and Jacob."

That admission quickly claimed Trini's attention. She looked up at her role model. "Oh? What have you heard?" Her sisters huddled around the kitchen sink, where Mamm led the conversation.

"That he's taking you to and from work every day." Excitement dripped from her voice. "Everyone knows that you two go way back."

Trini took in five sets of curious-looking eyes and became fully aware that the purpose of this visit was to garner every detail about her and Jacob Lantz.

She sighed before dishing up a generous-sized helping of pork roast and cabbage for herself. As she made her way to the small, round table, she briefly glanced back and tried her most casual pitch.

Before opening her mouth, she thought carefully because she knew how important it was to prevent any image of her and Jacob as a couple. For years her family had tried to fix her up with single men in their church. And it was no secret that Mamm had made it her personal mission to find a husband for her youngest and only single daughter.

As Trini listened to her family chitchat, she acknowledged that her accident and Jacob's role in it had stirred up every scenario imaginable. She'd already heard from Serenity that the bishop's wife had claimed to have seen their hands touch when Jacob helped her from his buggy.

Abby had relayed to Trini that she'd even heard that Jacob planned to ask Trini to court him as soon as she recovered. Absorbing reality, Trini made herself comfortable at the table while her mother joined her on the opposite side. Her sisters busied themselves but were clearly listening.

She could hear cabinets close and glanced at Emma pulling a mop from the storage area next to the refrigerator. Trini quickly realized the need to protect her lists and spoke in a tone that got everyone's attention. "I appreciate all you do for me; I really do. I must be the luckiest girl around to have so much help. Clean and organize all you want, but please don't touch my lists."

The scent of lemon furniture polish soon filled the air while Emma and Sarah dusted the living room end tables. Mildred sprayed the windows, and her paper towel squeaked as it moved up and down on the glass. Within a matter of seconds, Trini's home smelled like cleaning agents. The delicious taste of baked pork soon became less appetizing as the chemical scents stymied her appreciation of the home-cooked meal.

"Trini? What do you have to say about the rumors?" From experience, Trini was fully aware that her relentless mamm wouldn't drop the subject until she was satisfied she had answers.

Trini let out a sigh after swallowing a bite of cabbage. "I hate to spoil your excitement, but there's nothing between Jacob and me other than a strong friendship that started when we were kids."

Mamm was quick to reply. "I'll never forget how you talked about him after he went back to Lancaster County."

Sarah chimed in. "Jah, and if the grapevine is reliable, he never forgot about you."

Trini couldn't hold back a laugh.

"Gut thing you've got us, Trini," Sarah chimed in happily while she swished the feather duster over a wooden chair arm. "My heart breaks whenever I imagine you going through something like this alone." She paused to draw her free hand over her chest.

Trini bit her tongue and silently ordered her lips not to curve in amusement. To Trini, having a clean house wasn't really important— at least not right now. It wasn't even on a list. Right now, however, she had no choice. Like it or not, her home would soon be spotless.

Although her family intended to be helpful, they could also be overwhelming. Trini pressed her lips together thoughtfully. *Today is one of those times.*

Emma glanced up as she polished the living room's oak floorboards while the lemon scent floated lightly through the air. When she came dangerously close to the piles Trini had organized, Trini held up a hand to stop her sister from touching them.

"Just a moment while I move these." Trini's cast slowed her down a bit. Keeping her left wrist straight presented challenges. She motioned to the corner where she'd piled her items. "This part of the house is out-of-bounds."

"Okay. We hear you." Emma continued moving toward the granite. Trini's favorite part of the kitchen was this small island. Above, pots and pans hung from ceiling hooks.

While laughter and chitchat filled the house, Trini considered having her sisters pitch in with her projects as well. She mentally assessed her sisters' quilting abilities. Numerous Englisch customers had mentioned their theory that all Amish women could quilt. With as much kindness and tact as she could muster, Trini had countered their assumptions. Take Emma, for example. Because quilting wasn't something that could be done fast. It was a skill that required patience. Therefore, Emma would never make a good quilter.

Trini, however, was known in their tight-knit community for her quilts' smoothness and themes. Her continuity from corner to corner and everything in-between was impeccable. She'd offered her expertise to her sisters, but despite Trini's efforts, she hadn't had any luck.

"Trini?" Sarah's voice expressed concern. "Imagine these walls free of paper." She lifted her chin and motioned toward the lists. "Why don't you move your lists to one section of the room?" Before Trini could answer, her sister went on in an excited tone. "Just think how clean the walls would look without all the clutter."

Trini tried an appreciative smile. But inside, her heart was picking up speed to a nervous pace. Her lists kept her on track, and if just one of them went out of place, she could be thrown off schedule. "Thanks for your input, but I've tried that tactic, and"—she offered a small shrug for emphasis—"it didn't work."

Ruth stepped to Trini and spoke with what Trini was sure to be faux affection. It was the very tone she used to convince Trini to do something she didn't want to do. She took a seat next to Trini and laid her palm gently on Trini's shoulder. "Trini, we offer advice because we want what's best for you."

Trini loved her brood, each one of them, but she preferred to make her own decisions.

Emma finally breathed in and smiled a little. "Trini, we're so excited that you finally have an interested suitor."

The unexpected admission nearly stole Trini's breath. "Oh no."

Sarah lifted her chin to meet Trini's eyes. "In case you haven't noticed, your biological clock is ticking."

Mildred nodded. "Jah. And now, because of the fall, you have Jacob's full attention."

Ruth jumped back in. "Trini, we don't want your kitchen to scare him away."

Trini closed her eyes to try for composure. She felt the attention of everyone in the room. Then she cleared the knot from her throat, looked up, and spoke. "First of all, ladies, I appreciate your interest in finding me a husband. I can see why you think that I have Jacob at a place where I can reel him in. But. . ."

She looked at Mamm before exchanging individual looks with the others in the room. "As far as Jacob, I doubt if he cares that my walls are cluttered. And to be honest, it doesn't matter to me if he does or doesn't." She lifted her shoulders in a shrug. "I'm not husband searching right now. I'm interested in finding out who I am. What I can contribute to society."

Trini bit her lower lip, fully aware that she was the baby of the family and the only unwed sibling. But she yearned to be appreciated for what she offered others. And in their tight-knit Amish church, marrying and producing offspring was fundamental. *If I do as they expect me to, I'm no longer unique.*

Frustration edged Emma's voice as she flattened her palms against her thighs and gave a frustrated hop. "But Trini, don't you see?"

Trini shrugged again. "See what?"

"This is a perfect and rare opportunity for everything to fall into place." The pleased expression on Emma's face further convinced Trini that leaving the strict faith was the right choice for her. Although her family loved her, their efforts to make her life choices crossed the line. Still, she didn't aim to hurt their feelings. They simply didn't know better.

"You can finally join the church. At the same time Jacob does." She threw her hands in the air and squealed. "It will all be so wonderful!"

Trini softened her voice to an understanding tone that she hoped would stave off further ideas about her and Jacob. "I'd prefer not to force things to happen."

Ruth pleaded. "But Trini, if you don't help him to see that you're the wife for him, there are plenty of other single women in church who will do it."

Sarah chimed in. "Claim him, Trini, before someone beats you to it."

Mamm nodded and offered Trini the expression that made her the most determined to stay independent. "Trini, sometimes our family knows what's best for us. And this time, please trust our judgment."

Trini lifted a brow and met her mother's relentless gaze. "And that's to marry Jacob?"

"Jah!" The unanimous response echoed throughout the house. Her family looked at her, obviously eager for a reply. Trini's gaze drifted from Ruth to Mildred to Emma to Sarah and finally to Mamm.

Their expressions made her fully aware of how much she was about to disappoint her family. If they felt this strongly about getting her hitched to Jacob, how on earth would they accept her move to the Englisch world?

———————————— ⚓ ————————————

The following evening, Jacob met Trini at her shop. After completing her closing list, they proceeded outside. As she locked the entrance, he told her about the checkups the local vet had given Survivor as well as their two new standardbreds from the sale barn. He and his brothers were eagerly awaiting two new buggies they'd ordered.

As they stopped at the street, from around the corner, a youngster sped by on his bicycle. Jacob glimpsed the kid from his peripheral vision just in time to pull Trini out of the way.

The boy missed them both by inches. "Sorry!"

Jacob looked down at Trini. His arms were still around her waist. A nervous laugh escaped her throat. She was shaking, and Jacob was quick to note the breathlessness in her voice as she met his gaze. "You just saved me from a reckless driver!"

They laughed together. But as he looked deep into her eyes, the dancing flecks behind them mesmerized him to the point where he couldn't look away. An unfamiliar emotion stirred inside him. Whatever that sensation was took away his breath. And it claimed his voice.

Trini's eyes reflected surprise and uncertainty as they continued their tight embrace. Finally, she dropped her arms to her sides. He released his hold on her.

He finally found his voice. "We barely escaped an accident."

She smiled up at him. "I'm still alive, thanks to your quick thinking." As she stepped forward again, disappointment welled inside him. The embrace and the sudden emotion had quickly evaporated. Now he was back to reality as cautious steps took them across the road.

As they approached his buggy, Jacob tried again for something to say. But all he could think about was his fast-beating heart and the incredible sensation that had filled him when he'd held her in his arms. He wondered if Trini had experienced the same wondrous sensation.

Inside the buggy, Jacob and Trini absorbed the small bumps on the county road leading to her house. An uncertain silence ensued while he considered his feelings for the woman sitting beside him. He had always planned to marry her. At least, since he was five.

But now he'd been awakened, quite by accident, to something more between them. Immediately, he recognized the new sensation. *I'm attracted to her. I hope she can't read my thoughts. The last thing I want to do is to scare her away.*

He let out a breath of relief when Trini broke the silence. The softness of her voice prompted him to swallow an emotional knot. "Jacob, I owe you so much." She lifted her palms and glanced at him. "I don't know if I've adequately thanked you for all you've done for me."

Happy that the embarrassing silence had been broken, he looked at her long enough to smile with affection and address her concern. "Of course you've thanked me. Numerous times. But you must remember that it was my footsteps that prompted your fall."

"Accidents happen, Jacob. There was no way for you to have predicted that you would cause my fall. But what really matters is the sweet kindness you've shown me and how you've gone out of your way to make sure my chores get done and that I make it to work and back home every day." She lowered her voice so that it was barely audible. "Thank you."

He heard her take in a small breath as she turned to him. "Jacob, you truly are special."

Survivor slowed and turned onto the long dirt drive that led up to Trini's back door. When the horse stopped, Jacob helped her down the buggy's metal steps. But instead of immediately walking her to her door, he kept his hold on her and looked into her eyes, taking in the smooth, creamy complexion of her skin. He wondered if it felt as soft as it looked.

She returned his gaze with what seemed to be a comfortable, mutual understanding. He doubted there'd be another chance to pull her out of the path of a bicycle. And as he studied her, he said a silent prayer of thanks for this rare opportunity.

The beautiful shade of her delicate brown eyes absorbed his attention. While he took in the green flecks that danced with what appeared to be caution, he wondered what she was feeling.

He softened the pitch of his voice. "You're unreadable—you know that?"

While birds chirped in the background, and Honey could be seen in the distance expelling consecutive long neighs, he glimpsed the quick rising and falling of Trini's chest. Her flecks changed to what appeared to be a tumultuous dance.

Several heartbeats later, her breath caught in her throat as she spoke. "Why are you trying to read me, Jacob Lantz?"

"Because I like you, Trini. I'm trying to read your signals." After a slight pause, his voice cracked with emotion. "But they're mixed."

To his chagrin, she didn't respond. He yearned to hear an admission of love from her. At least of fondness. But she said nothing.

The breeze moved a stray hair from underneath her kapp to her cheek, and he slowly lifted his hand to take that one lost strand between his fingers. Her eyes followed his slow, deliberate movement as he used great care to tuck the piece back underneath her tight covering.

When he stuck the hair under the cloth, his fingers lingered.

She stayed very still while he returned his hand to his side. "Your hair is as soft as I guessed," he whispered.

As they kept very still, his observation of her continued. "It smells like peach." He didn't budge. Neither did she.

She parted her lips as if she intended to speak, but no words came out. Something within him wouldn't allow him to move. As he studied Trini's face, he became more perplexed about her thoughts. "So tell me. . .what's going on inside that beautiful head of yours?"

She responded in what came out as a whisper. "I'm trying to figure that out."

Using his softest touch, he tilted her chin up with his fingers so that their gazes met. "I'll settle for just a hint."

Trini broke the spell when she lowered her eyes, but when she looked up again, the flecks behind her irises appeared to dance to a wild, uncertain beat.

"Trini, I've always liked you, you know."

She smiled a little. "I've always liked you too, Jacob."

With a gentle movement, she stepped back. Trying to hide his disappointment, he knew what he wanted more than anything in this world. Trini's love.

"Jacob, as I was telling you earlier, I really do appreciate everything."

After a short silence passed, she added with more seriousness, "Truly, I do."

His heart warmed, but he tried to hide his disappointment at the sudden change of mood. "That's nice. And as far as your thoughts?" He offered a gentle shrug of his shoulders. "We've got our entire lives ahead of us to get to know each other. And I'm looking forward to the future more than ever."

Sensing that it was time to leave, he stepped toward the mailbox and pulled out some letters and a box. At the side door, he handed her the thick stack before opening the door and motioning her inside.

Her hands shook as she took the mail from him. She thanked him, and they said a simultaneous goodbye. As Jacob's horse clomped to the end of Trini's drive, emotions swirled inside Jacob's head until he thought he'd go crazy.

I'm deeply in love with Trini. But something has changed in her demeanor. I don't know why, but she seems a bit distant. My prayers will be answered when I make her my wife. But I sense that there's something that stops her from giving in to how she feels. There seems to be an invisible barrier that keeps us apart. If I'm not privy to her thoughts or her needs, how do I reach her?

CHAPTER SEVEN

Inside her house, Trini closed the door and squeezed her eyes closed to regain her composure. As she prayed for calmness, her entire body shook with a strong attraction to Jacob and an even stronger fear that the contents of this one particular package could have disclosed her big secret.

She opened her eyes and ordered herself to breathe. *Thankfully, the box is still sealed shut.* After pressing her lips together in a straight, thoughtful line, she pulled a pair of scissors from a drawer near the sink and carefully slit open the neatly addressed box from her brother. Her heart pumped so fast, she was sure it would jump right out of her chest.

Before opening the top, Trini glanced out the window to make sure Jacob was gone and no one else was nearby. Satisfied she was alone, she reached in to pull out the contents. The box gave no clue as to what it contained, but she knew exactly what was inside. A cell phone.

Without wasting time, she carried the phone that was forbidden within the strict confines of her Amish church down the hall and into her bedroom. She proceeded to wrap the phone inside a pair of socks and place it in a box in the corner of her closet.

Her broken arm began to throb, and she returned to the kitchen to retrieve an ice pack from her refrigerator. At her oak table, she pulled out a chair, carefully placed the cold pack on her left wrist, and began to write with her good arm on a notepad.

Making lists always calms me. And right now my emotions are on a roller coaster, just like the one I rode at Six Flags when I went through rumspringa.

My problems are real. Before Jacob moved into his aunt's home, I already had plenty of decisions to make. But now that Jacob is spending so much time with me, I'm more confused than ever. That's not like me. Not at all. I don't like guessing. That's why I write lists. I've done nearly everything on my master list, but it hasn't made it any easier to get ready to leave this life. And now I'm in deeper than I care to be. It's all because of how I feel about Jacob. What's really going on?

The fast beating of her heart finally began to slow to a moderate pace as she jotted things that really didn't matter on tomorrow's list. It was then that her thought process began to take root. The ice began to produce relief.

As Trini closed her eyes, she began to think through pieces of the afternoon. Her focus eventually landed on the tight, unexpected embrace outside The Quilt Room. Using her best reasoning skills, she tried to make sense of the chaos inside her.

It all happened so quickly, there was no time to think. But there was something about the way he looked at me. His expression was full of emotion. Of tenderness. And when I looked into his eyes, I matched his sentiment as strongly as he must have felt. We were so close, our noses nearly touched. It was only an embrace, and a very innocent one at that, but when we held each other. . .

She parted her lips in awe. *It was as if his eyes spoke to me. I read so much love and passion in those deep blue depths, the intense emotion stole my breath for a moment. And when Jacob helped me down the buggy steps right here at my house, I still sensed such a strong connection with him that I couldn't even think straight. What is wrong with me?*

Then the vivid recollection of him handing her the box that contained her new cell phone made her shoulders tense. *I knew I'd have to stay strong to get through this. There's no easy way to leave my upbringing. But Jacob doesn't know what's inside this box. So for right now, no worries, Trini.*

Early Saturday afternoon, Trini checked her list to ensure that The Quilt Room was ready to close. As she drummed her fingers against the table next to the cash register, she read out loud: "Money in envelope for deposit Monday morning. Inventory restocked. Baby quilt packaged and ready for UPS pickup. New design for birthday quilt in the works. Temporary help called for Tuesday during therapy. Bathroom cleaned."

The bell above the entrance sounded, and the door opened. "Hello!" Jacob said as he strode toward her. "How was your day?"

"Hi!" She nodded. "Gut." Looking around, she spotted her shop key and retrieved it. She proceeded to pick up her purse before she pushed open the gate that separated her work counter from the customer area.

She took in Jacob's appearance. Black trousers, blue shirt with the sleeves rolled up to his elbows, suspenders, brown leather work boots. As their eyes met, she acknowledged that she was a very blessed woman to have this kind man's attention.

She dropped her sketch pad, and Jacob bent to pick it up. As he did, he looked at the birthday design she was working on.

After eyeing her drawing with narrowed brows, he glanced up as he handed her the nearly finished picture on the oversized pad. "Are you custom-making this for someone?"

As she took it and looked down at it, she nodded before their gazes reconnected. "What do you think?"

"First of all, who's it for?"

With her right hand, she took one side of the paper while he held the other. "It's for an Englisch girl's eighteenth birthday. She loves fashion."

He chuckled. "That must be difficult for you. Does she know you're of the Plain faith?"

They laughed together. "At first it was a bit daunting," Trini admitted. "But now I'm almost finished. My customer offered me some suggestions, and my Englisch sister-in-law helped me too."

Jacob nodded in approval. "Trini, your work is very impressive."

"Denki." She lowered the pitch of her voice to a more serious tone. "Do you mean that?"

He glanced at her drawing again and smiled. "I can't offer a professional critique, but according to my eyes"—he raised a brow before grinning—"it's quite appealing."

"Thank you, Jacob. Your compliment means a lot."

She pointed to the bottom of the quilt picture, but as she started to comment on it, the tip of his fingers brushed hers. Automatically, she looked at him. His expression was thoughtful. Reserved and serious.

For a moment, she lost her train of thought as her heart did a somersault, and she was sure that her chest rose and fell much more quickly than what was appropriate. To distract from his gentle touch and her embarrassing reaction to it, she shoved her work into her oversized handbag. "Shall we?" she asked.

He motioned. "Ladies first."

They stepped across the street toward the carriage. When a car turned the corner, Jacob gently nudged her back to speed up her steps. Again, her heart reacted erratically to his touch.

Inside the buggy, Trini tried to calm her emotions. *Why am I reacting like a young girl? Perhaps Jacob's attention is beginning to affect me. He's a very gentle, kind man. And good-looking, although I've always been raised to focus on the inside of a person. Forgive me, Gott.*

As the horse's hooves made an uneven rhythm on the blacktop,

Jacob asked, "Your brother is Englisch, isn't he?"

Her mouth parted in surprise. For some reason, she hadn't expected that question.

"You mentioned that your sister-in-law is Englisch."

Her shoulders relaxed. *Don't be so paranoid. I did say that. He's only following up.*

"Amos is Englisch, yes."

"Are you close?"

Trini fidgeted with her hands in her lap, knowing full well that she'd made a mistake by bringing her sister-in-law into the conversation. She would make a point of not mentioning her again.

A wave of guilt swept through her. Jacob was doing so much for her, and he seemed honest and open. Yet it was mandatory to guard her secret. If word got out before she left, all sorts of issues could and would materialize and perhaps cancel her move.

Several moments later, she realized that he was awaiting a response, so she would make it brief. "We're as close as we can be. I mean, he lives in Rhode Island."

"He left the Amish church?"

She nodded. "As you can imagine, it caused a rift in the family." She released a helpless sigh. "It's really too bad."

"I agree."

She took in his unexpected opinion. "You do?"

He looked straight ahead and nodded. "Jah."

For some reason, his response surprised her. And because of his honesty and his openness, she smiled a little and relaxed. "Not everyone thinks alike. Yet we're all Gott's children."

He chuckled. "At the end of the day, we're all kinder of Gott. In fact, we Amish are like the Englisch in many ways."

She frowned and waved her hand in front of him before dropping her arm to her side. "Jacob, are you okay?"

He laughed. "Of course. But don't you agree?"

Trini shook her head. "I can't say that I do."

After a long, thoughtful pause, Jacob lowered the pitch of his voice to a more confidential, serious tone. "Trini, our church has strict rules, I agree. But deep down, we're like normal people in that we don't all think alike. My brothers share my DNA, yet we don't agree on everything."

Trini didn't respond because she was digesting his take on the Amish faith, which, in her opinion, didn't allow for enough variation in opinion.

His voice hinted doubt. "I see that you're not convinced."

She glanced at him with narrowed brows. "Not at all."

He offered a decisive nod. "Let me try again. Just because we go to the same church and follow the Ordnung doesn't mean that we all have identical views. We don't. Not at all. For instance, I believe that Gott loves all of His followers."

"I think that's true. Jah." Trini acknowledged to herself that Jacob's point of view surprised her. In her family, Mamm had always reinforced the Ordnung and made it clear that leaving the Plain faith was absolutely not an option. That Amos had disappointed Gott.

"So you believe it's acceptable that my brother left the Amish church?"

"Trini, I love and fully support the way we believe and worship. But I also know that not everyone interprets scripture the same way. I would never consider leaving our church. It's a part of me, just like passing down my beliefs to my future children is vital. But I also understand that we can't and we don't all have the same views." He raised his palms. "That's life."

His lips turned up in a small smile, and he offered a slight shrug of his shoulders. "Gott created us all with uniqueness, I'm sure. Of course we're not all going to think alike. But in my humble opinion, I'm sure that Gott understands this. And He loves every believer and follower, even though we don't all worship in the same way."

His voice revealed the intensity of his emotions. "That's the beauty of it." Then he surprised her. "In my view, we're human beings first, Amish second."

A long silence followed. Trini breathed in. His last statement stunned her. It made her feel gut to know what an open thinker Jacob was. *He can think outside the box.*

A sudden, unexpected calmness overcame her, and she relaxed her shoulders. While she took in the scattered two-story homes that appeared in the distance and the healthy soybean and corn crops that seemed to go on for miles, she garnered a new admiration and respect for the man next to her.

He's open-minded like me. Yet I still can't share my secret with him. Even if he wouldn't judge me, I can't risk anyone finding out. There's too much at stake.

Suddenly she realized he was waiting for her to say something. So she did. "I wish my brother and his wife could be part of our family again. I know Daed would want that."

He rubbed his chin with his fingers. "Have you talked to your mother about this?"

She nearly laughed. "No!"

When he turned to her, his eyes expressed sheer surprise. "Why not?"

"Jacob, you don't know my mamm. Or my sisters." For a few moments, she considered her words. She had to be very careful not to give away anything about her eventual departure from their tight Amish community.

"Try me." His voice hinted for her to go on.

An oncoming car slowed, and Jacob veered his horse over to the side of the road. For a moment, the carriage was a bit uneven since the paved surface was higher in the middle.

"I love my mother. I adore my sisters. But Jacob, honestly, they are headstrong."

He laughed. "Funny that you'd say that." His reaction caused her jaw to drop. Jacob shrugged. "That must be where you get it."

Trini breathed in and drew a hand over her chest. "You think I'm headstrong?"

He darted her a wink. "In a nice way, of course." He cleared his throat. "Those lists of yours drive you to get things done."

"I'd never really thought of it like that."

"That's because you like to be in control," Jacob observed. "And that's why you write lists. Please don't take this wrong." He stopped as if deciding whether or not to go on. "But, Trini, don't you think that sometimes your lists take control of you?"

She laughed at the question. "No!"

Jacob's voice took on a more understanding tone. "That's one of the reasons I like you, I think."

She considered the interesting road this conversation had taken. Was Jacob right? Did her lists control her?

"I always did like you, Trini. I've never made it a secret."

Trini's heart picked up speed again. She was thankful that Jacob couldn't see her chest rise and fall. She knew that she really liked him too. But as she recalled the brush of their fingers in her shop and her reaction, as well as his touch on her back while crossing the street, she wondered about the definition of the word *like. When you just like a man, does your heart pump as if it's running a race?*

"Jacob, I appreciate you." She gestured with her hands. "And everything you do."

"Thank you, Trini. You don't know what that means to me." He grinned. "To what do I owe that compliment?"

She offered a gentle shrug.

He guided Survivor to the far edge of the blacktop as another buggy approached them. As they met, he waved. So did Trini. She quickly recognized the Bontranger family and immediately caught the excited expression on Suzanne Bontranger's face.

"There goes the rumor mill," Trini commented under her breath.

Jacob chuckled. "I take it you speak from experience?"

Trini sighed and nodded. "It's a little thing, really, but sometimes even the smallest things hurt the most."

He glanced at her and returned his focus to the road.

"She commented that my quilt shop took away business from the area's locals. Many times she's approached me about selling her quilts in my store."

"And?"

Trini shrugged. "I thought about it. Even prayed about it. But local customers and tourists hire me to design their quilts for specific occasions. It's a privilege to cater to their needs. I'm not an ordinary shop owner because I custom design for people."

She shifted to a more comfortable position. "I suppose it's like penning a book. The art has to come from the person who writes it. And that's exactly why I create my own art."

He offered an understanding nod. "I get it. You want to keep your creativity the reason people buy from you."

She thought long and hard before offering an agreeable nod. "Jah. I know I wouldn't have to. But my special designs based on the needs of my clients are the root of my success. I don't believe sticking to my work is selfish—it's my livelihood."

The buggy bounced lightly as Survivor moved toward the right to allow an oncoming car to go by. "I understand. And by the sounds of it, you're very dedicated to your craft."

Trini's home came into sight. From where they were, she could already imagine bright red tomatoes that would eventually color her garden.

As if reading her mind, he spoke while slowing the horse to turn into her long dirt drive. "Your garden—it's beautiful."

"Thank you, Jacob."

"Do you know what those tomato plants remind me of?"

She lifted a curious brow. "What?"

He chuckled, but his voice carried some sadness. "They remind me of my aunt's meat loaf."

The comment prompted the corners of Trini's lips to curve into a curious grin. "Who can forget Margaret's famous meat loaf?"

He gave a strong shake of his head. "I certainly can't. She always teased that there was a secret ingredient that no one knew about."

"I never did figure out what it was."

"You mean she didn't even tell you?"

"No."

He smiled mischievously. "I might be wrong, but. . ."

"Go on! Don't stop now!"

He chuckled. "Okay. We know that she used garden peppers, onions, and tomatoes."

Trini waited for him to go on.

As they slowed to approach her home, he offered a wry grin. "Ketchup, Trini."

Before she had a chance to respond, he continued. "I'm convinced that ketchup was her secret ingredient."

Trini considered his take on Margaret's prized dish. Then she nodded in agreement. "You may be right, but she didn't make her ketchup from just tomatoes. She also grew herbs, and she used them in her homemade ketchup."

Excitement edged his tone. "Did she share her recipes with you?"

Trini breathed in as she took in the straight rows in her garden. She pointed a finger. "Some. But her ketchup?" Trini shook her head. "That recipe was hers and hers alone."

Jacob gave a low whistle. "Then I guess it's safe to say that I'll never get to experience that delicious meat loaf again. At least, not in this lifetime."

Trini contemplated his words. As their buggy stopped, Survivor let out a loud whinny and swished his tail.

Jacob helped Trini down the steps, and she tried to shrug off the way the warmth from his hands made her heart do funny things. She needed an explanation. So she quickly reasoned that her reaction was due to two things: First, she wasn't accustomed to a man's touch. Second, she also liked the independence of taking care of herself, and what she was feeling was guilt at needing help.

As they stepped to her side door, a loud whinny from the distance made her turn. She laughed. "Our horses are spoiled."

He grinned. "And that's the way it should be." Jacob glanced at the garden. "You planted pumpkins?"

She eyed her plants and nodded. "Jah. But not so much for the actual pumpkins. I love the tasty blossoms."

"No kidding?"

"I'll make them for you sometime."

"That's a deal."

As he laid his hand on the door handle, he stopped, looking down at the sidewalk. He bent to touch one of Trini's gerbera daisies.

Before he could comment, she stepped in. "I know they're suffering. How can I explain to the rabbits that this isn't their dinner?"

He laughed. When he stood, he put his palms on his hips and breathed in. "We've got to save them before they're not salvageable."

"I know."

"Either you've got to transplant them into a pot. . .or put a protective fence around them." He shook his head. "If we can get them through this struggle, they'll be gorgeous."

Trini blinked at the sudden sting of salty moisture. Memories of Jacob's aunt and her flower bed stirred her emotions. Trini whispered, "They were your aunt's favorite flowers."

He swallowed a lump that had formed in his throat. "Thank you for sharing that, Trini. Then we've definitely got to put wire around them. At least tall enough so that the rabbits can't reach the leaves." His gaze landed on her cast. "I'll be back later with something to stop your thieves."

She waved her hand in dismissal. "It's okay, Jacob. You've got plenty to do without fixing my plants."

His voice lowered to a soft, serious pitch. "But don't you see?" Before she could answer, he whispered, "I want to."

When she met his serious gaze, her heart reacted...again. This time it wasn't due to his actual touch. Rather, it was the tumultuous way his eyes spoke to her. As she studied the flecks that danced with seriousness and longing, she parted her lips in awe. The fierce combination compelled her to keep studying them.

His soft voice pulled her from her trance. "Trini?"

She realized that she was staring at him. When she lowered her gaze to her sturdy black shoes, he didn't budge. Neither did she.

For some reason, there weren't any surrounding noises to interrupt the intense silence. Finally, she pretended things were normal between them. But deep down inside, she knew that they weren't.

"Trini, look at me."

She hesitated. Did she dare? She didn't know what it was about Jacob that could steal her voice. Her breath. Her entire being.

With one gentle motion, he placed his finger underneath her chin. He was so close, the light cinnamon on his breath lingered in the small distance between them. His clothes smelled like outdoors. She could even see tiny squint wrinkles around his eyes. They made him take on a more manly appearance.

His voice was barely more than a whisper. "You feel it too, don't you?"

The last thing she wanted was any romantic complication that would interfere with her plans to leave. *I must not lead Jacob on. I must not lead myself on. What I'm feeling...it's so wrong.*

She tried for a more light-hearted conversation and remembered what had started the uncomfortable moment that still hovered between them. At least, on her part it was uncomfortable. "The shade of your eyes, Jacob, is the most beautiful combination of blues that I've ever seen."

His voice was so soft, like a whisper, she could barely hear his words. "But Trini, there's more to it than that. Isn't there?"

CHAPTER EIGHT

Trini shuddered. As she listened to the sound of hooves and an occasional whinny eventually fade, she took a seat on one of her oak chairs. At the dining room table, she closed her eyes a moment to try to regain her composure. When she finally opened her eyes, she heaved a deep sigh.

I'm in a scenario that cannot end well for Jacob or me. What should I do?

A glance at a blank notepad and nearby pen prompted her to do what she always did when facing a dilemma. She reached for the paper and ink with her right hand and focused on the empty lines in front of her.

First of all, I must list the pros. Daed always taught me to focus on what I can control, not what I can't. And surely a positive attitude must help in some way:

PROS

1. Therapy is helping, and in a matter of a few weeks, I'll be able to permanently remove this cast.

2. Jacob is wonderful. He's so kind and helpful.

3. I have great sounding boards, Abby and Serenity— that is, if I'm willing to spill my secret.

4. It's amazing what I'm able to do with a cast on my arm. I'm putting in extra hours, I'm nearly on schedule, and I should make most of my deadlines.

CONS

1. I'm sure that Jacob seeks more than my friendship.
2. When I'm with him, sometimes I allow myself to feel the same about him.
3. I've got to take the reins where my heart is concerned. At the end of the day, I cannot have Jacob as well as the freedom of Englisch life. I have to choose.
4. Serenity and Abby are devout Amish women. As much as they care about me, I'm not sure how they would react to my secret. If I reveal my intent, I no longer have control over my plan. The moment I voice my plan, I no longer have a secret.

Trini sighed in defeat and lifted her shoulders in a helpless shrug. *My life is complicated.*

———————— ⚜ ————————

Later that day, Jacob and Stephen walked through the crops behind their house. Sickles in hand, they cut out weeds as they stepped slowly to the distant end of the bean field. Many of the surrounding Amish farmers hired the "bean walking" done. But Jacob enjoyed his time in the field. It offered him a sort of mental therapy.

Jacob extended his sickle to cut a butterprint weed. As he did so, Stephen's voice carried over to him from several rows over. "The crop's lookin' gut, don't you think?"

Jacob smiled. "Thanks to the farmers who planted after Aunt

Margaret's passing." After he swallowed the knot in his throat, Jacob went on. "It's just beginning to sink in that all of this is ours."

"Having a clean field was always important to her. And clean ditches. We'll come through for her." Stephen extended his sickle and quickly yanked it to snap a milkweed.

As they moved through the rows, the bright sun fell on the green leaves, making them appear a couple of shades lighter than they actually were. Both men wore hats to keep their skin from burning under the scorching sun. As Jacob continued to work, the leaves brushed his hands and arms.

"So how's Trini?"

Jacob considered the innocent question, fully aware that his relationship with the quilter was far from simple. The truth was he was unsure of how she felt about him. Sometimes she was hot. Sometimes she was cold. Reading what was inside her head posed a challenge. But for now, he needed something to satisfy his curious brother.

"Trini's broken bones are healing. And she's keeping up fairly well with her work. Therapy sure has given her a boost." After a thoughtful pause, he added, "That, and her strong determination to return to normal."

"I'll bet. I've heard that those are the keys to recovery. Hey, I was thinking about asking her to make a special quilt for Mamm. For Christmas."

Jacob nodded and proceeded forward. Beads of sweat dribbled down his chest from his neck.

"I'm in. You know Trini creates her own designs."

"And it's a gut thing! I'm dry on ideas." He cleared his throat. "Time away from Mamm has given me an even greater appreciation for what she's done for us."

"I hear ya."

Stephen cleared his throat. Jacob swatted a fly away from his face.

"By the way, just thought you should know that. . ." He cleared his throat and glanced Jacob's way. "Word's gotten around that you and Miss Trini were sitting too close to each other in your buggy."

The statement sparked a laugh from Jacob. "That's hilarious."

"You weren't?"

"We sat in the buggy together, jah. There's not a lot of elbow room, you know. So it could have appeared that we were close. Actually, our shoulders didn't touch, if you're looking for specifics."

Stephen chuckled. "I'm not judging, you know. In fact, I expect that you and Trini will get real close real fast."

Jacob glanced at him to go on.

Stephen chuckled. "You'd better, anyway, if you plan to marry her. You know what you want, Jake. Why waste time?"

Jacob reached for a patch of smartweed and smiled at his younger brother. "Jah. But I'm responsible for her fall. And that, dear brother, makes me indebted to her."

Stephen responded with a chuckle. "But that's not the only reason you're her personal chauffeur." Amusement edged Stephen's tone. "Next time I see your house sketch, I'll bet there will be even more rooms. And by the way, I can't wait to become an uncle."

They both chuckled.

As Jacob snapped a milk thistle, he decided on a straightforward approach. The lack of a breeze sent more beads of sweat rolling down his face. He didn't bother to wipe them away.

"I love spending time with her. I hate to bear the responsibility of breaking her arm, but I'm certainly reaping the benefits of her fall."

They could see the end of the field. "And how about her? Is she reaping the benefits too?"

Jacob hesitated. While he paused, a bee buzzed in front of him, and he propped the long hook at his side and shooed the buzzing insect away with his hat. As soon as the bee was out of sight, Jacob put his hat back on and walked on with the tool. He took several steps without finding a weed.

He grimaced. "Stephen, I don't know if Trini likes me for more than a friend. And to be honest, it's frustrating." He shook his head in dismay.

Stephen stopped and turned to Jacob. Stephen's voice held genuine sympathy and understanding. "I'm sure she likes you, Jake. What is there not to like?"

As they laughed together, a breeze picked up, and the sun hid underneath a large, fluffy cloud. "Let's enjoy this sunshine break while we can," suggested Stephen.

"Okay. We're almost to the end of the row. And I could use some water."

They worked to the ditch then sat down on the incline and drank from their jugs. The only sound was water sloshing as the men turned their containers upside down and drank.

"Awww!"

"On a hot day, nothing beats a cold swig of water."

"Yep."

After a couple more swigs, they braced their jugs between their thighs. The view of the field prompted a happy, satisfied sigh from Jacob.

Stephen wiped his brow and turned toward his brother. "I'm looking forward to tomorrow."

Jacob nodded in agreement. "If the Amish women here cook like our Lancaster women, I can't wait." He paused to swat a fly away from his nose.

"I assume you'll be taking Trini?"

"Hopefully."

"What's that supposed to mean?"

Jacob paused to enjoy the welcome breeze that fanned his face. He removed his hat, placed it on the ground next to him, and ran his fingers through his damp hair. He popped his knuckles before addressing the question.

"You know, Stephen, my wants are simple."

"They always have been. How about Trini's wants?"

"She's complicated, Stephen. Especially for an Amish woman."

"Really?"

"Uh-huh."

"Okay. So let's talk this out. What makes her so complex?"

Jacob stood, put the plug back in his water jug, and grabbed his hook. Stephen did the same. Together they counted six rows apart and proceeded with weeding the beans.

"For one thing, she's a serious list maker."

The light sound of Stephen's hook cutting a butterprint was followed by Jacob's slicing a lone cornstalk. "That's nothing out of the ordinary, now is it?"

Jacob thought about the question. "Probably not. But there's something so intense about the way she sticks to her lists, Stephen."

He laughed. "Sounds like she takes them pretty seriously."

"She likes to control her life." Jacob paused to wipe a bead of sweat from his brow. "I would tell you that I wish she wasn't so intense, but. . ." He chuckled. "Ironically that's one of the things I like about her."

"Maybe she thinks her lists keep her on task?"

"I guess so. And she's extremely independent."

Stephen caught up with him several rows over, and they walked some distance without finding weeds. "Of course she's got to be somewhat independent, Jacob. I mean, she owns a business. And she lives all by herself out here in the country. There's no one to take care of her, Jake. No one except for Trini Sutter."

"But here's the thing. I like taking care of her. I *want* to take care of her."

"Whoa, brother. Slow down. You don't want to scare her off."

"Are you kidding me?"

Stephen shook his head as their hooks met midrow. "Jacob. . ." Stephen chuckled. "You barely know her. Give her some time."

"That's not true. I've known her since we were kids."

Stephen laughed harder. "Think of how long ago that was. Don't forget that you went fifteen years without seeing the girl. Now, I realize you've always known what you wanted. You still do. But Jake. . ." He paused. "Most people aren't like you. Not in that respect, anyway."

"But that's just it, Stephen. We are opposites, yet we are alike. Like me, she wants to know exactly what she's going to do, every step, so that everything goes as planned. She doesn't like surprises."

"Oh, Jake. No, no, no."

"What?"

"You love surprises." He cleared his throat. "Let me ask you this." Jacob waited for him to go on.

"Have you ever really thought about why you like her so much?"

Jacob considered the question. Even when he simply thought about Trini, his heart picked up to a speed that he was sure must be illegal. "When I was a kid, she took me under her wing. And I know it might sound crazy, but her reassurance and kindness stuck with me all these years."

Stephen's voice was edged with skepticism when he finally responded. "Does she still take you under her wing?"

Jacob chuckled before his voice took on a serious tone. "We'll see. Right now the roles have reversed."

Stephen extended his hook to quickly snap three weeds. While the hot sun illuminated the sky, Jacob considered his relationship with Trini. The more he thought about her, the more his adrenaline kicked in.

A breeze moved some plants while a butterfly landed on a leaf. In the distance, a horse-pulled buggy traveled the county road. Jacob thought of Trini and looked forward to their next ride.

He couldn't wait to replace her struggling gerbera daisies on both sides of her walk. He'd thought about trying to revive them but wanted her to enjoy the flowers as much as she could. Some tangled beans blocked Jacob's path, and he cut through the vines with one swift motion.

"I wish Trini enjoyed being pampered."

Stephen let out a low whistle. "Oh, but don't you kind of enjoy her independent spirit?"

Jacob chuckled. "Jah."

"Let me ask you this. If Trini liked you taking care of her, would you still feel so strongly about her? Or would it ruin the challenge?"

An amused grin curved Jacob's lips. "Point taken. Trust me. This has nothing to do with a challenge. I know you're trying to tell me that I can't have her independent spirit and also have her dependent on me."

The sun disappeared behind a cloud, and the light dimmed. Jacob sighed with relief.

Stephen stopped a moment to adjust his hat. When he caught up with Jacob, he stepped over several rows of beans and joined him.

"Jacob, I've never courted a woman, but I'm not blind to relationships. Logic tells me that you're never going to have everything you want." He blew out a breath and shook his head while he bounced his sickle off his palm. "So do yourself a huge favor and get used to Trini's independence. Embrace it. You've got to take all of her as a whole. And you can't ask her to be someone she's not."

"But I wish I could make her see that what I feel for her is gut in every way. That she can enjoy things in life that aren't on her lists. And most importantly, that if she follows her lists the rest of her life, she might miss some very valuable moments."

Stephen parked his sickle next to him. "You're in a difficult situation, brother—that's for sure." Stephen cupped his chin with his hand. "You know what I'd do if I were in your shoes?" Jacob looked down at his boots before meeting Stephen's sincere expression. "I'd keep on doing what you're doing. But if you truly want to court her, be honest with her, Jake. Tell her that you see the two of you together in the future. Ask her point-blank if she sees the same thing." He shrugged. "There's no need to walk the relationship road alone." He lowered the pitch of his voice. "Of course, that's just my humble opinion."

Before Jacob could respond, Stephen hopped over the bean plants until he was back in his row. Jacob's heart melted while he absorbed his brother's advice. He acknowledged how blessed he was to have two siblings who cared so much about him.

When the two continued down their respective rows, Stephen's voice interrupted Jacob's thoughts. "I can only advise the way I see it. But the truth is that Trini is a single Amish woman. Now I understand that she might be a bit different from the norm, but I can honestly say that I think the two of you will be great together."

Jacob beamed. "Really?"

"Really. Think about it, Jake. Sure, she might not meet the normal expectations of an Amish woman. That's okay. She's unique. But at the end of the day, I don't know one Amish woman who doesn't want marriage and a family. And as far as that goes, Trini's no exception. Tomorrow you'll spend the afternoon with her at the church potluck."

"If you wanted a future with Trini," Jacob asked, "what would you do differently?"

Stephen laughed.

"What's so funny?"

"I'm sorry. It's just that you're asking someone who's in the same boat as you are."

Jacob stopped. "You?"

Stephen nodded when Jacob glanced his way. "I've got my eye on the town florist."

The news sparked a grin from Jacob. "Serenity Miller?"

Stephen's voice took on a shy tone. "Jah. You know. . .the one who came by with the alterations lady." When Jacob glanced his way, the sun came out again and lit up Stephen's face. Jacob didn't know if the mushy expression his brother wore was from the bright light or if Stephen was experiencing exactly what he felt.

———————— ⚜ ————————

The following afternoon, the Glicks' front yard was lined with standardbreds and black buggies from the blacktop all the way to the back of the two-story white house. Jacob gave Trini a hand as he helped her down the steps. When she had both feet on the ground, she ran the palms of her hands over the front of her long navy dress to help flatten the wrinkles.

"It's the perfect day for a cookout, don't you think?" Abby commented while Jacob helped both her and Serenity down too.

Serenity smiled. "It's hard to believe June's almost here!"

The faces of Trini's friends were flushed with joy and hopefulness. And Trini didn't need to ask why. Serenity had confidentially confessed liking Stephen Lantz. And Abby was more determined than ever to carry through with Margaret's wish that she become Mrs. Gabriel Lantz.

In the distance, smoke rose from open grills. Folding chairs skirting lines of card tables and picnic tables covered the lawn. The delicious aroma of barbecuing meats floated through the air, reminding Trini how much she'd always relished church gatherings.

She smiled as she and Jacob followed her friends to the crowd. As they walked, happiness flooded her heart until tears stung her eyes. Trini blinked to rid the salty sting.

Today is special. I get to spend the day with my family, friends, and the man I adore. Before, I never really gave much thought to these wonderful gatherings. And there have been many. But in a few months,

I won't be around these people. I won't even live here. Will I have this many friends in Rhode Island?

As they walked, Trini tried to reason with these unexpected emotions that tugged at her relentlessly. *Of course, I won't. It's taken me my entire life to garner all these relationships. But I will have many newfound freedoms. And that's what I will cherish most about being Englisch.*

"Earth to Trini?"

Jacob nudged her.

"What?"

"We were talking about Aunt Margaret's horse from years ago that liked to hear her sing. What was his name?"

Trini smiled. "Oh." She snapped her fingers until it came to her. Then she flung her hands up in a satisfied gesture. "Moonlight!"

Serenity and Abby turned to face Jacob and Trini. "That's it!"

Abigail laughed. "And Moonlight wouldn't eat until Margaret sang to him."

Jacob joined in the laughter. "That's hilarious! Really?"

Serenity chimed in. "Jah! And remember how spoiled he was?" Before Trini could say something, Serenity practically bounced with excitement. "He would always let out a whinny at the end of each trip. And that was for an apple."

Jacob's eyes traveled from Abby to Serenity before they finally landed on Trini's face. When their eyes met, her heart picked up to an excited speed. But she didn't look away. She couldn't.

As she took in the beautiful flecks that hovered behind the blue in Jacob's eyes, emotion nearly robbed her breath. But it wasn't his eyes that pulled her into a place she didn't recognize. It was Jacob. It was everything about him.

"Trini?"

His gentle voice brought her back to reality. Serenity and Abby were some distance ahead of them.

"Trini? Are you okay?"

Suddenly embarrassed, she offered her most convincing nod. "Jah. Everything's fine, Jacob." Trying for normalcy, she said, "I just realized how hungry I am."

As his expression revealed both disappointment and surprise, she went on. "I didn't eat breakfast this morning."

Smiling a little, he nudged her in the direction of the gathering. "Then we'd better fix that."

But as they proceeded to the gathering, Trini acknowledged that there was something very wrong. And unfortunately, food wouldn't solve the problem.

CHAPTER NINE

Stephen looked on as Serenity and Abby walked toward the crowd. Serenity strolled with ease, as if she didn't have a worry in the world. Something about her was so comforting and relaxing. And she had many more assets as well. His heart skipped a beat as he took in her calm smile from a distance.

Carrying chairs from the house to the outside dining area, Stephen let his gaze linger on Serenity. Her blond hair was neatly covered by a kapp. Something about the ease she conveyed and the way she seemed to be in a deep conversation with her friend prompted the corners of his lips to gently curve into a half smile.

From where he stood, he couldn't see the soft blueness of her eyes. But it didn't matter. He'd memorized it the moment she'd introduced herself to him at Margaret's house.

A firm hand on his shoulder made him look up. Gabe darted him a wink. "You need a hand?"

"Thanks."

"Nice day for a cookout."

Stephen agreed.

Abby and Serenity approached them, and Stephen greeted them, glancing at Gabriel as he introduced the women to him.

Serenity offered a polite nod. "It's so nice to finally meet you, Gabriel."

Abby's voice sounded a bit out of breath. "It's gut to meet you."

As some kinder nearly bumped into Abby while they played chase, Gabriel narrowed his brows and focused on her. "I must say, Abby, that we are most appreciative of the beautiful quilt."

He lowered his tone. "You can't imagine how we feel knowing that it was our aunt's very last project." After a slight pause, he added, "That makes it even more special."

Abby beamed. "I hoped you would love it as much as I do."

"That you can be sure of," Gabriel said.

He turned to Serenity. "And you made those delicious desserts?"

Serenity blushed. "Jah."

Gabriel grinned. "Denki. They were absolutely mouthwatering."

Serenity bobbed her head in a thank-you.

Stephen placed his chair next to an empty chaise and focused on Serenity. "Serenity, I was wondering if you would take a short walk so we can get to know each other better."

After a slight hesitation, she blinked her thick, dark lashes. "Stephen Lantz, it would be my pleasure."

Early the following morning, Serenity breathed in the fresh smell of pines as she made her way up the incline behind her house. The light pine fragrance was one of her favorite scents. Not only because of the delightful aroma but because the natural smell from the large trees helped her to relax and to practice positive thinking.

From where she walked, she glimpsed Margaret's house. *But it's really Stephen, Gabe, and Jacob's home now. But in my heart, it will always be Margaret's.*

As her heart pumped to a rigorous beat, she took a deep breath. "Five positive things for the day," she said to herself.

She came to the part of the dirt path where full-grown trees on both sides nearly came together. Her path darkened. She stopped to take a branch in her hand and gently run her fingers over the long needles. Afterward, she sniffed the handful of green before slowly pushing some branches out of her way to move forward.

What are my five positive thoughts today? She was awestruck by the way the morning sun and shadows made the gorgeous panorama in front of her appear the color of jade. She thought of yesterday's gathering at the Glick farm and smiled.

Number one: the welcome lunch for the Lantz brothers reinforced how fortunate I am to have so many people in my church who care about me.

She thought of poor Abby's unsuccessful attempt to win the oldest Lantz brother's attention and closed her eyes while she winced painfully. In her years of studying positive thinking from local library books, she had learned that often something good comes from something bad. *So what good could possibly come from Abby's over-the-top behavior to win Gabriel Lantz's attention?*

As she lifted her dress to prevent the cotton material from rubbing against a large stone to her right, she carefully put her mind to work. *I can't save Abby. She's so headstrong. Years of spoiling by her parents have allowed her to think that whatever she wants can be hers.*

Serenity shook her head in despair. *Poor Abby. I must think of something gut that may result from her embarrassing admission to Gabe that his aunt had yearned for him to marry her.*

Serenity bit her lip. *Think hard. Maybe there is a way for Abby to redeem herself in Gabe's eyes. I am not privy to what goes on inside his head, but his facial expressions and common logic told me that Abby did not achieve the desired impression and her efforts definitely backfired.*

Serenity decided to put that goal on the back burner. *If Abby still insists on marrying Gabriel, I'll enlist Trini's assistance to help me think of a realistic plan.*

What is positive thought number two? I get to enjoy this beautiful view on this wonderful day.

Number three: I work on the same street as my two best friends.

And whenever we meet, I can tell them things that no one else would even try to comprehend. I've always confided everything to them. She looked down at the ground before correcting herself. *At least, almost everything.*

Number four: I love what I do.

A noise startled her. Serenity stopped and caught her breath. Propping her hands on her hips, she looked around. She listened. She stood very still and gently separated the branches in front of her to enable her to see what caused the stir in the brush.

After she'd waited awhile, she decided that her imagination was too active. *No one's here but me. This area of Illinois is safe. There has never been a murder or kidnapping in this neck of the woods.*

After she'd convinced herself that everything was okay, the noise sounded again. This time, she recognized it as footsteps.

It could be an animal. Maybe it's a deer. She sighed in relief. *They're harmless. I'm being ridiculous.*

Suddenly, she came face-to-face with another human being. She screamed, and a set of strong arms braced her.

"Serenity?"

She clutched her hands to her chest in shock as she stared into a set of familiar-looking deep brown eyes. "Stephen?"

Her heart pounded with a strange mixture of fear and relief. As she closed her eyes to reclaim her composure, she laughed. Her reaction was automatic. She wasn't sure why she laughed.

When she opened her lids, their eyes met. Stephen had the most compelling eyes she'd ever seen. Not that she'd had the opportunity to be this close to many, of course, especially not of the male species. But the dark depths of Stephen's eyes seemed to absorb her entire heart and soul. She reasoned that the shock of running into him here in the woods exaggerated her reaction.

She pulled in a deep breath. As she did so, his grip on her relaxed. But his hands lingered on her where her dress sleeves met her arms.

His soft voice offered a soothing, reassuring tone as she continued to breathe for calmness.

"St–Stephen, what on earth are you doing here? You scared me to death."

His easygoing tone reassured her as she felt the warmth of his breath on her face. The heat of his hands penetrated her thin cotton dress and lingered. He moved his palms down the sides of her arms.

"I'm sorry, Serenity. The last thing I wanted was to scare someone. Especially you."

As a light breeze stirred the trees, Serenity finally regained her composure—except for the way her pulse zoomed. She wasn't sure if this was because of the sudden fright she'd experienced or if it was the result of his gentle manner.

Whatever the reason, here they were. And the sequence of events had unfolded to result in this comforting, yet exciting, situation.

Finally, his arms dropped to his sides. She asked him the obvious question: "What are you doing here?" At that moment, her focus landed on his binoculars, which hung by a thick black strap around his neck.

He pulled in a breath, and his uncertain expression led her to believe he didn't want her to know. His eyes hinted skepticism. The curve of his mouth conveyed doubt.

She continued to regard him for an answer, and she pointed to the binoculars. Finally, he motioned to the path she was on. "Mind if I join you?"

Temporarily forgetting this particular walk's purpose, she shook her head. "Not at all." Then she added in a hushed voice, "If you tell me why you're here and what you're doing with those." She touched his binoculars and smiled a little.

They proceeded. When they came to another overgrown spot in the middle of the dirt path, he pushed away the brush and held it so she could make her way past it.

On the other side, the bright sun beamed down on his face. As she looked up at him, she noticed that his expression was uncertain.

An unexpected qualm edged his voice as he adjusted the strap holding the binoculars. "Can I trust you with my deep, dark secret?"

Eager to hear what it was and feeling privileged that he would share it with her, she offered a quick nod. "You've got my word that I won't tell." She stepped around a large tree root that protruded from the ground. "What is it?"

He looked down at her with a wry smile. His eyes sparkled with excitement. "I'm looking for a red-headed woodpecker."

She stopped and moved her hands to her hips as she absorbed his surprising admission. "You're a bird-watcher?"

He lowered the pitch of his voice. "Guilty."

She laughed. "Stephen Lantz, I never would've guessed." She looked at him with curiosity. "But I don't understand."

"What?"

She frowned a little. "Why is it a secret?"

He hesitated. "First of all, do you think there's anything wrong with it?"

She considered his question before giving a strong shake of her head. "Not at all. In fact"—she smiled—"I'm impressed."

The pitch of his voice lifted, conveying both relief and approval. "You are?"

"Jah! It's just funny. I never would have expected you—such a big, strong guy—to be a bird-watcher." Feeling a bit awkward, she shrugged. "I don't know. . .the two just don't seem to go together."

Obviously pleased with her assessment of him, his face lit up in a satisfied smile.

She hesitated as she considered her newfound secret and the man who had insisted that she keep it to herself. "But why don't you want anyone to know?"

When he didn't reply, she glanced up at him. "You're blushing!"

He ran his free hand over his face. "Oh boy. You're finding out a lot about me real fast."

She paused a moment before her tone hinted seriousness. "Don't worry, Stephen. I find your appreciation for nature impressive."

"You do?"

"Uh-huh."

They stopped as both of their homes came into immediate view. Serenity pulled in a deep breath and released it while she hugged her hips with her hands. "This is my favorite spot."

He appeared to take in the beautiful, full oaks that towered over them. The sun hitting the leaves made the foliage take on a heavenly appearance. Serenity lowered the pitch of her voice so it was barely more than a whisper. "Look, Stephen!" She pointed. "There's a goldfinch!"

A surprised expression floated across Stephen's face as he followed the direction of her finger. "You're really into this, aren't you?"

She tried to keep her excitement hushed so that the bird wouldn't fly off. "I guess, in a way, I'm a bird-watcher too. Without binoculars."

He looked at her as if awaiting an explanation.

"I always look for it. It's beautiful, Stephen. The yellow coloring is so rich."

Stephen pulled his binoculars to his face and appeared to focus his lenses. For several moments, they watched the tiny bird in silence. When it began to sing, Serenity whispered, "Have you ever heard anything so sweet?"

His arms brushed hers as he handed her the lenses. Then he came around behind her to help position them over her eyes. "Here. This is how you focus. It takes a little practice."

With great care, she used her right finger to focus the lens until her view of the goldfinch was crystal clear. She gasped while taking in the colorful bird. "This is amazing," she said under her breath. "I've never in my life seen such rich colors."

He agreed. "And this is a female bird we're looking at—did you know that?"

She held very still. "How can you tell?"

"Because the male has a black dot on its head. Without that marking, it's hard to tell the female from the male."

Serenity couldn't stop watching the bird. When it finally flew away, she removed the binoculars with great hesitation and returned them to Stephen. "Thank you for that, Stephen." Her words came out in what was barely more than a whisper. "That was my day's inspiration."

He looked at her as if waiting for her to continue. "Is that what you're doing out here? Inspiration?"

They continued to walk in the clearing. She nodded. "You could say that."

"Wait a minute. I told you my secret. Now you owe me one of yours."

She laughed. "I do have a secret. I mean, it's just something I keep to myself."

"Want to share it?" He waved a hand. "It's none of my business. But if you change your mind. . ." He winked. "I'm a gut listener."

She hesitated while contemplating what to say. She'd never discussed her secret with anyone, but for some reason she felt comfortable sharing it with Stephen. Instinctively she knew that whatever she told him would be confidential.

They stopped, and he refocused his binoculars. When he returned them to his chest, he spoke in a tone that was half-reassuring and half-apologetic. "Serenity, you don't have to share anything you don't want to with me. I'm sorry if I put you on the spot."

She smiled up at him. "Apology accepted." When their gazes met in mutual understanding, his expression was so sincere, she knew it was time to reveal her secret. "It's okay, Stephen. You can be my confidant."

His face broke into a smile. For some reason, she was glad that her sudden and unexpected admission pleased him. She liked him. From the moment they'd met at Margaret's house, Serenity had sensed an unusual bond with him. She wasn't sure why. Perhaps it was the way his eyes seemed to talk to her. Or maybe it was the encouraging tone of his voice. Whatever the case, she was sure she'd found someone she could trust.

She lifted her palms in a helpless expression. "I don't want to bore you."

He held a branch for her as they moved back to another trail. "I doubt anything you could say would bore me." He cleared his throat. "Besides, no one knows about my bird-watching except for you." He winked.

She nodded. "I walk for my health. When I was young, I was quite sick. The illness robbed me of all my energy, and local doctors didn't find anything wrong with me."

After a slight hesitation, his voice expressed sympathy. "That must have been discouraging."

She nodded eagerly. "Jah. Very. And a couple church members even said I was fabricating my sickness." She shrugged.

He frowned.

"You see, I couldn't walk to a buggy without stopping to rest. Needless to say, I didn't attend church for months. Or school."

She lifted her palms in a helpless gesture while she stopped to look up at him. "Stephen, it was awful. And I was afraid I'd never recover, despite the number of prayers coming my way."

Sympathy edged his pitch as he glanced down at her. "I understand. And I believe you. Was it just the fatigue?"

"No. I was ill for a very long time. No energy. Headaches. Sore throat. Even nonstop hiccups."

He lifted a curious brow. "Hiccups too?"

She nodded. "I had the Epstein-Barr virus."

He shook his head. "I've never heard of it."

"I guess you could compare it to mono. Anyway. . ." She picked up her pace.

"But you're okay now, right?"

"Jah. For the most part. But I have to be careful to get enough rest and eat right because during my lengthy time with the virus, it attacked my autonomic nervous system."

His eyes widened.

She laughed. "It's complicated. And it took me four years to recover from it. Lack of energy was my biggest setback. Eventually I went to a Chicago doctor who knew what I had and what to do about it."

She realized that she had perhaps put too much on him and decided it was best to end the story. "There's actually more to it than what I've told you. But basically, I feel that Gott has blessed me with gut health again. And for that"—she drew her palms to her chest and teared up—"I'm so grateful."

He stopped. So did she. They looked at each other before he finally broke the silence. "Wow. Just looking at you, I would never have guessed what you've been through."

Relief swept through her. "Denki, Stephen. Gott gave me library access to learn about all sorts of herbs and natural remedies. Homeopathic ways to stay healthy."

His voice conveyed both surprise and joy. "That's wonderful."

As they walked, Serenity glanced over and took in his thoughtful expression. As they approached another incline, he turned to her. As they studied each other, she absorbed the depth and compassion in his brown eyes. Under the trees, they seemed to have darkened a shade.

The longer their gazes held, the more Serenity was convinced that a strong, unexplainable bond had developed between her and Stephen Lantz. *This is so unexpected. And wonderful.*

CHAPTER TEN

Two knocks on Trini's door startled her. She was still thinking of Abby's failed attempt to win Gabriel at last week's church potluck as she turned off the water, dried her hands on the nearby white towel, and glanced up at the wall clock. It was six, an unusual time for a visitor on a Saturday morning. When she answered, she smiled at Jacob.

"Gut morning," he said, lifting an amused brow.

"Morning, Jacob." A long silence ensued while they looked at each other. The warm June breeze floated in through the open door. She offered a little shrug. "Jacob? Is everything okay?"

He chuckled. "Jah. Everything's gut for two reasons."

She waited for him to go on.

"Number one, it's Saturday, so I thought we could spend some time together."

She smiled. "Sure. It just so happens that someone's filling in for me today while I get things in order at home. What's the second reason?"

He paused. "I have a little surprise for you." He lowered his voice and stepped toward her. "Okay, Trini. I'm going to show you what it is, but on one condition."

"There's a condition?"

He nodded. "Close your eyes."

She agreed. "Okay."

To her surprise, he took her right arm and put his free hand gently against the small of her back. "Don't worry. I won't let you fall."

Trini's heart did a wild somersault as he guided her. She swallowed. She was sure that he must be able to hear the nervous, fast speed of her beating heart.

"We're at your steps. I'll help you down—just trust me." After a slight pause, he added in a reassuring tone, "Have I ever let you down?"

She couldn't stop a grin from forming. "Never."

Satisfaction edged his voice. "That's what I like to hear."

He steadily led her down the two steps just outside the side porch.

Curiosity made her pull in a breath. "How long do I have to keep my eyes closed?"

"Just a few more seconds." Their bodies touched. She knew that she was inappropriately close to a single Amish man, a man she wasn't even courting. And she acknowledged her obvious physical attraction to Jacob.

In her church, it had been instilled in her from an early age that a person needed to focus on another person's heart. That attraction to the outer beauty was wrong and could lead people down the wrong path, a road of sin that ultimately could never ever result in anything lasting and godly.

But all in all, the chemistry between her and Jacob conveyed something that could only be construed as warm and kind. And loving. She bit her tongue.

He stopped her, but surprisingly, his hand on her back remained. And his right hand around hers seemed quite comfortable.

She impatiently tapped the toe of her black shoe. "Can I open my eyes now?"

"Go ahead."

As she did so, he motioned to healthy-looking gerbera daisies in small planters next to her struggling plants. The moment she glimpsed the beautiful flowers, her half smile turned into a full-grown grin. "Jacob Lantz, you are truly special."

His eyes lit up. She didn't think she imagined that his breathing picked up as well. She looked into his eyes and nodded. "You rescued me when I fell. Now you're salvaging my plants. What would I do without you?"

He beamed. "If you'll allow me, I'll plant them for you."

She nodded. "Of course. But only on one condition."

He lifted a curious brow.

"That you eat breakfast with me." She lowered the pitch of her voice to a more confidential tone, even though no one else was around. "I have fresh coffee and homemade doughnuts, and I'm just icing the last batch."

"Then that's a definite yes!"

She motioned him inside.

"Do you mind if I wash up first?"

She led him to the hall bathroom. As he turned the spigot, she spoke while stepping back to the kitchen. "I'll put them on the table while you clean up."

After he closed the door, she could hear the running water. In the kitchen, her heart warmed. Jacob was definitely gut for her. And she truly liked him. *I more than like him. And that's exactly why I need to make sure he knows our relationship is strictly friendship. Don't forget that.*

During the past few weeks, she might have unintentionally indicated to him that there was more between them than friendship. And in her heart, she knew there was. But she had to nix any ideas on his part that there could be a man-to-woman relationship. *How do I do that when my heart pumps a million times a minute when he looks at me?*

He joined her at the table, where they sat down opposite each other. He sipped from the porcelain cup and nodded in satisfaction. "Just what I needed."

"I hope you like the doughnuts."

He took a bite and smiled. "You're full of surprises, Trini. Little did I know when we pushed each other on my aunt's swing years ago that you'd grow up to be such a gut cook."

Her cheeks warmed. "Now you're making me blush."

He looked down. When he finally looked up, his voice was barely more than a whisper. "I like it when you blush."

"You do?"

He nodded. "Please take this as a compliment. You're a very independent woman. But when you blush, it makes me feel like. . ." He stopped.

She set down her mug and leaned forward. "Like what?"

He waved a dismissive hand and changed the subject.

As they continued conversing about gerbera daisies, the bean crops, and the neighbors who had planted Margaret's field, his discontinued sentence etched itself into her mind. *I wonder what he was thinking and why he suddenly decided to change the subject.*

After breakfast, they continued outside, where he dug up the sorry-looking daisies. She held out a cardboard box. "Here. Put them in here, and I'll take them."

He grinned. "Out to the trash they go."

She hesitated and smiled a little. "I'll try to revive them first."

When he glanced at her, she added, "I think Gott would want us to offer them a second chance—don't you?" She looked at the box of daisies and added, "Even though they look pretty sorry!"

The two shared a laugh.

As he planted the new flowers, she helped to cover the roots with the fresh topsoil he'd brought.

"Do you have a pitcher? A good soak should give them the boost they need."

She stepped to the porch, retrieved her blue plastic pitcher, and proceeded to the kitchen sink to fill it with water. Once outside, she handed him the full pitcher and offered a small smile. "I'll let you finish the job. I sense that you might just offer them that special touch they need to thrive."

Suddenly, Trini grimaced.

Jacob stopped what he was doing and gave her his attention. "What's wrong?"

Trini tried not to appear unappreciative of his kind efforts. She gestured with her hands as she knelt next to him. Touching a bright green leaf, she looked down as she spoke. "Now that these beautiful, healthy daisies are in the ground, what's to say they won't also become a grazing ground for rabbits?"

He stood and looked down at her. All the while, she waited for his admission that these flowers would end up resembling the old batch.

He winked at her and held up a hand for her to be patient. "Have faith, my Trini. I've got that problem covered."

While he turned and made his way to his buggy, she considered what he'd just said and, especially, how he'd said it. *"My Trini."* Her pulse did a little dance while she absorbed what his words might indicate. The bright sun kissed her face. She closed her eyes a moment to enjoy everything about the morning.

To her, his words implied that she was his. There was no other interpretation. She deliberated their significance and her honest reaction to them.

She breathed in a deep sigh and slowly expelled it. At the same time, she was an odd combination of jubilant and sad. Jubilant because it meant the world to her that he thought of her as "his." In her heart of hearts, she'd never met a man as kind as Jacob. Except for her daed.

The more time I spend with him, the more difficult it will be to leave him. I have to let him know that the most the future can hold for us is a strong friendship. That reality prompted a deep sigh of regret. Suddenly she felt out of energy, and her countenance fell.

When he returned, he held up his hand to display a small roll of metal fencing. He stopped in front of her, knelt, and looked at her face-to-face. "Hey, what's wrong?"

Embarrassed and ashamed that she seemed unappreciative of his efforts, she wasn't sure what to say. In fact, no appropriate words came to her. She wanted to tell him the truth. To talk to him about her plan. She had to. Yet she couldn't. And she couldn't lead him to believe that she wasn't interested in him as a man. First of all, that just wasn't true. Second, she'd hurt his feelings.

"Trini?" As she stared into his beautiful blue hues, she imagined what the Caribbean must look like. She'd seen pictures. His shade must match the color of blankets that God gave to babies in heaven. There was no word strong enough to describe it. She teared up.

She didn't even look toward the pasture when she heard Honey giving a long, drawn-out neigh.

He softened his voice. Their faces were so close, his breath fanned her eyelashes.

"Trini? Say something."

She tried for words. None came. With gentleness, he took her by her good arm. His gentle touch reassured her. The concerned expression on his face touched her soul.

"Does your arm hurt?"

She shook her head. "A little. Not bad."

He walked her to the wooden bench that overlooked her garden and dusted the seat with his hand before helping her to sit down.

He turned toward her so that their knees touched. She so appreciated Jacob and everything about him. He pulled a handkerchief from his pocket and handed it to her. "Here. Dab your eyes."

She did as she was told.

Then she forced a smile as an oak leaf floated gracefully down from a tall tree and landed on his thigh. He gently took the greenery in his hand before dropping it to the ground.

"Jacob, I owe you an apology." She cleared her throat before speaking from her heart. "Right now, I'm feeling a bit stressed."

He lifted a concerned brow for her to continue.

Her words came out in an unsteady rush. "I know anxiety is wrong. Because when we stress about things, that means our faith in Gott isn't strong enough. We should always know He cares for us. My faith should be stronger."

After a short pause, she lowered her voice. "A church speaker once said that, and it always stuck."

His compassionate, understanding smile deepened. "My Trini. That's why I brought the bright-colored flowers. You've been through a lot. And you want to know something?"

She nodded.

"You can always count on me. I'll never leave your side."

The statement that she was sure had been meant to console her made her pulse jump in immediate alert. She'd made their situation worse by giving away her feelings. She had to set things straight. And this was the time.

She took in the straight rows in her garden before turning to him. "Jacob, you know I appreciate all you've done for me."

He drew in a breath. "You deserve the best, Trini."

And little does he know that my life will never be normal again. And I anticipate things will get worse when I announce my departure. Oh, what am I doing? Be independent. Strong. Don't worry. Everything that needs to be done is on my list. Now, all I have to do is carry out those things. Don't think too much.

Suddenly her spirits began to lift. *Make this be okay. Jacob is very understanding. If I'm honest, we will get through this.*

She tried for the right words. "Jacob, I apologize."

"There's nothing to apologize for, Trini. Actually, you know what?"

"What?"

His cheeks pinked as he spoke in a soft tone. "Whenever you need kind words or anything, I love being your support."

Her heart fluttered. "You do?"

He nodded and paused to tuck a stray hair back underneath her kapp. His touch was so comforting, she wondered what it would be like to just stay here and let Jacob take care of her.

His voice pulled her from her thoughts. "It's just something in my DNA, I guess, that makes me want to protect you. You know what I learned from helping Mamm?"

"What?"

"That taking care of someone you love benefits the caregiver too. Doing chores is an important part of Amish life. I mean"—he lifted a hand and dropped it to his thigh—"as we both know, there's a lot to do when you're part of the Plain faith. Most things need to be done by hand. But as I tried to get my mother through the hard years after Daed left, I began to see that there was something much more important than getting things done on the farm and even making enough money to eat and pay bills."

She looked at him, not trying to hide her surprise. "Really?"

"Actually, I didn't come up with it on my own." His voice choked with emotion. "Mamm told me."

"What did she say?"

"When she was tucking me in one night, she thanked me for being me. Told me that the things I did for her nourished her soul."

Trini narrowed her brows while she contemplated Jacob's honest admission. She couldn't fathom what it meant or how on earth a boy could *nourish* someone's soul. "That's a very sweet thing for her to say." After Trini adjusted her body into a more comfortable position, she realized that her own mamm had never paid her such a compliment. Any compliment.

He chuckled. "What? You don't believe me?"

She pressed her palms against the bench to sit up straighter and better view his sweet expression. "Oh, I'm sorry. No, it's not that at all. Of course I believe you."

He turned, lifted his legs to the bench, and bent them at the knees so that they folded underneath his body.

The bright sun warmed her face. She would love to free herself of her kapp and let her hair fall carelessly over her shoulders. She would love to wear blue jeans and tennis shoes, as she had during rumspringa.

They looked at each other. As they did so, he laughed. Trini wasn't sure what was so funny, but realizing her heart felt so light and playful, as if she were a child, she laughed too.

"Do you remember when we laughed like this at Aunt Margaret's house?"

She laughed again. "Jah. Only we were on the ground. It was at the base of the oak tree by the swing." As she recalled that sweet day, a sudden seriousness overcame her, and she lowered her pitch. "How could I forget? That was one of the best days of my life."

His grin became a bit more serious, and his tone more intense. "Do you remember what we did?"

She nodded and drifted back in time to that brief, magical part of her childhood she'd spent with the boy who was now the man opposite her. And the expression on his face requested her to answer his question.

"We played tic-tac-toe with sticks in the dirt." She paused and pressed her lips together before talking in a tone that was part amusement, part serious. "And we had a deal that the loser would make the winner lunch."

"And you made me a peanut butter and jelly sandwich. And the most delicious lemonade I've ever tasted." He hesitated before narrowing his brows and lowering his voice. "Want to play again?"

She forgot about her lists. All concerns that her family take her seriously evaporated. Before she knew it, she and Jacob were opposite each other, lying on the ground, sticks in hand.

"Want to toss a coin to see who goes first?" he asked.

"Jah."

He pulled a quarter from his pocket. "Just so happens I have some loose change. Okay. Heads or tails?"

"Tails!"

He tossed the quarter into the air, and it landed on the dirt in front of them. "Tails, it is."

She began to draw an *X*, but he stopped her. "One more thing."

She stopped.

"Let's play the best out of five?"

"Agreed."

After they'd both nodded, she made the first *X*.

Trini felt like a young girl as they started their fifth game. And she was fully aware that she was behaving like one too. But she quickly reasoned to herself that this was a gut thing for her mental health. And fun.

"I won," she declared gleefully as she sat up and then stood. She paused a moment to consider the consequences. "You don't really want to make lunch, do you?" Before he could speak, she went on in a soft voice. "You don't have to."

He stood. At the same time, they brushed their hands together to rid the dirt. He motioned her toward the house. "No worries." He winked. "I might surprise you."

She laughed. "But you don't know what's in my kitchen."

"You're taking this much too seriously," he responded with another wink. "Just trust me."

For several moments, they gazed at each other. As she took in the gentle blueness of his eyes, something tugged at her heartstrings. She shivered.

His expression turned to concern. "Are you okay?"

She pretended she was and offered a firm nod. But in reality she wasn't. *I'm too fond of him.*

Inside the house, she opened some cabinets and her generously stocked refrigerator to show him her inventory. Afterward, he led her to the table and pointed to a chair.

"Now, Ms. Sutter, all you have to do is sit back and relax." He winked.

Finally, she offered a nod of encouragement. "If you insist."

He looked down at her and conveyed an unreadable expression. Again, an excited shiver trickled up her spine.

"While you find your way around in my kitchen, I'll jot down some things to order for my shop."

"Deal."

As Trini wrote on her notepad, her thoughts were focused on Jacob and the fun they'd just shared. He was right about one thing: she hadn't planned their game or the conversations they'd shared. Yet their time together had definitely been good for her soul. First of all, she'd needed the laughter he'd sparked. Trini, by nature, wasn't a worrier, but the stress of getting things in order to leave her Amish life had been a heavy weight on her shoulders. And since she needed to be extra careful not to aggravate her broken arm, not working at full capacity had contributed to her duress.

Second, she had more energy than she'd had in a long time. She yearned to live again and feel gut about herself. Now that she'd laughed again, she realized that Mamm's seemingly constant disapproval, as well as her sisters', had tugged at her naturally happy spirit.

They hadn't intended to hurt her, of course, yet that was exactly what had happened. Trini was fully aware of her beloved mother's struggles. Raising so many children couldn't have been easy. And losing her true love had taken its toll on her.

The sound of something hitting the floor made her jump up out of her seat. She glimpsed Jacob bending over. He looked up. "Sorry! But you'll forgive me, jah?"

A laugh automatically escaped her throat. She reclaimed her chair. "Of course. But I may have underestimated your culinary talents. Something smells pretty gut."

She glanced his way, and he darted her a reassuring grin. "Just be patient. And trust me."

Trini grinned. She was fully aware that patience wasn't one of her strong character traits. But she wanted to make sure he knew that she rooted for his culinary success. She was extra careful to make Jacob feel gut about himself because obviously he took great care to make her happy.

"Take your time, Jacob."

She heard a sizzling sound and guessed what he might be making. She licked her lips, acknowledging she was very hungry. All the while, uncertainty began to stir within her. While she was with Jacob, everything might seem easy. But because of her well-laid plans for her future, her life was far from simple.

She considered her feelings for Jacob and bit her bottom lip. She'd never been in love before, but as she glanced at him working to one side of her, she was sure that she was falling in love with him. And what a great catch he was!

She wasn't absolutely sure of his feelings for her. But could it be that his attentions were simply because of feelings of guilt at having caused her fall? He'd admitted he was responsible and had assured her that he'd help her to recover.

She pressed her lips together thoughtfully and further contemplated Jacob's motive behind spending time with her. *He's genuinely kind and giving. So if he'd caused Serenity or Abby to fall, would they have been the beneficiaries of this good man's assistance?*

She decided they would. *But something inside me tells me that Jacob still feels about me the same way he did years ago. I comforted him at the lowest point in his life, and he never forgot it.*

To Trini's surprise, the mere thought of Serenity or Abby benefiting from Jacob's attention sparked a jealous sensation inside her chest. She closed her eyes a moment. *Please forgive me, Gott.* She put down her pen and folded her arms over her chest.

Then she recalled how he'd referred to her as "my Trini." *It's not my imagination that Jacob Lantz is seriously interested in me. And if I joined the Amish church, there would be no better man for me. Because I genuinely care for him.*

She breathed in a deep breath and released it. *What is the worst that could happen to Jacob if I left?* She drummed her fingers against the table and frowned. Finally, she rested her right hand in her lap before releasing the Velcro straps on her removable cast and pulling them a bit tighter so that the fit was more secure.

If Jacob truly plans to make me Mrs. Lantz, my departure will crush him. Especially if it takes him by surprise. She acknowledged the great need to tell him before anyone else knew.

His low voice startled her from her reverie. "Close your eyes."

She did as told. "Okay."

She could hear a plate meet the table. "You can open them now."

She did. And she nodded in approval at the grilled cheese. She noticed that his hands slightly shook.

"Jacob, this looks delicious!"

"Really?"

"Jah. Not only that, but the bread is just a tad browned with lots of butter." She smiled up at him. "Perfect! How did you know that's how I like it?"

He chuckled while stepping back into the kitchen to retrieve his own sandwich. When he sat down opposite her, he snapped his fingers and quickly jumped out of his seat, moving to the kitchen a second time. "I forgot our lemonades."

When he returned and appeared to make himself comfortable

across from her, she lowered her eyes and spoke in soft appreciation. "Thank you, Jacob. You're so very kind."

He smiled at her. "Let's bless our food."

They bowed their heads for silent prayer and started their meal. She proceeded to cut her sandwich in half. "This is an unexpected treat."

He picked up part of his sandwich, tasted it, and nodded in satisfaction. "I can taste the delicious butter." He chewed his bite and followed it with a drink of the lemonade. "It's as tasty as Aunt Margaret's."

She paused, recalling his late aunt's delicious butter. "I'm afraid I can't take credit for the butter. Abby makes it." When he looked at her, she confirmed, "Of Abby's Alterations."

"Of course. The nice lady who gave us Aunt Margaret's last quilt." He stopped and pressed his lips together as if recalling something. "Which reminds me. . . I have a hem in my trousers that needs to be fixed. I'll stop by her shop."

"She'll be happy to help." After a slight pause, Trini went on to put in a good word for Abby. "She's one of my best friends." After a slight pause, she went on. "And Serenity." She swallowed a bite and followed it with a drink. The ice cubes clinked against the glass as she returned it to the table.

"Do you know what I'm going to do to repay you for this delicious, unexpected lunch?"

He waved a hand as if to dismiss her idea. "That's not necessary."

She leaned forward a bit to ensure that he could see her sincere expression. "Oh, I insist. I'll make you a wet-bottom shoofly pie. Just for you."

His eyes lit up.

"It's a recipe from Abby." A short silence ensued before Trini added, "Out of my besties and I, Abby was closest to your aunt."

He looked at her to go on.

As Trini wiped her hands with the white napkin that Jacob had placed next to her plate, she realized that not having been raised here, Jacob wasn't privy to a lot of the local relationships. And because Trini thought so much of Abby, she wanted to ensure that Jacob knew how much her friend had meant to his late aunt and how close they'd been.

A thoughtful expression filled his eyes, and he leaned forward. "You've piqued my interest. Please tell me more about your alterations friend."

Trini sat back in her chair a moment and tried to think of the moment when Margaret had taken Abby under her wing. "Margaret thought of Abby as a daughter."

The statement seemed to please him. He smiled a little. "Why Abby? I mean, I know my aunt was close to you."

"It's true. I loved your aunt very much. And she loved me." She paused before softening her voice. "But looking back, Abby needed her. She needed someone to listen to her ideas and love her unconditionally."

Jacob wiped his mouth with his napkin. "Doesn't Abby have parents? A family?"

Trini nodded. "She does. Parents, anyway. She's an only child, you see."

He offered a slow nod of understanding. It appeared as though he continued to consider the relationship.

"Anyway, and this is just my opinion. . ."

His eyes twinkled with amusement. "Your opinion means a lot to me. Go on."

"I don't say this with malice—only from my observation. Abby's parents are good church people. They are very involved in helping our community. In fact, her mamm volunteers a lot of her time to help at our nursing home here in town."

After Trini had said that, she added, "A number of Amish stay there after surgeries. The workers are trusted and friendly, and going through rehab"—she gave a light shrug of her shoulders—"you can imagine how much easier it would be than taking the horse and buggy to therapy every day. That is, if in-home therapy isn't available."

He nodded in understanding. "That makes sense. But what does that have to do with my aunt taking your friend under her wing?"

Trini shifted in her seat for a more comfortable position. "Abby's mamm?" She looked down at her half-finished sandwich before looking back at Jacob. She tried for the right words. "You know how some people are really gut with kids?"

He nodded.

"At the same time, some tend to be better with older people?"

"Are you saying that Abby's mother isn't good with kinder?"

Trini considered the question. The last thing she wanted was to give Jacob a bad impression of Abby's folks, so she tried especially hard for the right words.

She shrugged. "Not exactly." While she hesitated, a bright beam of sunlight came in through the window and lightened the brown stain on the table a notch. The even ticking of the wall clock was the only noise while Trini finished her sandwich and wiped her lips with her napkin.

When she looked at Jacob, she glimpsed keen interest in his expression. And she knew he depended on her to help catch him up to speed with the church members he was trying to get to know.

She took a sip. "I guess the point I'm trying to make is that Abby—well, she didn't really have a sounding board in her mother."

The tone of Jacob's voice reflected understanding when he responded. "I understand."

"You do?"

He nodded with a grin. "It's funny. When people have children, they quickly learn that they're not really trained to be parents. I mean, I think that if you have your kids' best interests at heart, you can't go wrong. But from what I've seen over the years, parents learn to parent at the same time their children learn from them."

She considered his take on parenting.

"Jacob, that's a very sweet, astute thing to say."

He smiled a little. "I don't know if it's astute, but that's how I feel. And when I have kids of my own, I'm sure I'll make bloopers along the way, and hopefully my offspring will forgive me and know that I'm not perfect. But I will do my best to raise them, encourage them, and most of all, make sure they know they're loved."

His take on parenting nearly stole her breath. Instinctively, she was sure that there would be no better daed than the man opposite her. Another unexpected emotion pulled at her heartstrings. Because the more she got to know him, the more she understood that, in life, everything wasn't black and white.

Recalling their unfinished topic, she backed up. "I think, as far as Abby's parents and Margaret, they all played a role in the wonderful woman she eventually became. But your aunt?"

He looked at her to continue and caught sight of a crossword puzzle book on the table, open to a puzzle that she'd started. He pulled it toward him.

"There was something extraordinarily special about her, and without a doubt, she was truly a blessed gift to us three girls—but most especially, Abby." Trini lowered her voice and attempted to hide the strong emotions that were so fresh inside her from the relatively recent loss of her neighbor.

All the while, Jacob appeared to take in the puzzle. Trini's voice cracked. "Margaret always seemed to understand Abby." She shook her head, and the tone of her voice lightened. "It's amazing how someone without children could truly see things through their eyes. And now that I look back at her relationship with Abby, Serenity, and me. . ." Trini offered a shrug as Jacob filled in a word in the crossword puzzle. "I firmly believe that she considered Abigail the daughter she'd never had."

Several seconds of silence passed while he seemed to absorb her last statement. Finally, he responded, his eyes meeting hers. "You don't know what that means to me to hear you say such sweet things about my aunt."

He held up the puzzle. "Inspiring."

She lifted a surprised brow.

"How did you know that?"

He winked and returned the book to its original place on the table. "You gave me that one."

She tried to understand.

"It's you, Trini. You're inspiring."

While she took in his obvious compliment, he scooted his chair back from the table and stretched his legs. "But there must have been something more that bonded them. I mean, for them to have had such a special relationship."

Trini nodded. "It was sewing. Abby loved to sew, and Margaret did too. They also loved to knit and crochet."

"I'll never forget my aunt knitting every night when she stayed with us."

"In that way, they're very much alike. Abigail has a natural talent for being able to sew that is nothing less than amazing. And as far as clothes for the Englisch?" Enthusiasm crept into Trini's voice while she told Jacob of numerous dresses she'd made for young girls. "I think sewing kids' clothes is Abby's strongest talent."

His expression softened. So did the pitch of his voice. "Maybe she dreams of sewing for her own children."

Trini didn't think it was in Abby's best interest to tell Jacob that she had already made bibs for the ten babies she hoped to bear. Or that she had planned her wedding to Jacob's oldest brother long before the brothers had moved to Arthur.

She loved Abby the way she was, and the last thing she intended was to make it sound as though Abigail was desperate to marry and bear children. In her heart, Trini hoped that Gabriel would make that dream come true.

But she thought the best way for Abby's dreams to materialize was to have them transpire from Abigail's efforts, with no interference from anyone.

Trini went on. "Jacob, did you know that your aunt helped launch Abby's Alterations?"

"No kidding!"

Trini nodded. "It's true. And if I recall correctly, Margaret even thought up the name. She made sure Abby succeeded. After the store opened, of course, Abby needed her business to earn a profit. And Margaret's keen instincts told her that word of mouth and referrals were needed to get things going."

Jacob agreed. "That's true. There's a lot more to making a great business than merely selling a product."

"To Abby's benefit, few within the neighboring towns didn't know your aunt."

His eyes sparkled. He sat up a little straighter and planted his palms on his thighs. "She had her hand in a lot of projects, didn't she? When she came to see us in Pennsylvania, most of her focus was on us boys and ensuring that we were nurtured with love. But every once in a while, she'd mention some project she was working on. Most everything she did was church related, of course."

"Not many in central Illinois haven't heard of Abby's Alterations. And Abby's busy, of course. But she works long hours to return projects in a timely manner. She knows that even though she's good at what she does, people don't like to wait. And there's plenty of competition that would be very happy to take some of her thriving business."

That admission sparked a grin on Jacob's face. "That doesn't surprise me at all. I mean. . ." He paused to reach for her plate, which he stacked on his, and stood.

Looking down at her, he spoke in a tone that conveyed love and gratitude. "Is there anyone within a hundred miles of here who didn't know Margaret Lantz?"

He chuckled. Trini laughed.

As she did so, an unfamiliar sensation swept through her that warmed her heart. Although she couldn't pinpoint the particular emotion, this new feeling was so sweet and so reassuring, Trini never wanted it to go away.

She wasn't able to think of what it might be, but she surmised that it was a mishmash of her birthday, Christmas, and how she'd felt when her mamm had once complimented her on a quilt.

As Jacob stepped away from the table, Trini closed her eyes, trying to capture and contain everything she was experiencing. A love and zest to keep Jacob here with her forever welled inside her. It was a rush of excitement filled with comfort, compassion, and love.

She opened her eyes, recognizing how open and honest Jacob was. She even sensed a vulnerability on his part that yanked at her heartstrings. After he left, she needed to absorb their conversation and make sense of her reaction.

But one thing was becoming clearer to her the more she chatted with him and got to know him. She needed to tell Jacob that she was going to leave the faith. And the town. And the state. And him.

She heard light steps from his boots on the wood floor as he headed to the sink. She considered him further. *He can think outside the box. He's understanding. And he'll understand when I explain my plan to him. There's no doubt in my mind. Tell him. Now.*

She slid back her chair and joined him in the kitchen. For a brief moment, they looked at each other in mutual understanding. As she peered into his deep blue eyes, she noticed that his flecks were the most unusual gray she'd ever glimpsed.

The moment was broken when he retrieved a small scrubber from next to the spigot and prepared to wash the dishes. Trini pulled the Velcro from her cast and laid aside the plastic. Drying dishes would be more comfortable without it.

Jacob filled the sink with water and a squirt of dish soap and began moving the scrubber over the top plate. "I think I have an idea what Abby's like. But how about Serenity? Is she like you?"

The question was asked with such innocence, Trini couldn't stop a big grin from forming. "No. In fact, it's funny that the three of us are best friends."

"Why?"

She shrugged. "Because we're all so different. And I say that with love for both of them. Abby's quite headstrong. In a good way," Trini added. "I'm the list maker and the most focused of the three. And Serenity?" Trini thought a moment. "I would say that she was named appropriately. Serenity reminds me of the word *serene*. And that's exactly what she is. She's calm. Quiet. People from miles around pay her to do wedding and funeral flowers."

"She must be talented."

"She is. But there's something about Serenity that makes her unique. She's very focused on her health. You'll never find Serenity drinking caffeine. Every week when we meet in the back of my store, she always brings her own bottled water and herbal teas. Sometimes she even brings fruit to snack on."

As Jacob ran the water over the dish, he glanced at Trini. Then he handed it to her. "She sounds like an interesting person."

Trini dried it and set it on a towel. "She is."

Trini paused to decide how to explain. "She's really into herbs and what plants can do for her health."

Tell him. Now. There won't be a better time.

As they worked together, the sun floated in through the window above the sink. Trini enjoyed their light conversation. Most especially, though, she liked Jacob. Still, she needed to tell him her plans. *The longer I wait, the harder it will be. I should do it now. What will he say?*

I don't think he'll be angry with me. Of course he won't. He doesn't have a temper. Despite her logic, she still struggled for the right words.

After the last dish, they dried their hands. Trini turned to him. She lifted her chin a notch. "There's something I need to tell you."

He looked at her with affection and surprise. "Let's take a walk. Because first, there's something I need to ask you."

His statement made her pulse skip a beat. Dutifully, she stepped out to the porch with him, and they continued onto the dirt path that led to the barn. As they walked past the beautiful new daisies, he stopped and, with a gentle motion of his hand, tenderly pulled her to him.

As she took in his serious demeanor, she parted her lips, and her chest began to rise and fall more quickly.

"Trini, my feelings for you aren't a secret."

She tried to order her heart to slow down.

The color of his cheeks took on a light shade of pink. She glimpsed his hands, which he made into a fist in front of him. She could see his fingers shake.

An alarm went off inside her. At the same time, he proceeded to tell her how glad he was to be back in Arthur. And most especially, to be her neighbor.

A long silence ensued while she wondered what else he'd say.

"Trini, do you remember the card I made you when I was five?"

The question sparked a nervous laugh on her part. His tone and the way his voice shook told her that this conversation was getting serious. *No!*

"How could I forget it?" The recollection of his sweet gesture filled her heart with deep appreciation and respect for him. She swallowed an emotional knot before continuing. "You drew me a heart."

He beamed, obviously happy she remembered.

She cleared another emotional knot from her throat. A bead of sweat trickled down her chest.

He swallowed. "Underneath were four words: 'Will you marry me?'"

Trini could guess what was coming. And she could do nothing to stop it.

"I still love you, Trini." His voice quavered. "When I saw you on the ladder, I knew that what I felt for you nearly two decades ago was as real today as it was when we were kids."

She tried for the right words to stop him, but before she could open her mouth, he went on. His expression was so genuine, so very sincere and sweet, she became lost in his eyes. Her own eyes teared up, and she blinked to clear them.

"I still love you, Trini. Only it's a mature love." He softened the pitch of his voice. "I'm going to ask you again. Only this time, it's for real. Such a long time away from you has confirmed what I really knew a long time ago."

He got down on one knee. "Will you marry me, Trini?"

CHAPTER ELEVEN

Jacob didn't have an answer. Later that day, inside Margaret's barn, he propped the large, heavy doors open in order to allow what was left of the day's sunlight to brighten the otherwise dark structure.

His mind was on the afternoon. And Trini. The gerbera daisies. The tic-tac-toe game. The lunch. The enlightening conversation. But thanks to the appearance of her family, his proposal had been interrupted and he still didn't have a response.

Inside the large barn, he ascended the rough wooden steps that led up to the hayloft. Survivor let out a loud whinny. A chicken scurried across the floor to the open door.

In the hayloft, he pushed himself up and quickly brushed his hands together to rid them of straw dust. A rat slipped into a hole in the wall. From the small window, he glimpsed Trini's backyard.

He gripped the twine on a bale of straw and lifted it. With one swift motion, he let it fall to the cement floor.

The horse responded to the sudden thump with another loud whinny before clomping its hooves. Looking down at Survivor's stall, Jacob assured the standardbred that what he was doing was for the animal's benefit. "I don't think you'd be happy without straw, would you?"

The noble animal neighed and glanced up at Jacob, who laughed.

"I suppose you want oats too." After catching a breath, Jacob continued the one-sided conversation. "I bought you fresh oats. But first things first. And that means cleaning your stall so that you have the first-rate living arrangements you deserve."

Jacob gripped a second bale of straw by its twine. After releasing his grip, he listened to the *plop* as the horse's bedding met the concrete. Again, Jacob brushed straw dust from his hands. For a few seconds, he stood and looked down.

He couldn't stop a grin while taking in the warm ambience and the special things that made his Survivor's home different from every other Amish barn he'd set eyes on.

On the far wall, opposite Survivor's stall, hung a large wreath that Margaret had made from scratch with other churchwomen. She'd used twigs and evergreen branches from her own backyard. A special warmth filled Jacob's chest as he imagined her creating the piece for her rescued horse to look at. Years ago, Survivor had overcome a serious virus. Since that miraculous day, Margaret had named him appropriately. A chuckle escaped Jacob's throat as he shook his head. He couldn't help but wonder if Survivor actually enjoyed her efforts. Whether or not he did wasn't really what mattered. The point was that his dear aunt had made the wreath with love and good intentions.

Something came to him. It was what she used to tell him. *"When you do something with love and good intentions, it's never in vain. Because when your heart gives in a spirit of love, you reap more benefits than the recipient. Doing for others is a way of nurturing your own heart and soul."*

Jacob wiped moisture from his eyes as wind chimes hanging from the ceiling moved with the gentle breeze that blew through the wide entrance. Margaret had insisted that animals needed many of the same things that humans needed in order to feed their souls. Thoughtfully, he acknowledged the sweet, special soul that earth had lost and heaven had gained. An uncomfortable knot suddenly blocked his throat, and he swallowed. He hugged his hands to his hips as he focused on the wall above the oversized barn doors where a large, framed cross-stitch of Survivor hung. It was often true that horses looked alike. This piece, however, left no doubt that it was this particular standardbred's face. The long nose was dark brown with light tan speckles, just like the animal's. And the large chocolate-brown eyes were dotted with sprinkles of green.

The picture prompted a chuckle. While he bent to carefully step down, Jacob glimpsed the large wicker basket of sugar cubes on the top shelf close to the ladder.

The sound of hooves clomp-clomping against the floor caught his attention. Jacob looked down at Survivor. "You know what your problem is? You lack patience."

Survivor repeated the aggressive clomp-clomping and threw his neck up while expelling a loud, demanding whinny. Jacob laughed and carefully made his way down the wooden ladder. Without wasting time, Survivor approached Jacob and nudged the deep pockets of his trousers.

Jacob was sure he was being ridiculous by catering to this spoiled horse, yet obediently he stepped to the shelf that housed the sugar cubes and quickly emptied several white cubes from the box into his palm.

All the while, Margaret's beloved horse clomp-clomped to a more impatient, demanding beat.

Pushing out a sigh, Jacob said, "Here you go." Without wasting time, the animal greedily sucked up the sweet treats.

Jacob made his way to the wall for a rake and a pitchfork, then put them in the old blue wheelbarrow, which he pushed toward the horse stall.

"Move over, friend, and I'll set you up with the best barn suite in the county." He raked the old bedding into a pile next to the stall's simple gate, then began loading the wheelbarrow with the dirty straw. He whistled while he worked.

As he transferred smelly piles into the wheelbarrow, he thought of Trini and what her answer would be. Instinctively, he was sure it would be a yes. Jacob took a keen interest in gauging what others felt. And the afternoon with her had sparked only positive vibes. He'd observed the happiness in her eyes while they'd played tic-tac-toe in the dirt. Her tone had conveyed joy while they'd shared memories and ideas. He smiled at the thought.

Finished with his task, he propped the rake against the fence and opened the gate. He pushed the wheelbarrow out of the stall, closed the gate until it clicked, and made his way outside to the burn pile.

Having emptied the wheelbarrow, he placed the two fresh bales of hay in the stall. Survivor, obviously excited to have his company, continued to shove his nose in the direction of Jacob's pockets.

"After my work is done. Be patient."

Jacob retrieved a pair of clippers and snipped both twines. The straw immediately separated into two piles, and Jacob began to evenly spread it throughout the stall. Then he rubbed Survivor's long nose while he assessed his work.

Afterward, he opened the gate, closed it behind him until the latch clicked, and stowed the wheelbarrow and the rake.

While he stepped to the large barn doors, an emotional sigh left his throat, and a strange, wonderful sensation welled in his chest until he thought it would burst. *I enjoy being here because my aunt loved her horse. When I'm in the barn, I can feel her presence.*

Back outside, he shoved the doors closed one by one. A hinge creaked. He carefully moved the boards that ensured that both doors were locked and tested that they were secure before he headed toward the house.

While he walked, the sun created colorful streaks in the western sky. He took a moment to absorb the beautiful hues that nearly stopped his breath.

While he took in the gorgeous colors, he glimpsed the faux owl perched on top of a clothesline post near the garden to scare the birds. The wishing well. The swing where he and Trini had once connected.

He continued to his aunt's home. As he came closer, he could just barely see Trini's side door that led into her kitchen. Right outside that entrance was where he and Trini had looked at each other with obvious affection as he'd asked her to spend the rest of her life with him this afternoon.

He closed his eyes to create a clearer vision of her creamy complexion. As he considered the woman he loved, he could almost smell the light, fresh scent of her navy dress and the peachy fragrance of her shampoo. He imagined the beautiful autumn shade of her eyes.

Remembering his nervousness when he'd proposed, he smiled a little. His heart pumped with new excitement as he imagined her soft voice responding with a definite yes.

On Monday, Trini made a decision. Most of the night, she'd been awake contemplating Jacob's question, her secret plan to soon join the Englisch world, and the need to tell Jacob about it. Initially, she hadn't intended to reveal her plan to anyone until right before she left.

But after taking in the hopeful, eager expression in Jacob's eyes and hearing the genuine feeling in his voice, she knew she had an even bigger responsibility to him than she'd originally realized.

He didn't deserve that she would soon leave their tight-knit Amish community. Their faith. The last thing on earth that Jacob deserved was being denied a wedding he seemed to want very much.

I will miss Jacob. But I've planned this move for years. I can't have Jacob and be Englisch. Jacob's dream is to marry an Amish woman and raise a large brood. He especially looks forward to his family piling into one buggy and riding to church together.

Trini's heart sank at the thought of having to break the news to him that she wouldn't be with him in the buggy. *I should have done it Saturday when I had the chance.* A lone tear slipped down her cheek, and she stopped it with her right hand.

She caught a breath, pulled her new list from her work purse, and read out loud the words she'd printed early this morning. "Tell Serenity and Abby about Jacob's proposal. Then tell them why I must say no. Lay out my plan to Serenity and Abby. After I unveil this information, ask how I should break all of this to him."

Thank goodness our weekly Quilt Room meeting was moved to this afternoon. Serenity and Abby will understand. I will unload this cumbersome information. They're my two best friends. The more difficult part will be explaining to Jacob and getting him to comprehend.

The shop clock let out a noon chime. Without wasting time, Trini began tidying the back room. *I have to tell them. Today. And tonight I will tell Jacob.*

Thirty minutes later, Trini claimed her usual chair in front of the quilt frame. Serenity and Abby were already threading their needles. *Don't rush it. My turn to talk will come soon enough. I can't appear nervous. They will be shocked. This is the most difficult thing I've ever done.*

Trini began cutting around a plastic stencil. Serenity started the group conversation. "I'm really glad we're meeting today." She glanced over at Abigail. "Abby? How are things between you and Gabriel?"

Abby shrugged.

Trini lifted a curious brow. "And what does that mean?"

A strange mixture of defeat and hope edged Abby's voice. "It's okay."

Serenity chimed in. "Be positive, Abby! As time goes on, he

will most likely be more inclined to want to talk to you and get to know you."

Abigail smiled a little. "Leave it to you to think of that."

Trini grinned. "I agree."

Serenity paused a moment before her voice took on a more serious pitch. "How about we pay the Lantz boys another visit? You know, with more delicious dishes. You know what they say about finding a way to a man's heart?"

Trini answered. "It's food."

Abby sighed. "Over and over, I've thought about what to say to him."

Trini's heartstrings pulled. She knew Abby so well. And her determination stemmed from something inside her that yearned for love.

Abby turned to Trini. "What would you do if you were in my shoes?"

The question caught her off guard and she sucked in a breath. When she noticed the curious stares from her two friends, she laid her work on her lap and thought hard about the question.

Finally, she answered. "I'm the last person on earth to advise on something like this." She looked at Abigail. "However. . .because you're one of my two best friends, and also, because I love you like a sister, I'll try to help." Trini pressed her fingers against her chin and closed her eyes for a moment.

What would I say to Gabriel Lantz if I wanted to marry him and I barely knew him? She opened her lids and knew exactly what she would do. "Abby, first of all, I'd make a list of things to converse about."

Before Abby could respond, Trini went on. "You know, things like the crops, church, and especially his late aunt. I think because the two of you were so close, that might be a way to get close to his heart."

Abby nodded.

Trini considered what she'd said and lifted her palms in the air.

"That's exactly what I would do. And of course, make sure he knows that you're the go-to person for any hemming he might need."

Abigail sat very still. When she finally responded, doubt accompanied her voice. "I thought you might come up with something clever. Something to encourage him to see more of me."

Serenity shook her head and continued her work.

Trini smiled at Abby, who appeared both disappointed and stunned. Trini's heart ached, so she tried again. "Abby, we are different personalities, so I'm not sure my approach would work for you. But my logic tells me this: The Lantz brothers come from humble roots. I doubt that Gabriel Lantz or his brothers are looking for someone clever. I think. . ."

She paused to shove a loose strand of hair off her face. "First, get to know him. At the same time, he needs to get to know you. After that, perhaps you can engage in simple conversation."

Serenity piped in. "The thing is, Abby, that you already know him because Margaret shared so much with you. But he hasn't had someone telling him about you."

Trini spoke in a sympathetic tone. "At the end of the day, Abby, Gabriel will have to like you just the way you are. And he will. But don't be in a rush."

Abby hesitated a moment as if uncertain of whether to continue the topic. "How do you get Jacob to keep seeing you?"

The unexpected question nearly stole Trini's breath. When she noticed that both sets of eyes were on her, she explained. "Remember that Jacob and I met when we were kids. But my situation right now. . . Jacob feels responsible for my broken arm."

As Trini considered her very complex situation with Jacob, what he didn't know, and what she had yet to tell him, her hands began to shake. Her scissors, stencil, and fabric fell to the floor, and she bent to pick them up. As she sat up, a lone tear slipped down her cheek. She quickly wiped it away. But all too fast, another tear slid down.

"Trini, are you okay?" Serenity's voice was filled with shock and emotion.

Abby followed with concern. "I'm sorry, my friend. I think we need to focus on you. There's more to this than meets the eye, I'm guessing?"

Trini didn't know what to do. She couldn't risk anything stopping her plan. At the same time, she couldn't hurt Jacob. *I need to share this burden. I can't handle it alone.*

"Trini?" Abby's voice pleaded with her.

"We're here for you," Serenity assured her in a soft, emotional voice.

Trini finally took a deep breath and began to speak. "I'm dealing with a very unique and sensitive situation." She folded her hands over her lap. "I don't even know where to start. But a lot is riding on my secret, and I trust you both." She hesitated. "But I need your word that you will not repeat any of what I tell you."

Serenity's usually calm voice hinted excitement. "Of course, I promise. Your secrets are always safe with me." She blew Trini a kiss.

Abby added an eager nod. "You can tell me anything. And my lips are sealed." She closed her mouth and ran her index finger over it.

Trini got up out of her chair and stepped to the main shop area to ensure that no one was there. Satisfied that her revelation wouldn't be overheard, she returned to her seat and crossed her legs at the ankles.

A bit unsure of how her friends would take what she was about to tell them, she looked at Abby and then Serenity. Her breath caught in her throat. "Okay. Here goes."

She started by talking about Jacob and his desire to take their relationship to happily ever after.

Both friends gasped and drew their palms to their chests. Abby blurted, "Trini! It's what we've dreamed of all our lives!"

Serenity chimed in. "I'm so happy for you! Why on earth did you wait to tell us?"

Trini couldn't stop an amused grin. She wagged a hand to stop their reactions. "There's more."

Serenity nodded eagerly.

Abby made an invisible circle with her hand in a fast motion. "Please don't keep us waiting. Go on!"

Trini nodded. "Okay. So thankfully, some of my sisters pulled up in their buggy the moment his words came out."

Abby's tone was breathy. "So you didn't tell him yes?"

Trini shook her head. "I appreciate both of you. And you're my closest friends. That's one of the reasons it's so difficult to tell you this."

Serenity's expression grew more serious. Abby leaned forward a bit and tapped the toe of her sturdy black shoe in an uneven beat against the wood floor. Her jaw was set.

A long, tense silence ensued while the women sat very still. Trini's knees shook. Then, determined to say her piece, she lifted her chin and squared her shoulders. "I'm leaving the Amish life."

While she listened to the simultaneous intakes of breath, a bright ray of sunshine floated gracefully in through the window and landed on Trini's ream of thread. The dark blue shade became sky blue. *There. I said it.* Trini expelled a deep sigh of relief. Her shoulders relaxed.

There was no verbal response. Only two stunned expressions. Suddenly Trini regretted sharing her secret. She silently acknowledged that she was stuck in a situation in which she saw no ending that would please everyone. *I need guidance. Hopefully my two suddenly silent friends will come up with something to help me.*

She had expected her friends to have plenty to say about her departure from the Plain faith. She had anticipated that they would waste no time explaining why she couldn't leave. After all, they were devout churchwomen. Like her, they had roots so deep and strong within their church that breaking them would be extremely difficult.

Trini glanced at Abby. Then Serenity. Both women sat very still. Their eyes expressed shock and dismay.

Serenity was the first to break the silence. "Trini, forgive me for my lack of response. I'm still absorbing what you just told us." She breathed in and expelled the air. "I. . .I just didn't expect this. I'm in shock."

With a slow motion, Abby rose from her sitting position. She walked right over to Trini and extended her arms. Trini rose to accept her embrace. Fighting tears, Trini held on tightly to her dark-haired friend. When they both dropped their arms and took a step back, Abby's voice cracked with emotion. "You're serious?"

Trini nodded.

Abby's voice cracked. "Oh my. Honey, I understand why you've kept this to yourself." She hesitated and lifted her palms in the air in a helpless gesture.

Serenity joined the twosome and flung her arms around both Trini and Abby. A strong silence of love and understanding passed between the three. Trini didn't need them to say anything right then. She felt the support she'd sought. No words could accurately describe what she was feeling.

Serenity's voice was soft and filled with emotion. "I'm here for you. And I'm not going to judge you in any way."

"Me neither," Abby echoed.

A huge sense of relief filled Trini. She thanked them. "I've been so afraid to say anything."

"When are you leaving?"

"September. But the reason I'm telling you today is because I have another pending issue. One that will be deeply affected by my actions."

Serenity looked at Trini and whispered, "We've got to be extra careful that no one gets wind of your plan, Trini."

Abby quickly agreed. "But where will you live?"

Trini's voice was barely more than a whisper as she explained that her brother was helping her and that there was a sewing shop near his house where Trini could work.

Abby and Serenity shared a glance. Serenity broke the silence. "Trini, are you sure this is what you really want?" She gestured with her hands. "I mean, look at this beautiful store. And your family loves you. Do they know?"

Trini shook her head.

Abby continued. "That's why they're overly demonstrative in helping you." Her tone was soft. "I'd give anything to have my parents that interested in me."

Trini considered Abby's comment and pressed her lips together in a straight line. Abby had a tendency to feel left out, which was most likely why she could come across as a bit pushy. Still, Trini needed to be heard for who she was. She yearned to know that she could support herself and make her own decisions without family interference.

In their small circle, Abby's voice hinted of uncertainty and dread. "But you said there's more?"

Before Trini responded, Serenity cut in. "What about Jacob?"

Trini decided to continue. As long as they kept their voices down, even if someone walked into her shop, they wouldn't overhear her next bombshell. It felt like it had taken the entire afternoon to explain the first half of her dilemma. *Now I have to tell the rest.*

Trini took a deep breath. "Here's part two of my problem. As I said, Jacob asked me to marry him. Thankfully, there was an interruption. But I can't marry Jacob. And I've got to tell him why."

Abby claimed an empty oak chair near Trini's, leaned back, and fanned her face with one of the stencils. "Whoa!" She held up a hand to stop Trini. "This is a much deeper conversation than I expected."

Serenity faced Trini, and her eyes doubled in size as her voice wavered. "Trini, you mean that Jacob doesn't know you're leaving?"

Trini dropped back into her chair and looked straight ahead. "Exactly."

Serenity bent directly in front of Trini, took her hands, squeezed them, and lowered the pitch of her voice. "Okay. You've given us a lot to think about, but here's what you absolutely have to do before you do anything else."

Trini looked at her to go on.

Serenity's words sounded a command. "You've got to tell Jacob. And while you're at it, you might want to tell him you love him."

Trini's jaw dropped. "What?"

Abby rejoined them. "Trini, do you love the man?"

Trini lowered her eyes before meeting their gazes. She finally offered a conciliatory nod. Serenity seemed to think out loud. "So why don't you stay here and forfeit your plan?" Before Trini could get a word in, Serenity continued. "Marry him!"

Trini considered the potent question. *Why not stay here and marry Jacob?* A warm rush swept through her.

Abby stepped in. "Okay. We're going to solve this problem right here and now. First, here's what I need to know. Any chance you'll change your mind about leaving?"

Trini looked into Abby's curious eyes. "I've had it on my list for over a year. And the planning. . ." She shook her head. "You can't believe everything I've done so it can happen."

Never had Trini glimpsed such a determined expression in Serenity's eyes. "Trini, please leave your list out of this." She waved a dismissive hand in front of her. "Let's just pretend that you never wrote it down. If that were the case, would you reconsider and stay here?"

Abby interrupted. "Trini, you can move and be more independent. But you know what?"

Trini looked at her to go on.

"You will *never* find another Jacob Lantz. You love this man. And true love is rare." Abby gave a strong shake of her head. "I'd think long and hard about your plan."

Trini's eyes teared, and she blinked at the sting. "I won't change my mind."

Abby glanced at Serenity before turning back to Trini and fixing her eyes on her. "If you're sure about that, then you need to go to Jacob with this. As soon as possible, Trini."

"Tonight," Serenity jumped in. "Tell him!" Serenity's voice took on a hint of optimism. "Maybe he'll come up with a compromise. I don't know, but what I'm sure of is that if this good man has invested his heart and soul into you and wants to take care of you the rest of his life—"

"That's just it," Trini responded. "I can take care of myself."

Serenity's voice filled with sympathy. "Of course you can. Now I'm no expert on love, but I can tell you that if you're determined to leave the church and everyone you've grown up with, you need to give serious thought to what you're giving up too." After a slight pause, she took Trini's fingers and held them.

Abby rested a hand on Trini's shoulder. "This is something we can't decide for you, Trini. And we can't do it for you. But I vote with Serenity. You can't keep this from Jacob any longer. And if he loves you, he'll understand. But I've known since the day you broke that arm"—she pointed to the cast—"that you love Jacob. Be honest with him. And hopefully he'll be able to talk you out of the move. Or. . ."

Serenity shrugged. "Maybe he'll think of something that Abby and I can't."

Trini's voice was merely a whisper. "Thank you, Abby. Thank you, Serenity. I don't have the answers. But what I can promise you is that by this time tomorrow, Jacob will know why I can't marry him."

CHAPTER TWELVE

Something was seriously wrong. The following morning, Jacob took note of the odd way Gabe acted. He avoided Jacob's gaze. He even skipped his typical second cup of coffee. Jacob knew his brother well. And many things seemed off.

The expression in Gabe's eyes was a weird mix of dread and uncertainty. The lines around his mouth were etched in a devastating position, the way Jacob remembered from years ago when Mamm had broken the news to her boys that their daed had left.

Before Jacob could inquire to what the problem was, the back door slammed shut. Jacob startled. When Stephen stepped inside their beloved aunt Margaret's house, Gabriel didn't use his typical words whenever Jacob or Stephen entered his space.

Gabriel's typical welcome was, "Hey there!" But this morning he said nothing. His body language lacked his usual energy and optimism. Jacob stepped directly in front of his older brother.

"Gabe?"

No verbal response.

"You're acting really strange."

The only sound was the light whir of the fan blades spinning above them. The breeze gently lifted a corner of a piece of mail on the table.

The aroma of freshly brewed coffee filled the air. From where he stood, Jacob could see an opened carton of cream on the countertop.

Then the floorboards creaked as Stephen joined them in a small circle. To Jacob's astonishment, Stephen's mood matched Gabriel's somber demeanor. In response to this silent yet obvious statement that both brothers made, Jacob met their serious gazes with forced confidence.

He focused on Stephen first. "Okay, guys. Something's up. What's going on?" Then he turned to Gabe. After shoving his hands into the deep pockets of his trousers, he stood very still and continued to stare at his brothers.

A long, tense silence passed until Gabe laid his hand firmly on Jacob's shoulder. His voice was soft and filled with an odd combination of doubt and certainty. "I think you'd better sit down."

Stephen and Gabe shared a concerned glance before Gabe motioned to the nearest oak chair. Obediently, Jacob sat and slid the chair back from the table. He extended his long legs in front of him and tapped the toe of his leather boot against the floor. Breeze from the fan caressed his forehead.

When his brothers stayed silent, a bead of sweat trickled down Jacob's chest. He felt his heart beat faster.

Gabriel looked down at Jacob while Stephen pulled out a nearby chair and cleared his throat. "First of all, I want to remind both of you what Aunt Margaret used to tell us about believing everything we hear. She told us to confirm what we hear before repeating it."

Jacob shrugged. Patience was one of his strong traits, but as he contemplated what his brothers obviously knew that he didn't, he raised his voice. "Whatever you heard can't be that bad."

Stephen and Gabe shared another glance before Gabe let out a sigh. "Rumor has it that Trini Sutter is going to leave our town and become Englisch."

———— ⚜ ————

She still couldn't believe Trini's news. Serenity breathed in fresh air while she walked the dirt path through the woodsy incline behind her house. As she focused on relaxation, she silently hoped to cross paths with Stephen this morning.

She frowned as she thought about Trini's unexpected revelation. Of all the things Serenity had expected to hear from her friend, deciding to leave the Amish was nothing Serenity would have imagined.

Last night she hadn't slept much. Trini's admissions had kept her awake, tossing and turning. Serenity was fully aware of the tricky position Trini would be in if anyone found out—anyone, that is, besides Serenity and Abby. If Trini's secret was exposed, she'd face terrible scrutiny.

Serenity cringed as she imagined the outright gossip that would run rampant if the confidential information reached even one set of ears outside The Quilt Room. Technically, Trini should not be shunned because she had not yet joined the Amish church.

Serenity and Abby had joined immediately after going through rumspringa. Thinking back on Trini's delay in joining, Serenity wondered if her friend's desire to become Englisch had gone back several years.

No stress. Relax. Think of something to stay calm. Stress causes all sorts of health problems. Breeeeathe!

Serenity smiled as she began to count her blessings out loud. "I am healthy. I am loved. I am a child of Gott."

Serenity took small, quick steps, careful not to trip over tree roots that stuck up out of the ground. She blinked as the sun came through a break in the trees. The warmth of nature's light prompted a sigh of happiness.

She adjusted her vision when shade from the trees stymied the short-lived brightness. A voice startled her, and she nearly dropped her water bottle as she quickly turned.

"Stephen!"

She wasn't sure why there was an odd catch in her voice. She'd been dying to run into him.

"I'm sorry. I didn't mean to scare you."

"Oh, I'm fine." Her gaze migrated to his binoculars. "Any sightings of your red-headed woodpecker today?"

He shook his head before smiling. "Not yet." He motioned. "Mind if I join you?"

"It would be my pleasure to have your company." Serenity usually kept her thoughts to herself, but this morning she decided on honesty and openness. "I'm actually glad to meet up with you. I like your company."

The curve around the corner of his lips lifted two notches, and enthusiasm edged his voice. "That's gut to know." He paused before adding, "Because I enjoy yours too."

"Denki." She sighed. "To be honest, I've got a lot on my mind today."

"Anything you'd like to share?" He darted her a quick wink while they glanced at each other. "I'm a good sounding board. And although I may not have answers, you can trust me to keep whatever you tell me confidential."

Her heart warmed as she considered his offer. She didn't know Stephen well, but her impressions of people usually proved to be correct. And although she had promised Trini to keep her secret, that didn't stop her from dying to confide in someone.

As Serenity had absorbed Trini's unexpected revelation overnight, she'd acknowledged that her independent friend was quite capable of decision-making. But this time Serenity wasn't so sure Trini's goal could be easily accomplished. And unlike Serenity and Abby, other members of their church would not be as understanding.

After a few steps over a clump of tree roots, Stephen spoke, his voice taking on a more serious tone. "There's something on my mind too. And because you're such a good listener, I hope you don't mind hearing me out."

His unexpected admission surprised her. She stopped to take a drink from her water bottle and make sure she had screwed on the cap tightly. As she took a big step to avoid another clump of roots, his hand steadied her. On the other side of the roots, she expected his arm to drop from her side. But it didn't.

Serenity came to a stunning observation. She truly felt something for Stephen Lantz. She didn't know him well, but her feelings for him. . .they were real. Whatever he needed, she would try to help.

"Stephen, I would be honored to listen to whatever's on your mind. I wish I could run my concerns by you." She shook her head and stopped a moment to catch her breath. When she started again, she could hear her own frustration as she conceded, "But I can't."

His voice was low and soft. "I understand."

He stopped to focus his binoculars. Several moments later, he handed them to her and pointed to one of the trees. "You've got to see this. It's another yellow finch. Absolutely beautiful."

As she adjusted the lenses, he helped her locate the bird. "It is gorgeous. The color. . . Absolutely amazing that Gott created so many different creatures. I've never really given thought to all the species of birds."

"It's a lot to take in."

She returned the binoculars to him. Neither spoke as they proceeded up the uneven path until they reached a clearing where they could look down at their houses.

Stephen motioned to some large rocks next to a small creek that snaked through the trees. He waited for Serenity to sit. After she got comfortable—as comfortable as she could get, anyway—he surprised her.

"Serenity, you know Trini Sutter well, jah?"

He sat on a rock next to her. The question momentarily stopped her breath. Trini was the last thing she wanted to talk about with Jacob's brother today. Keeping her friend's secret was of utmost importance. The information Trini had confided to her and Abby would be high risk if it were to get out.

Serenity glanced at Stephen and realized he was waiting for her answer. "Jah. But why do you ask?"

Stephen turned closer to her. "I trust you with what I'm about to confide in you."

She quickly offered a reassuring nod. "I'm a good secret keeper." Her heart pumped a little harder.

Stephen cleared his throat and fidgeted with his hands as he adjusted his hips on the stone. "My brother Jacob is in love with Trini. He intends to make her his wife." Before Serenity had time to respond, he held up a hand and wagged it in front of him in a dismissive gesture. "I know. We haven't been here long. But my brother—from a very young age, he has always known what he wants. So I'm really not surprised that he's already decided to marry her. His feelings for her go way back to when they were kids."

Serenity knew that. But she let him go on.

"Anyway, Gabe and I heard a rumor." His serious expression changed to an optimistic expression. "Hopefully, it's just that. Because if it turns out to be true. . ." He closed his eyes a moment while shaking his head. When he opened his lids, their eyes connected.

"We heard that she's leaving our church. That she's even moving from Illinois."

Serenity's heart pounded with a dangerous combination of certainty and uncertainty. She deliberately didn't respond.

In silence, his eyes penetrated hers. He lowered the pitch of his voice so that it was nearly a whisper. "It's surely not true?"

While she thought of a reply, a large patch of clouds veiled the sun, and the colors of the landscape darkened. The sunny, happy ambience had transformed into a conversation that put Serenity on edge.

She searched her heart. *Stay positive. The predicament you face isn't your fault. But this wonderful man is obviously distressed at this rumor, which really is true. And you have to say something to help him.*

"Stephen, whether I know what Trini plans or don't, it's not my place to tell you. But I think if Jacob wants the truth, he needs to ask Trini in person."

After a slight hesitation, he countered, "I'm sure he will."

The sun reappeared, and Serenity noticed the small worry creases around Stephen's eyes. Lines around his mouth were etched into a frown.

"It hurts to see my brother worry."

To help ease his mind, she picked a dandelion that was next to her and handed it to him.

The gesture prompted a chuckle on his part. "What's this for?"

"I have this philosophy. It comes from trying to accept things I cannot control." She grinned at him, and he smiled back. "Keep in mind that I arrange flowers for a living. Their beauty and fragrances help keep me focused. So whenever I'm on edge about something, I look at all the intricate details—the petals, the coloring, the leaves. And as I take in the delicate structure of any flower"—she gently ran a finger over the golden top—"I know that if Gott can make this, He will bring a resolution to my concerns."

Stephen appeared to digest her assessment of life and way of dealing with worries.

Serenity delicately stroked the top of the flower and gently took it from him. "Most people consider this a weed."

Amused, Stephen grinned. "Jah." He paused. "I suppose you don't?"

She pulled the flower to her chest. "Do you know that this can be used for medicinal purposes? Of course, you would want to be careful that the crop you pick hasn't been sprayed with pesticides."

That last statement prompted him to laugh. She studied him for a moment. With the bright sunlight hitting his face directly, she noted that his eyes were the most beautiful shade of brown she'd ever seen. Their autumn-brown flecks made one dynamic shade that tugged at her heartstrings.

"I often roast the roots and drink dandelion tea. It's actually much healthier than coffee."

"Serenity?" His voice was soft and urgent.

"What, Stephen?"

The light flecks were suddenly very still. "I like being with you."

She softened her voice with genuine affection. "I like being with you too, Stephen."

Several moments passed in silence. Next to this man, Serenity felt safe and secure. Serenity had never been interested in marrying. She'd dealt with her own issues for many years and had steered clear of men within her church. She had her reasons.

But spending time with Stephen had awakened something new and exciting and comfortable inside her. Something that was so honest and hopeful. Unlike Trini, Serenity had never yearned to venture outside her Amish community. She was content with a simple life as a member of the Plain faith. To her, the secret of being happy was never wanting for anything.

Now, as she talked with Stephen, she found herself wondering what it would be like to be his partner. He was very easy and refreshing to talk to. And the more she conversed with him, the more she suspected that he too enjoyed blessings that Gott had planted here on earth for enjoyment.

Serenity never had understood why people poisoned their yards with chemicals for the sake of killing weeds. She preferred an organic landscape, and she had never minded cleaning the thistles and other weeds with her blue-handled spade.

"Stephen, I can tell you're concerned about Trini breaking your brother's heart. So many things that happen in our lives are out of our control. Sometimes issues can seem unsurmountable. But

I can tell you this."

He lifted a curious brow. "I'm listening."

"From what I know about Jacob, he's a wonderful man. And I love Trini. I knew your aunt well, and from time to time, she shared tidbits of information with me about you and your family. Trini's fall has resulted in many changes in her life. And I firmly believe that if it's Gott's will for Jacob and Trini to be together, they will be."

After appearing to contemplate her theory, he said, "You make it sound simple."

"It is and it isn't." She shrugged. "But sometimes our answers don't come as quickly as we'd like."

He played with a leaf for a moment. As he seemed to observe it, he said, "Let's say that Jacob learns the rumor is true." He sighed and looked down at the ground. "What should he do?"

The answer came to Serenity. As the creek gurgled and a large dragonfly landed on a milkweed, she sat up straight, hugged her knees with her arms, and turned so that her gaze met Stephen's. Something came over her. She wasn't sure what it was and swallowed an uncomfortable knot that blocked her throat. She didn't know why she cared so much about this man whom she barely knew. Yet she did. And although she couldn't directly help Stephen with his brother's quest to be with one of her very best friends, she could send him to the person who could help.

"Jacob needs to ask Trini."

They both looked straight ahead. As Serenity rethought the advice she'd just given Stephen, she was fully aware that her words had sounded very simple. And actually, the action that needed to be taken was easy.

Her direction to Stephen, however, would most likely bring great disappointment to Jacob. And the end result might spark an enormity of complications. But as Serenity sat in silence next to Stephen Lantz, she wondered how on earth this secret had escaped the small back room of The Quilt Room. She hadn't told. She was sure that Trini hadn't said a word to anyone else.

Did Abby spill the secret? No. Serenity knew firsthand that although she and Abby held different views on many different subjects, she could trust her dark-haired friend with anything.

But someone else knew that Trini planned to emancipate herself from the Amish church. Who was it? And how did they find out?

———————— ⚜ ————————

That morning Jacob knocked on Trini's door. Usually he looked forward to talking with her. Today, however, he wasn't sure if he was ready to hear her response to the awful rumor. Still, he had to address it. If the rumor was indeed true, he needed to know so he could deal with whatever came next.

"Jacob, gut morning."

She motioned him in.

Did he imagine that uncertainty edged her voice? Was his mind playing tricks on him as he observed that her demeanor was different than usual?

"Trini, I'm glad to see that your cast is off. How's your arm?"

"Therapy has worked wonders. I still have a little pain every once in a while, but look." One by one, she moved her fingers, beginning with her thumb. Her expression revealed both relief and happiness. "Do you remember when I could barely move my fingers?"

"Jah."

He recalled his purpose and thought a moment while he decided how to broach the rumor. While he contemplated his dilemma and the answer he wanted, she motioned him to the table. "Please. Let me bring you a cup of coffee. I just made a fresh pot."

She motioned to the French press and the freshly ground coffee in a pile on her wooden cutting board.

"I'd love a cup. Denki."

He pulled out a chair. The legs squeaked as they slid over the wood floor. While he seated himself, she stood on her tiptoes to reach two mugs in one of her cabinets. He could smell the delicious coffee aroma. When she joined him, she smiled before taking her seat.

"Your new gerbera daisies are growing fast."

She stirred some sugar into her coffee before putting the small spoon on a napkin. The metal clinked against the porcelain mug. "They are beautiful." She lowered the tone of her voice. "That's thanks to you, Jacob."

"It was my pleasure."

A bird pecked at the window while they sat across from each other. Jacob cleared his throat and tried to conceal his nervousness. "Trini, there's something on my mind. Can we talk?"

The question seemed to take her by surprise, and she paused. "Of course."

The bird stopped pecking, and the room became eerily quiet.

"It's about the question I asked you a couple of days ago."

He noted the way she looked down at the table to avoid his eyes. At that moment, he knew the answer. But Jacob loved this woman who seemed so determined to do things on her own. And he would never let her go without a fight.

When she glanced up, her cheeks flushed. "Jacob, I have some explaining to do. It's rather involved."

He smiled a little. "Please. I'm listening."

Letting out a sigh, she told him all about the months her Englisch brother in Rhode Island had helped her to prepare to leave Illinois and work at a fabric store near Providence. As he listened, his heart sank.

She continued that, for some time, she'd wanted to venture out into the world. That she had her own mind and a good work ethic, and that she didn't need so many people trying to make her decisions for her.

As he took in every word, Jacob acknowledged that her difficult plan could only evoke obvious disapproval within their community and create more problems for Trini than he suspected she could begin to imagine.

He sat very still while he listened with dismay and fear as she tactfully conveyed that the Plain faith didn't allow her enough room to express her individuality. That a strong need inside her had been pushing her to prove that she was able to excel on her own. That there was much she yearned to experience. Fear welled inside his chest until he finally shifted to a more comfortable position.

When Trini stopped speaking, they stared at each other while the second hand on the wall clock kept an even beat. When he was certain that she'd finished having her say, he got up and stepped around the table to join her. He knelt beside her and looked up at her creamy complexion. To his surprise, her eyes reflected something he'd never seen in them. They were darker than usual. And a sense of newfound seriousness emanated from them.

He softened his voice. "I appreciate your honesty." Then, after a moment of hesitation, he added, "I just wish I'd heard it from you first."

A look of shock passed over her face. She gasped, and her eyes widened. She pulled her arms to her chest and stood. "You already knew?"

Jacob explained.

Afterward, he took in her reaction. "You're shaking."

She nodded. "Jah. I've been preparing for this for months. And I should have shared this with you earlier. I'm sorry." Her voice cracked with emotion. "Will you forgive me?"

An understanding smile lit his face. "Forgiven." He let out a small sigh and said, "Please. Sit back down." For long moments, he considered this revelation, then spoke. "So it is true."

Her cheeks suddenly lost their color, and she breathed in, moving her palms to her thighs and extending her fingers. "Someone must've overheard me tell Abby and Serenity. I wonder who."

Suddenly he realized that she hadn't been aware that her secret was out. "My brothers got wind of it in town yesterday. That's why I came over this morning. To verify." He shrugged. "And I did."

"But, Jacob, the only two people I've told are Serenity and Abby. And they promised not to say a word to anyone." She softened her voice so that her words came out barely audible. "I trust them."

"Trini, eventually we'll know who told. But for now, let me help you."

The surprised expression in her eyes that also conveyed fear made him love her even more. She didn't drop the subject. "Jacob, who told your brothers? And how did they know?"

He thought a moment. "I'm not sure. I think they heard it in town."

She began fidgeting with her hands, and she looked down at her lap while she spoke. "I've been so careful not to give away my plan. Because, although the Amish are forgiving people, I'm sure that many in our church will not understand. Worse, they might take it out on my family."

He shook his head. "I don't have any idea who told." He rose to sit in the nearest chair and scooted closer to her so that they were face-to-face. He could see that Trini was afraid by her body language. And he was also fully aware that he still loved her.

"Trini, there's something else we need to discuss."

"What?"

He softened his voice. "I asked you to spend the rest of your life with me."

After he swallowed a knot in his throat, he whispered, "I love you, Trini. I still want you to be my wife."

A tear slipped down her cheek, and she bent so that their faces were very close. He could smell coffee on her breath. He wiped away the tear with his finger, then took both of her hands in his.

"Trini, do you love me?"

She looked away before turning back to him. "What does it matter? You want to marry an Amish woman and raise a large family." She shrugged and pulled her hands from his. He missed her touch. Her warmth. He wanted to hold on to her forever and erase everything she'd told him this morning. Because her plan doomed his hope to marry her. But he wouldn't give up.

"Trini, when it's all said and done"—he shrugged—"it doesn't really matter who told your secret." When she began to disagree, he held up a hand to stop her. "What matters is your happiness. Your life. Trini, I love you." His voice cracked with emotion. "Do you love me?"

Teary-eyed, she nodded. "I love you so much, Jacob. And I'm so very sorry about all of this." She lowered her voice to a guilty whisper. "Especially that I wasn't up-front with you."

He smiled weakly. "It's okay. Right now things might seem hopeless. But in my heart, I still believe we belong together. But if and when we marry, I want everything to be right between us. Today our timing is off. Down the road. . ." He lifted a shoulder. "Who knows?" He paused. "Let me help you."

She inhaled, eyes wide with surprise. "You want to help me?"

In response, he offered a slow, firm nod of his head. "I will be by your side." He thought of his aunt Margaret and her optimism and positive outlook. He stood and motioned Trini to stand with him. She did.

She was so close to him, he could see the quick rise and fall of her chest. "I remember something my aunt used to tell me. To be honest, I'd never really thought about it until now."

"What is it?"

"When I was little, she used to say that when I yearn for something that makes my life complete, I should never, ever give up on that dream. That dreams are worth the wait."

Trini smiled a little and nodded. "She was a wise woman. But Jacob. . ." She lifted her shoulders in a defeated gesture. "Why would you still want to marry me? I never joined the Amish church, and I'm ready to spread my wings, as they say. And unless you plan to become Englisch. . ." Looking directly into his eyes, she softened her voice, and it pulled at his heartstrings.

He considered the potent message she'd just conveyed and felt an ache in his heart.

She choked with emotion. "The last thing I wanted was to break your heart."

He tried for the right words. At least he'd been warned before she'd told him. Still, his heart pounded and his palms were sweaty. Yet despite all of this, he knew what he wanted.

When he observed her expression, he glimpsed pure turmoil. The flecks in her eyes were a dusty haze. It reminded him of a summer storm. But he reasoned that was a good sign because it conveyed to him that there was still hope for them as a couple. He wasn't sure how much, but he was grateful for even a small amount.

"Trini, I will stay an Amish man. No matter how much I love you, leaving the Amish church would strip me of my core."

She stood very still before finally offering a small nod of understanding.

"At the same time, I don't want you to marry me unless I can have all of you." He cleared his throat. "Trini, I fell in love with you years ago. I fell in love with you as an Amish girl. In my view, it's a large part of who you are. And if you became Englisch. . ." He offered an uncertain lift of his shoulders and shook his head. "You wouldn't be the same Trini I love and adore. Do you understand?"

She appeared to absorb his view. She offered a small smile. "Jah.

But, Jacob, you said before that one of the things you love about me is my independence. And that goes along with my longing to become Englisch."

He gave a firm shake of his head. "You're right. And you're wrong."

She didn't respond.

"I love your independent spirit, yes. But you follow the Ordnung."

In the distance, he could hear Survivor neighing. Honey echoed the sound.

"And in my heart, I believe the Englisch world will eventually lose its appeal for you. But it might take time for you to see that."

She raised her palms. "I'll have to test the waters, I guess."

After a long silence, he released a breath. "In due time, everything will work out. But right now there's something that concerns me. My instincts tell me that our tight-knit community will not be happy about you leaving."

She nodded. "I'm aware that I'm about to face wrath from our church. I anticipated that." She threw up her hands in a frustrated gesture. "I just didn't expect it to be this soon." She let out a sigh as small lines around her mouth deepened in seriousness. "I have no idea how this got out."

"It will come out soon enough. But right now, we can't worry about that."

Her pupils dilated in surprise.

"My main concern is your well-being, Trini."

Jacob contemplated the seriousness of her situation. And of his. Right now she needed him. He narrowed his brows and lifted her chin a bit with his finger so that he was sure he had her full attention. "I insist on helping you through this."

Her eyes shone with both gratefulness and surprise. He barely noticed the rooster that crowed outside. He vaguely glimpsed the dust ball through the front window that Survivor made as he stomped his hooves with repeated impatience.

Smoke from a distant ditch fire rose in the distance beyond the dining room window, before eventually morphing into the air and disappearing. While a tense silence loomed between them, Jacob noted the neat layout of Trini's yard and guessed she'd planned it on one of her lists.

The clotheslines were parallel, and the end posts were the same distance from her home, as if she'd measured their spots. The vegetable-garden rows were perfectly straight, and the distance between the plants appeared as if they'd also been carefully measured.

A new sense of appreciation edged her voice when she finally softened her expression. "Jacob, I don't even know what to say." She looked down. When she finally looked up to meet his gaze, her eyes were moist. They reminded him of the morning dew on his aunt's hibiscus plant next to the porch steps at home.

"I very much appreciate your kindness." She paused. "I never expected you to be so understanding. And I wish with all of my heart that you'd heard about this from me and not from someone else." After a slight pause, she added, "Again, I'm sorry."

He smiled. His heart seemed to grow at her remorse. "You're forgiven. But about your plan—if I'm going to help get you through it, I'll have to know the details. When are you going to leave?"

She sighed. "Initially it was September. But now it looks as though it will have to be soon."

"What about your quilt store?"

"I'll sell it."

He waved his hand toward their surroundings. "And this?"

She bit her lip. "Same thing."

His voice cracked with emotion as he looked down at her and said, "Trini, there's something I want you to know."

Her eyes invited him to go on.

"I'm aware that you're independent and that you've obviously given your plan a lot of thought. But in the long run, it's my hope that you'll reconsider." He wiped moistness away from his eyes. "Please, Trini. When you're gone, keep me in your life." He whispered, "Please."

CHAPTER THIRTEEN

Later in her kitchen, Trini's hands shook as she tore her day's list from the pad and looked at it. A knock made her look up. *Maybe Jacob has come back.*

She answered the door. And straightened her shoulders as Mamm and six sisters rushed inside. By the expressions on their faces, they sought answers. With great concern, she motioned them to the kitchen table.

Mamm and two sisters remained standing as Mamm waved a hand in dismissal. Her voice quavered with emotion. Her arms shook. "Trini, there's a rumor going 'round."

Beside her, Elizabeth's mouth was open, her eyes wide. While Trini took in the desperate expressions on her family members' faces, which ranged from disbelief to great fear, their words started coming.

"Trini, please say it isn't so. You'd never leave us." Anguish filled Mamm's voice.

Elizabeth chimed in. "Word's all over town. They're sayin' crazy things about you, Trini."

Esther jumped in. "That you're leaving our church. Even Illinois."

Sarah cut in. "Please. We want to hear from you that it's not true. So we can set the record straight."

Trini could feel her blood leave her face. All the time she'd made plans to move to Rhode Island, she'd never really acknowledged how strong and emotional her family's reactions would be. Now, as she read their faces, watched their body language, and listened to the fear in their voices, she realized that what she was about to do would be more difficult for them than she'd expected. These people were her own flesh and blood. She could only start to imagine how others in her church would react. *No one is going to stop me from doing this.*

Trini breathed in, squared her shoulders, and lifted her chin in forced confidence. "I'm sorry. What you heard—it's true."

She hadn't prepared herself for what would come next. Mamm's voice shook with despair. Trini had never witnessed this serious level of devastation on her mother's face. Not even after Daed had passed on. They looked into each other's eyes before her mother broke down in tears. "No! Please, Trini! Don't leave us. We love you!"

Elizabeth began to cry.

Sarah stepped up next to Mamm and tried to comfort her. As she wrapped her arms around her mother, she glanced at Trini. "You don't know what you're doing. Your life is here." Then she extended her arms so everyone was included. "Your church is here. You have no idea what you'll be up against in the Englisch world."

Suzanne raised her shaky voice. "Trini, you haven't given this enough thought. We're your world. We won't be there to help you."

Esther wiped away tears as she grabbed Trini's arms and pleaded with her. "Trini, we love you. Please reconsider."

Mamm wiped at a tear, and her voice cracked with emotion. "Trini, I beg you to stay," she stammered. "What if you get the flu?" Before Trini could reply, Mamm went on, spitting out her words at a speed that must be illegal. At least, for words. "Remember that time when you spent a week with a high fever? I made you chicken soup with homemade noodles."

Elizabeth jumped in. "And I got your medicine."

Sarah's voice vibrated with emotion. "And I made your favorite chocolate chip cookies with oatmeal because you craved them."

The impact of their statements was so powerful, Trini nearly stopped breathing. The room suddenly darkened as if the sun had slipped behind a cloud. Trini's arms chilled so that she had to wrap them around her chest to warm herself.

They all looked at her in silence. Finally, she said in an emotional tone, "You know how much I love you."

The heavy silence was almost deafening. Trini's voice caught in her throat as she tried to find the right words to console her family—and herself, because of the pain she had unintentionally caused them.

Trini faced an impossible situation. Their love touched her heart. And stunned her. Yet her desire for independence was so overpowering she yearned for the life her brother had helped her plan.

Her gaze traveled to each of her sisters before finally landing on her mother's face. Taking in the creases around her mamm's moist eyes, Trini filled her voice with as much sympathy as she could muster. "I love all of you. I also love my brother. I don't understand why we can't continue to be close to him. I have no doubt that I'll be safe with Amos and his wife. Of course, I'll miss you. But surely we can continue to keep in touch. I'll be doing what I know well. . .working at a quilt store in Providence."

Those statements seemed to die. Mamm's jaw dropped. Sarah and Elizabeth held hands and appeared as upset as they had been at Daed's funeral. Trini didn't know what else to tell them.

A long silence ensued. At last she spoke with a voice that was barely audible. She forced her words, and her chest ached with spasms. "This is something I have to do."

She lifted her shoulders in a helpless shrug. She tried positive thoughts. "It's not like I'm leaving the country. I'm grateful for your love, but I didn't choose the Amish life. I was born into it." She raised a hand to stop them from protesting. "For a long time, I've wanted to find my own voice in this world. I want to know who I really am. Here, I can't do that."

Trini pointed to her kapp. "I want to wear my hair down. And on a more serious note, I'm opposed to any kind of shunning, even though we don't often do it."

Mamm's voice was hoarse. "You know good and well how Gott expects us to live. And the bishop offers plenty of chances to those determined to disrespect the Ordnung."

Trini glanced at each of her sisters before finally focusing her attention on her distraught mother. "It's just not right to exclude those who need our love and support. Instead of avoiding them and not speaking to them, we should embrace them and help them."

She paused a moment before adding, "We need to pray for them, Mamm. For heaven's sake, we are Christians. I've never forgiven myself for avoiding Samuel Glick after our church shunned him. Afterward I prayed for Gott's forgiveness."

Trini stiffened, suddenly sure that she would never be able to convince her family to think differently from what had been instilled in them from birth. But these women were her own flesh and blood, and she yearned to keep on good terms with them. She and her family had never had much in common, yet she cared deeply for them.

"Please." She drew her hands to her chest and closed her eyes as she begged them. When she opened her lids, her eyes stung with salty tears. She blinked.

"I love you all, but right now, more than ever, I need your support. My move—it won't be easy, but as long as I know you're behind me. . ."

The expressions Trini faced told her that support was not coming from this group. At least not today. Her heart pounded with uncertainty and fear of their reactions. "I know this is a shock, but in the long run, I hope you'll be happy for me."

Elizabeth lowered her gaze to the floor. Her voice was unforgiving. "Trini, you've always done your own thing."

The statement caused a shadow to fall over Trini's countenance. Couldn't her family just accept that she differed from them and offer love and encouragement? She would have done it had the roles been reversed.

After they left, Trini prayed for strength. She also asked Gott to help her family and her church understand. She compared Jacob's kind and supportive reaction.

As she listened to their horse trot out of her drive, her hands shook. Her bottom lip trembled. Forcing confidence, she headed outside and toward the pasture.

The fresh air lifted her spirits. Inside the barn, she loaded her pockets with sugar cubes and gave a sigh of relief as she continued to the pasture with Honey.

The horse immediately nuzzled his nose in her pocket. She pulled out a white cube and placed it on her palm, and as always, her standardbred accepted it. She'd always found it amazing that her horse's large teeth could take the cube without biting her.

Honey's gentleness prompted a smile. If Trini had large teeth like her true bestie, she didn't know if she would be able to accept sugar so gently.

Trini bent forward to plant a firm kiss on the long nose and looked into a set of large eyes. As she stroked the honey-colored hair, she spoke softly. "There's something I need to run by you, Honey."

The four-legged animal rubbed his nose against her cheek. Side by side, they walked toward the back of the pasture. "I'm in a bit of a predicament, my friend."

Honey let out a sympathetic whinny. At least it sounded sympathetic. Trini laughed and ran her hand over Honey's side while reflecting on what had just transpired and how her secret had escaped the four walls of the quilt shop.

"You know me better than anybody." She paused while she acknowledged her unconditional adoration for this beautiful animal. Of course, her horse couldn't make her soup when she was sick, as Mamm did. Nor could Honey assist at the house or at her quilt shop. Honey couldn't even help Trini make her lists.

"But you know what's more important than anything?"

This time Honey lifted his neck and neighed.

"It's the tight bond we share. I know you can't talk like me, yet you love and understand me. I'm not sure if horses are judgmental or if they're not, but whatever the case, my instincts tell me that you would never think badly of me for having different views than you. And even when there's an ice storm and I'm late feeding you, you always seem grateful to see me." Trini smiled. *Unconditional love.*

As they made their way around the wooden fence, Trini took in the countryside's beauty. Her shoulders began to relax. Her neck became less tense. Many of the huge oaks that stood in the distance were over a hundred years old. In the summer, they provided protection from the sun during the day. But in the fall, oh. . .their glorious, luminous colors. Trini paused trying to resolve her dilemma for a moment and instead imagined the trees decked out in autumnal hues. She breathed in the heavenly country scents and said a quick prayer of thanks to Gott for providing her such joy.

"Honey, something happened that is tearing my heart to pieces." She explained the emotional visit with her family. "I don't have their support, Honey. And it makes me sad. But I have never been able to please them. I anticipated that they'd be upset, but I didn't expect that they would be as distraught as they were. If I leave, things aren't perfect. If I stay, nothing's perfect either."

As they continued walking around the fence, Trini's head swam with the things her family had said to her just a short time ago. When Jacob popped into her thoughts, she mindfully reviewed his support and love for her.

"Honey. . ."

The animal pawed the ground and dust flew. Trini closed her eyes while the dust settled. When she opened her lids, she waved her hand in front of her face so that the remaining particles wouldn't get in her eyes.

"What surprises me most is Jacob's overwhelming support for me at what I'm about to do." As she recalled his concern for her, Trini's heart warmed. The pulse on her wrist did a little happy dance. "I know how he feels about me, Honey. But for some reason, I didn't expect him to be so understanding and encouraging." She paused and lowered the pitch of her voice. "He's worried about me. He even warned me about the strong opposition I would face."

She glimpsed a white SUV far off down the county road as it passed a black buggy. "Since my brother moved away, I can't recall when anyone so much as mentioned his name. Amos told me he's written our sisters and Mamm numerous times over the years, but to my knowledge, no one has responded." She shook her head in dismay. "That's just wrong." She grimaced. "Am I making a mistake?"

Honey gave a strong shake of his head to ward off a fly that buzzed around his mane. As he began to trot, Trini quickened her pace and pumped her arms to keep up. As her heart beat faster, her mood improved. Fresh air always lifted her spirits. As she moved, she nearly forgot about the tumultuous visit with her family. But she couldn't get Jacob out of her mind.

She smiled as she pictured the concern on his face. She could nearly hear the gentleness of his voice. She'd always liked him, but today her perception of him had changed in a positive way. And her love for the middle Lantz brother was undoubtedly stronger than ever.

She had misjudged him. A lot. For some reason, she had expected him to respond to her plan with complete disapproval. But to her surprise, he had supported her and was troubled about the aftereffects that her news could spark.

She warmed at the knowledge that Jacob genuinely cared for her. And today she knew that he was her true friend through thick and thin. "Like you, Honey."

She would miss Jacob. She bit her bottom lip.

But Jacob also wanted to take care of her. She was sure that his daed's absence had made him ultraprotective. That was a gut thing. But it was also what Trini yearned to escape. She was fully aware that many single women in her church would love to marry Jacob. No doubt, he would make a great Amish husband.

The thought of leaving him behind brought on sadness. He'd confessed that he'd stay Amish. So joining her as an Englisch husband was not an option. *But for several years, my goal has been clear to me. I can't have my freedom from the Amish world and have Jacob. And that's not going to change.*

The country smells filled her senses. She took in the fields all around her. Amish houses were like dots in the middle of the vast countryside.

As she and Honey headed back to the barn, Trini took a moment to caress her horse's long nose. She pulled the last remaining sugar cube from her pocket and fed it to him.

I will miss you. I will ask Serenity to keep you until the sale of my store and my house are complete. Then I'll purchase a small country home in Rhode Island. "Leaving you behind won't be easy. But trust me. Be patient, and we'll be together again."

I will be okay. But I'll have to say a lot of prayers for Gott to help me to endure both the sadness and the criticism I'm about to face. But I'm strong. And I'll stay strong.

————— ⚜ —————

Mary Sutter couldn't sleep. She could not imagine life without her youngest. *How will she survive in an Englisch world? Who will be her sounding board when she needs guidance? Dear Gott, please don't let my baby leave me. Amen.*

Mary's body shook. She closed her eyes and tried not to cry. As she contemplated her shocking situation, oak branches caressed the sides of the house and squeaked lightly against the siding. Moonlight beamed in through her window and landed on the foot of her bed.

I've lost my only son to the Englisch. Even though he left several years ago, his departure seems like yesterday. A shiver crept up her arms and landed in her shoulders. She rolled them to rid the unwanted sensation.

The aroma of pork roast and cabbage floated up the winding stairway and filled her room with a delicious scent. *I bore eleven children, yet here I am, alone in this big house.* She squeezed her eyes closed, trying to block the pain. But closing her lids did not quell the emptiness and the void looming inside her.

I miss my husband. I miss my son.

She recalled Margaret Lantz and blinked at the salty sting of tears. *She never had children. She never married. She lived in a two-story house alone, and she never gave any indication that she was lonely or sad. I never sensed that she longed for company. Tonight, as I face my worst fear of losing my baby, I have to admit that Margaret must have experienced loneliness too. She hid it well.*

Mary thought of the three Lantz nephews and smiled. *They seem like good, honest men. And they will keep their aunt's spirit alive.*

As Mary tossed and turned in her bed, her focus migrated to Jacob and her plan to call him her son. Her heart warmed but also ached. *I've always been aware of the strong bond between Jacob and Trini. When they were young, she talked about him for months after he'd traveled back to Pennsylvania. I'll never forget his sweet proposal to her with a heart on it.*

She recalled the generous attention Jacob had offered Trini since his move here. Her motherly instincts told her that there was much more to his time spent helping Trini than merely compensating for the guilt of having caused her fall.

I have nine other daughters. Twenty-two grandchildren. I'm blessed with a large family. I suppose I can't expect 100 percent from each of them. But I try hard to ensure that they're loved.

Her thoughts drifted back to Trini, and Mary caught a lone tear before it slid down her cheek. *She's my miracle baby. The doctors told me I couldn't bear another child. Yet Gott blessed me with Trinity.*

She has always been independent. Growing up, she was determined to handle everything herself even though she had a brother and sisters who tried to do things for her. Samuel and I provided her extra attention. Looking back, Trini always sought our approval. She raised the best vegetables. As far as her relationships with her nieces and nephews, she spent more time with them than anyone in the family. And despite so many quilt shops in the area, Trini, at an exceptionally young age, started and grew a successful business. It shouldn't surprise me that she owns the most popular shop around.

She squeezed her eyes closed and pressed her palms together. *I can't let her go. Dear Gott, please tell me how to stop my baby from leaving me. I've always tried to be strong for her, but now I realize that I need her more than she needs me.*

Mary's mind traveled back to Trini's childhood days. The youngest of eleven had always stood out. Mary tucked her toes inside her queen-size quilt and pulled the extra pillow next to her to hold it for reassurance.

Trini is capable. Maybe that's why she's so independent. As I think back on church gatherings and family get-togethers, I can see clearly that Trini was her own woman. Growing up, she differed from other Amish girls. She'd question some of the rules that we live by while others her age needed no explanations. And she was determined to do what she believed was right. Like when one of our horses was to be put down, she begged her daed to let him live. And she'd gotten her wish. In the end, the sick standardbred made a miraculous recovery.

She has a soft heart. And a terribly independent spirit. She respects viewpoints that don't agree with hers. At the same time, she lets her thoughts be known. And I admire her.

When Trini had launched her quilt shop, Mary had yearned to assist her daughter. But for some reason, Trini hadn't sought or accepted Mary's intent to be part of the new business. Because of that, Mary had been deeply hurt.

I'm her mamm. Of course I expect to play a role in her life. Yet Trini hasn't ever come to me for guidance. In fact, Trini rarely sought out advice or help from anyone. Still, Mary yearned with all her heart for her youngest daughter's love. And most especially, she wanted to be needed.

While the cool nighttime breeze floated into the room through the open window, crickets chirped. Mary reasoned that most likely Trini would do fine wherever she went. But it was the horrendous thought of losing her that Mary feared more than anything.

Trini has no children of her own, but when she does, hopefully she will realize that my needs as her mother are real. And wanting her to lean on me isn't such a bad thing, is it?

Coyotes yip-yipped in unison, making it sound as if there were hundreds outside the house. Still, Mary realized that most likely only two or three created all the noise.

After, Mary yawned then released a deep sigh that was a sad mixture of hopelessness and defeat. She could assess Trini's character as much as she wanted. The issue, however, was that Trini obviously had solid plans to leave. And once her daughter ventured out into the Englisch world, it would be difficult to convince Trini to return to her humble roots. The move would undoubtedly result in a life that held pleasures and opportunities the Amish weren't privy to.

Mary turned onto her side and sighed. *I should have seen this coming. Surely there's a way to keep her here. Over the years, I've tried so hard to advise her. I've been here for her. But now I realize how very different she is from her sisters. She doesn't need me. I need her.*

Her breathing slowed. She yawned again, but her mind was wide awake, and she continued to focus on how to get Trini to stay in Arthur.

I know my youngest daughter. She's addicted to list making, and I'm guessing that she has had this departure on a list for some time. But there must be a way to thwart her plans.

Minutes later, Mary's eyes popped open. She swung her legs over the side of the bed and sat up. *I have an idea.*

CHAPTER FOURTEEN

On Sunday, Trini half heard the pastor's message as she sat between family members at the home of the Millers. She'd always been amused by how the men sat on one side of the room and the women huddled together on the other side.

The remainder of her thoughts were on what people must be thinking of her. She usually didn't focus on others' opinions of her, but today she did. She was fully aware that by now the entire Amish community was aware of her plan. And she still didn't know who had told her secret.

The second Jacob had helped her down from his buggy, she'd sensed that all eyes were on her. As she thought about her situation, she wanted to roll up her sleeves. She yearned to remove her kapp and allow her hair to cascade over her shoulders. She'd like to be most anywhere except here.

She clenched her hands together, gently planted them on her thighs, and focused on the front of the room to pretend an interest in the sermon. *I predicted that I would be the topic of many conversations when word got out about my move. But little did I know that it would be this soon. Because I haven't made my secret public knowledge. And I have no doubt that Serenity and Abby aren't responsible. Who told? I've got to find out.*

———————— ✦ ————————

Early the following morning, Jacob answered a knock on the door. Seeing who his visitor was caused his brows to narrow in surprise. "Gut morning, Mrs. Sutter."

"Morning, Jacob."

Before he motioned her inside, she handed him a fruit basket. He thanked her and set it on the table.

Unsure of her purpose, he hesitated, then he smiled and said, "Please, sit down."

"Denki."

She pulled out a chair.

As she did so, he stepped over to the countertop. "Would you care for coffee?"

She waved her hand. "No, but that's very kind of you to offer, Jacob."

He sat opposite her after placing his hot drink on a coaster. From across the table, he met her gaze.

"Jacob, first of all, I'll start by saying how very nice it is to have you and your brothers in our church." She offered a sad shake of her head. "Your aunt. . .we miss her so much. She contributed greatly to our community."

The admission brought a grateful smile to his face. "Your kind words are much appreciated, Mrs. Sutter."

"Please. Call me Mary."

He took a drink, returned his mug to the coaster, and regarded her with uncertainty. "To what do I owe this pleasure?"

She offered a half smile. "I won't bother you long."

He waved a dismissive hand. "Don't be silly. I've already dropped Trini off at The Quilt Room. But you must be here for a reason. What can I do for you?"

After releasing a sigh, Mary explained her distress over Trini's plan. After a long pause, she confessed that because of her strong love for her youngest, she might have unintentionally contributed to Trini's move.

"Why would you say that?" He accidentally brushed his coffee cup with his hand, and some liquid spilled on the table. "I apologize for asking, Mary. I know it's none of my business."

He got up and stepped quickly into the kitchen, where he pulled a hand towel from a wall hook before returning to his chair, where he quickly wiped up the small mess and laid the towel on the table next to him.

Her voice cracked with emotion as the coffee's aroma filled the air. "Jacob, Trini is my miracle baby. Before I became pregnant with her, I was told I couldn't bear more children." She laughed nervously. "Of course, after ten kids, you probably wouldn't think I would care so much. But oh, I wanted one more." She drew her hands to her chest and let out a sad sigh. "Surely you can understand why I consider her my special blessing."

Jacob absorbed her explanation and looked at her with empathy. "I understand. She is definitely a miracle."

Mary's eyes suddenly shone with tears. Desperation edged her voice, and she leaned forward. "Jacob, I can't lose her." Her hands shook. And Jacob realized that Trini was her mother's special child.

He wondered if Trini had any idea of the strength of her mamm's love for her. He guessed that she didn't. He recalled Trini's comment about how her mother and sisters always told her what to do. But he wondered if perhaps Mary Sutter was determined to advise her youngest because she cared about her so much.

As Jacob glimpsed Mary's horse and buggy from the front window, he cupped his chin with his fingers and considered what he had just learned. He picked up his coffee and took another sip. After he rested his mug on the table, he took in Mary's countenance. As he did so, his heart sank. It was impossible to miss sadness in her hazy brown eyes. Worry lines etched her mouth. As he took in her features, he noticed how Trini physically resembled her mother. Their eyes were the same color. Even the identical shape. Their brow lines followed the same curve. And both had high cheekbones. He wondered if Trini's mother also wrote lists.

When Mary resumed her concern, a newfound determination edged her tone. He quickly picked up on the anxiety that peppered her staccato words. "Jacob, I'm aware of the close bond you have with her."

She interlaced her fingers together in front of her before stretching her arms, which she slowly dropped to her thighs. At the same time, a sigh escaped her throat. "I'm not sure exactly how close the two of you are, but what I do know is this: Trini must consider you extremely special to spend the amount of time with you that she's spent."

He chuckled. "Her broken arm has put her at a disadvantage. And the accident was my fault."

She offered a small smile. "Perhaps it was, but I know my Trini. And believe me when I say that broken arm or no broken arm, that girl wouldn't give you the time of day if she didn't really care for you."

Mary's opinion sparked fresh hope in Jacob, and he sat up a little straighter and his heart pumped a little faster.

She looked down and cleared her throat. When she looked up at him, her tone firmed. "I'm pleading with you to help me convince her not to leave." After a short silence, she lowered her pitch to barely more than a whisper. "Please, Jacob."

Jacob scooted his chair back from the table, making a scraping noise on the wood floor. He considered her intent and looked at her with compassion and understanding.

"How do you think I can change her mind about leaving?"

"I don't know."

He offered a slow, certain shake of his head. "I can't."

Her eyes widened with surprise. Then she frowned, and her eyes begged for help. "But you can."

Jacob now understood why Trini believed that her mamm was a bit overly assertive. "No."

A long silence ensued while he finished his coffee and returned his empty cup to its coaster. He and Trini's mother studied each other. Finally, Jacob pressed his palms against his thighs, stood, and stepped around the table to join Mary Sutter. When he looked down at her, she glanced up with an odd combination of dismay and hope. With gentle firmness, he tried to convey his point with as much clarity as he could.

"Mary, we both want your daughter to stay. We're on the same side." His voice cracked with emotion. "I'm in love with her and have asked her to marry me."

Mary drew in a surprised breath and covered her mouth with her hand. "Oh, Jacob!" Mary dropped her hand to her side without looking away from his face.

"But honestly. . .I've had time to consider this difficult situation, and deep down inside, I don't think it's about us." Before she could respond, he went on. "I believe this is about Trini and her determination to prove that she can survive on her own. You're surely aware of her fierce independence."

He didn't look away. Neither did she. "I don't know why. . .maybe it's because she's the youngest, but Trini has a deep need inside her to prove that she can hold her own without our help."

He lifted a hand to stop Mary from cutting in. "I have no doubt that she can survive without us. In fact, I know she can. But I'm afraid that until she has actually done it, we won't be able to change her plans."

Mary's top lip quivered. "But, Jacob, if she goes to Rhode Island, she may never come back. Just like Amos." Her words picked up speed until she nearly spit them out. "I knew I should have pressed harder for her to join our church after she went through rumspringa."

He shook his head before answering in a voice that revealed both frustration and understanding. "I don't think it would've mattered. In fact, I'm glad she didn't."

Mary's jaw dropped, and she looked at him with a stunned expression like she couldn't believe he was saying something so outrageous.

He focused on her eyes. "Trust me. We're on the same page. It's going to be difficult to let her go—for both of us."

Mary raised the pitch of her voice. "Difficult?"

He nodded. "But"—he lifted his palms in a gesture of surrender—"we have no choice. I think the best thing that we can do for her"—he motioned to Mary before pointing to himself—"and the best thing we can do for us is to show our love and support. Especially before she leaves. Because when she's out east, she'll think of us and appreciate how we dealt with this situation." After a slight pause, he added, "I'm hoping she'll miss us and come back."

Mary opened her mouth to speak, but he stopped her by holding up his hand. "After she has a taste of living outside our Amish rules, and after she proves to herself and to everyone that she can hold her own in the world. . ."

Mary raised a curious brow while he paused.

His voice softened with emotion and hope. "I believe, in my heart"—he closed his eyes with great emotion—"she will come home." He lowered his voice to a whisper. "Home to where she belongs."

———————————— ⚜ ————————————

Wednesday afternoon, Serenity cut, sewed, and stitched with Trini and Abigail in the back of The Quilt Room while they talked about Abby's frustration with Gabriel Lantz.

Serenity's voice was calm and edged with hope. "Abby, for

goodness' sake, he just moved here. Relationships take time. Just continue to charm him." She winked.

Trini contributed to the conversation. "Abby, be grateful that he's still single."

Abby's offensive expression met Trini's gaze.

"I mean that. Things could be much worse than they are. I mean, he could have been married by now. Fortunately for you, he must not have met the right woman in Lancaster County. And *you*"—she pointed to Abby with affection—"you are going to marry Gabriel someday, but you have to be patient." Trini blew her a kiss, and in response Abby finally smiled a little.

Serenity couldn't stop an amused smile. She was fully aware that Abby's greatest struggle was staying patient. She'd always wanted things to happen at the snap of her fingers. And once she set her mind on something, she never changed it. In that respect, she and Trini were very much alike.

Serenity wondered if Gabriel Lantz had any idea what was in store for him. She imagined his shocked reaction if he knew that Abby had already sewn her wedding dress and bibs for the ten children she planned to bear with him!

She also believed that it was to Abby's advantage that he didn't know. If he got wind of Abby's plan and if he could see that she was already prepared for ten children—with him—the oldest Lantz brother would probably catch a ride back to Lancaster!

Serenity grinned.

Abby confronted her. "Why are you smiling like that?" Before Serenity said anything, Abby went on in her most defensive voice. "You think this is funny?"

Serenity held up a self-protective hand as she tried for the right words to calm her dark-haired friend. Serenity was an honest woman, but right now complete honesty would deeply hurt Abby. The last thing Serenity wanted was for Abby to lose confidence, so she used her best logic. "Abby, you have no idea how much I want you to marry Gabriel."

Abby's expression brightened. "Really?"

Serenity stopped what she was doing and drew her hands to her chest. "Jah!"

"I want that for you too, Abby." Trini joined in on the discussion. "I'd hate to see all those bibs go to waste."

The three laughed.

"I don't mean to change the subject, but"—Trini lowered her voice to a near-whisper as she looked from Abby to Serenity—"have either of you heard how word got out about my move?"

Abby shook her head. Serenity lifted her shoulders in a small shrug. "I've been wondering that myself." She let out a small sigh and directed her attention to Trini. "Have you told anyone besides Abby and me?"

Trini shook her head. "No. Last week, right here"—she pointed to the floor—"this is the only place I mentioned it. And I know that neither of you would ever betray my trust, but"—Trini shrugged—"I don't have a clue how the secret got out."

Serenity softened her tone, and her expression revealed concern. "We were alone when you spilled your plan." She looked at Abby and Trini for confirmation. "Isn't that right?" She lifted her hands in an uncertain gesture.

Abby motioned toward the entrance. "What I don't get is how someone could have stepped into this shop without that bell over the entrance alerting us."

Trini sat up straighter.

Serenity cut in. "We checked for visitors, and nobody was here."

Abby dropped a stencil and bent to retrieve it. Once she had it in hand, she focused on Trini. "I wonder if someone got in without that bell sounding."

Trini shook her head. "I don't think so."

Serenity got up out of her chair. "There's one way to find out."

She exited their small work area and entered the main shop, where she went to the door and stepped outside. The bell went off when she opened and closed the door.

She repeated the action. Same thing. She did it again. Only this time, when she opened the door from the outside, she did it very slowly. The bell didn't sound. She stepped back to Trini and Abby and offered a small shrug.

"That's our answer. The customer overheard just enough of our conversation to learn your secret." She nodded to Trini. After a short pause, she glanced back at the door. "Then they left."

Abby dropped her stencil again and bent to retrieve it. "It makes sense." Her voice was serious.

Trini shrugged. "I think you're right. Because that's the only time I voiced my secret."

Serenity got up to pour a second cup of herbal tea. The cinnamon scent combined with other fresh herbs filled the small area where they worked.

Abby addressed her choice of beverage. "That tea does have an interesting smell to it, Serenity. It's growing on me."

Serenity pivoted and stepped back to her chair. Right before she reclaimed her chaise, she winked at Abby. "It's delicious."

Trini grinned.

"So. . ."

The other two women eyed Abby with curiosity.

"How are we gonna find out who our eavesdropper is?" Abby pressed the subject.

Serenity's voice took on a determined tone. "It will come out. Eventually." She focused her attention back on Trini. "But in the meantime, how do we protect you?"

Trini lifted her chin and smiled a little. "No need to worry about me. I have strong shoulders. In my heart, I know I'm doing nothing wrong." After releasing a sigh, she added, "Abby, Serenity, there's just one more thing I'd like you to know."

Two sets of eyes regarded her in curiosity.

Trini drew in a breath and squared her shoulders. "Because of the unexpected knowledge of my departure, I've decided to leave sooner than I originally anticipated."

Serenity's voice reflected surprise, as did Abby's. "When are you going?"

Trini regarded both of her friends, aware that this would be their last time together. "Next week."

Providence, Rhode Island

Trini's dream had finally come true. It was only July 3rd, and the Englisch world belonged to her. At the Sew Shop in Providence, she advised a customer on a quilt. Although she was accustomed to designing her own patterns, for the time she was content to sell what was in stock. She was experiencing a transition that required big adjustments. And time.

Even though Trini hadn't brought much with her, buying new clothes, acclimating to her new job, and adapting to life with her brother and sister-in-law took more time than she'd planned on.

She smiled at the new jeans and pretty top Amos and Stephanie had gifted her. She glanced down at her deep jade blouse, with its large, gorgeous buttons, and smiled in satisfaction.

This is the start of my independence, and wearing Englisch clothes makes me happy. She'd experienced this kind of wardrobe during rumspringa, but now she wasn't merely trying the Englisch lifestyle. She was living it. Permanently.

Her customer finally heeded Trini's advice, and Trini led her to the checkout counter. Two weeks had passed since her relocation. But it hadn't taken long to get down to business. After all, sewing and quilting were what she knew well. And Trini reasoned that she was basically continuing what she'd done her entire life. As far as work, that is.

Of course, there were several differences. Here, low-key music played while customers shopped. Listening to the gentle melodies offered Trini a bit of unexpected comfort she hadn't expected.

The sound of the phone ringing was nothing new. In Providence, however, most who shopped here had cell phones and talked while they looked around. So far Trini hadn't met any members of the Plain faith, which didn't surprise her, since she was no longer residing in an Amish community.

Something she began to accept was how extremely quiet her Amish life had been. And the Amish went to bed much earlier than the Englisch. The moment she'd stepped into her brother's home, she'd quickly noted how enhanced the noise level was with the television and Alexa, which Amos and Stephanie often used. Trini found Alexa amazing. Even when she'd gone through rumspringa, she'd never experienced anything like it.

Her bedroom alarm clock played music. Morning music was something Trini wasn't fond of, so when she had an opportunity, she'd purchase a simple ring alarm clock.

Trini proceeded to the checkout area and pulled a small notepad from the drawer underneath the cash register. Focused on what needed to be done, she wrote on the black lines:

1. Put today's deliveries in a pile out of customers' sight.
2. Organize the numerous bolts of material so the prettiest are displayed in front.
3. Restock the spools of thread and the tools: scissors, needles, and crochet hooks.
4. Redo the front window's lackluster display.

As Trini glanced down at her list, she tapped the end of her pen against the paper. As she did so, she tried to relax a little. Despite being here by choice, she now lived miles away from the only home she'd ever known and in an entirely different culture from the one she'd been part of all her life.

There had been plenty of Englisch where she'd been raised. But this environment differed tremendously from the mixed town she'd come from. So far she hadn't seen any black buggies or horses. Nor had she encountered anyone dressed as Mennonite or Amish.

But that's what I wanted. A broader life where I can experience new things, make more choices, and learn exactly who I am. Life offers much more than I have experienced. Here there's more opportunity.

For years she'd wanted a fresh start, where she could develop into the self-sufficient woman Gott had intended her to be. She was grateful, of course, for her elders and others within her Amish church who had ingrained in her what she should and shouldn't do. She would utilize their guidance to make important decisions that would define the rest of her life.

The thought of exploring Providence made her heart beat with excitement. She looked forward to shopping at the quaint stores nearby. As soon as she worked out her finances, she would purchase a more extensive wardrobe. Garments with bright, fun colors that conveyed her optimistic personality. She did not miss her dark-colored dresses. Being Englisch enabled her to try different hairstyles too.

She looked down at her sturdy black shoes and frowned. Unfortunately, new shoes would have to wait until she sold her shop and home.

A buyer had already expressed interest in her home. She reasoned that selling her business might take a bit longer. In the meantime, she'd reached a fair agreement with a church member who loved the quilt business. This person was running The Quilt Room in hopes of eventually purchasing it.

Not everything here was better, though. Trini missed her yard. Her peach orchard. Most especially, she missed Honey. Fortunately, Serenity was keeping Trini's beloved horse. The thought made her smile in amusement.

She hoped that her healthy friend would be generous with sugar cubes because Honey would not be happy without them. Trini had made Serenity promise not to make Honey adhere to the same food that Serenity fed her own horse. Trini frowned. It was well known throughout Arthur that Serenity's horse was the thinnest standardbred in the area.

Trini lifted a thoughtful brow while she inventoried the bolts of beautiful fabrics. She closed her eyes a moment while she ran her hands over the soft, pale blue cotton material that had just arrived. When she opened her eyes, an idea came to her. *This shade is so beautiful, I'll display it in the window.*

The store owner had already left for the day, and the part-time worker was on lunch break. That meant that, for the moment, Trini had this large, beautiful store all to herself. While she organized fabrics, she garnered all sorts of ideas on how to redecorate the front to appeal to more shoppers.

The owner had already placed flyers throughout town announcing dates of quilting classes that Trini had agreed to teach. Releasing a small, happy sigh, she ran her palms over a jade-green fabric to rid its wrinkles.

So far, so good. Although she was surprisingly comfortable in her new domain, she was fully aware that her two besties were miles away. And their secret Quilt Room gatherings were something she very much missed.

Her throat tightened as she imagined Serenity sipping herbal tea and the light cinnamon scent that had floated throughout The Quilt Room. A grin drew up the corners of her lips as she wondered if Abigail had made any progress with Gabriel Lantz.

As Jacob entered her mind, Trini closed her eyes, acknowledging that he was the person she missed most. Until she'd traveled miles away from Illinois, she hadn't been aware of how much she'd truly coveted their time together.

She bent to cut open a box that had been delivered earlier in the day. As she pulled the four sides up, she glimpsed sewing tools. This particular store sold sewing machines, as well as material.

In Trini's view, any store could tout sewing machines. But it had always been her goal to make The Quilt Room unique with everything pertaining to quilts. The moment the customer entered the store, that person should feel at home. That included nice-smelling aromas. Sachets. Scented candles. And beautiful quilts that hung from the ceiling and on the walls.

Her thoughts wandered back to Jacob, and she stopped what she was doing, stood, stepped to the window, and pressed her palms on the sill, leaning forward to view the city.

Jacob, I do miss you. But living outside the Amish church's strict confines is everything I dreamed it would be. I can think freely without guilt. Providence is filled with kind people. At least that's my first impression. My brother and his wife gave me a quick tour of the area.

Suddenly, visions of Jacob floated through Trini's mind. Recollections of Jacob planting healthy gerbera daisies prompted a sad smile. She then envisioned him making her lunch. Riding to and from work with Jacob in his black buggy. Then there was the mental clip of him helping her up from the ground after she'd fallen from the ladder. She glanced down at the light scar left by the stitches.

She squeezed her eyes shut to savor the precious thoughts. The strongest, most passionate image she recalled was the moment he'd confessed his love for her and his sweet, honest marriage proposal.

I didn't want to hurt him. But in the end, I did anyway. Unfortunately, that came after he'd heard from an outside source that I was leaving. And I never learned who it was.

A frown took over her face. Jacob had offered her the world. His world. And she had turned it down. With determination she lifted her chin. She'd made the right choice.

After all, she'd given years of thought to leaving the church and many things had been considered. Becoming Englisch had been number one on her master list.

I've finally done it.

CHAPTER FIFTEEN

Arthur, Illinois

Trini was gone. From his buggy, Jacob glimpsed the FOR SALE sign in his true love's front yard. He swallowed a knot in his throat, silently commanding his aching heart to stop breaking. *She's gone.*

But reality didn't stop his anguish. Next to him, Gabe's lips formed a tight, straight line. Jacob didn't stare at his brother, of course, but he could easily glimpse his grim expression from the corner of his eye.

As they proceeded down the country road, Gabe's gaze remained fixed in the direction of Trini's house. He was uncharacteristically quiet as they traveled.

Jacob tried to focus on anything but Trini's home and the new sign. To their left, soybeans went on for rows upon rows. To their right, acres of field corn blocked their view from the road running parallel to the route they took.

"Jake?"

"Jah?"

"I don't know what to say about Ms. Sutter except that I'm truly sorry. I feel your pain."

Jacob offered an appreciative nod. "Thanks, Gabe." After a long silence, Jacob furthered the subject he'd not mentioned since Trini's departure. "It's strange. One of the reasons I love her is the very same reason I've lost her."

Gabe's voice took on a gruff tone. "As much as I long to offer my support, I'm probably not the best one to talk to. You know my thoughts on marriage."

Jacob nodded.

"But I'm ready to do whatever I can to help bring her back to you."

Jacob's heart warmed. "Thanks, Gabe. I know you are. But this isn't one of those situations that can be solved, unfortunately."

After a thoughtful pause, Gabe said, "Remember what Aunt Margaret used to say?"

Jacob frowned. "About what?"

Gabriel turned his left leg so that his body half faced Jacob. "About fixing things." He chuckled. "I'm not talking about material stuff. No, not at all. I'm referring to the advice she gave Mamm after Daed left us."

Jacob shook his head. "I don't recall, but I can say with complete authority that if Aunt Margaret indeed tried a way to bring him back, it didn't work."

Gabe and Jacob bounced in their seats as a buggy wheel hit a pothole. After that, a long silence ensued while Gabe sat very still. The expression on his face was difficult to read.

Jacob was sure his brother was trying to ease his suffering. But his efforts weren't successful.

"Aunt Margaret was a wise woman. I think any advice she offered is well worth repeating." Gabe's voice hinted at optimism. But despite his late aunt's great wisdom and Gabe's determination to encourage him, Jacob knew his situation. There was no way to win.

Gabe pressed. "You surely want to hear what it was—I mean, our dear aunt's advice."

Jacob edged his tone with amusement. He couldn't help it. Even if Gabe couldn't bring Trini back to Jacob, he seemed most resolved to convey something. So Jacob didn't argue. "I'd love to know what Aunt Margaret said, Gabe. Go ahead. I'm all ears."

"She said something to this effect: Life is a continuous process of adjusting to things we don't expect. But what separates the weak from the strong is the determination to keep trying." Gabe went on. "Jake, it's true, right?"

Jacob offered a slow nod.

Gabe just wouldn't let the subject go. "I've also read that most of the things in life that happen to us are out of our control."

"I appreciate that wisdom." Jacob chuckled. "So how does that help my situation?"

Gabe shrugged. "I don't know, but I think that acknowledging that we don't have control over most events in our lives kinda puts things into perspective." He added in a solemn tone, "That should be some consolation, huh?"

"Not really. As much as I hope and as many prayers as I send to our Creator for help. . ." He shrugged. "I'm having trouble letting go of her."

Gabriel sat up a little straighter when they veered to the right to allow an oncoming car enough space. "I'm still thinking about that potent sentence."

Jacob muttered under his breath, "Sounds pretty simple to me."

Gabe's voice was edged with optimism. "I've considered our aunt's advice numerous times. And when you really think about it, I see two sides. That is, her little tidbit of wisdom can be interpreted two different ways."

Jacob breathed in. He was usually the most patient of the three brothers, but the more his dark-haired sibling attempted to console him, the more frustrated he became. He rolled his shoulders to relax.

Gabe refused to let the subject die. "Jacob, it means that *most* things in our lives are out of our control."

Jacob turned to his brother long enough to throw him a stern glance to give it up. "I get it."

Gabe's voice hinted hope. "But 'most of the things' is not everything."

Jacob let out a breath. "Gabe, can we drop this?"

Gabe raised his frustrated voice and motioned with his hand. "Jacob, you're not getting it. What I'm trying to say is that your situation with Trini might not be out of your control. It might just seem that way." They veered to the right to allow an SUV to pass. "This is how I see it."

I can't stop him. Jacob decided to let his brother talk. *What's the point of arguing?*

"Trini has been Amish all her life. Now she's in an environment, I'm guessing, that will truly test her obvious love for the Plain faith."

"Gabe, her love for the Plain faith has been tested for years. It failed. And that's exactly why she left it."

Gabe shifted on his hips and began fidgeting with his hands.

A new firmness accompanied his tone. "Ms. Sutter might think she's on to greener pastures, but at the end of the day, no place is perfect. And no church is perfect."

Jacob bit his bottom lip. "Gabe, there's a For Sale sign at her house."

Gabriel threw his palms up in a helpless gesture. "Okay. If you're giving up, I can't help you."

Jacob could feel a smile forming. "I appreciate you trying to cheer me up. But in my heart of hearts, I know she's planned this change for years. And to me that means she's fully aware of what she's doing. Trust me, Gabe, she's had plenty of time to think about it." A few seconds later, he added, "It's not like she left on a whim."

Gabe softened his voice. "You're missing it, Jake."

For a moment, Jacob entertained the possibility of getting Trini back home.

"You're forgetting that during the years she planned her move, there was one thing missing from her life. You. So the wheels were already in motion when you stepped back into her life." Gabe moved his feet. "That woman loves you, Jacob. I don't know her well, but it only took a glance at you together to know that she's in love. And I don't care how long she's planned on moving to Rhode Island. In the end, you entered the picture. I am convinced that right now she's missing you. Here's the deal. She might not agree with everything about our church. There's no church in the world that she will be 100 percent in agreement with, believe me. In my humble opinion, her move will work to your advantage."

"Do explain."

"You know what they say about absence making the heart grow fonder?"

Jacob nodded.

"Being without you might very well make her love you even more than she already does. And when she realizes her true feelings for you. . ."

Jacob glanced at him to finish his sentence.

Gabriel's voice was barely more than a whisper. "My guess is that there will be an Amish wedding."

———————— ⚜ ————————

Inside the Pink Petal, Serenity did a double take at the Amish man peering into the cooler room of fresh flowers. She stepped over to him from behind the counter. When he turned to face her, she looked up at him with a surprised smile. "Stephen?"

He grinned back at her, and her heart fluttered a little.

"Morning, Serenity."

"Gut morning." When he closed the flower-room door, the coolness in the space they stood in began to warm.

She gestured with her hands. "You're the last person I expected to see here." She ran her hands over her work apron to flatten the creases.

"I was down the street and thought I'd check out your shop."

His admission made her heart flutter again. Her heart did a happy dance. "Would you like a tour of my store?"

He offered a nod. "Please." He hesitated as if having second thoughts. "That is, if you're not busy."

She smiled up at him. "You came at the perfect time. I just finished a birthday arrangement."

She showed him her stock behind the counter. Eucalyptus, carnations, all sorts of dried flowers, bows, ribbon, and a hundred other things she used to create her projects.

He cleared his throat and stammered, "Will—will you help me put something together? For a friend?"

She hesitated before nodding. "Of course. What kind of arrangement do you want?"

His brows narrowed as he pressed his lips together thoughtfully. Then he cracked a smile. "I'm not sure. I'll have to enlist your expertise on this."

"Okay."

He hesitated. "Why don't you tell me what you would like, as if you were making it for yourself? That way I can't go wrong."

His request took her by surprise. "You trust me that much?"

His eyes sparkled. "Jah."

"Now?"

"Uh-huh." A nervous chuckle escaped his throat.

Without responding, she made her way to her notepad by the cash register and tapped the pencil tip against the paper. "Okay. I'm happy to oblige. But first we need to establish a price. How much do you want to spend?"

He thought a moment. "The sky's the limit."

Her eyes widened at his obvious generosity. "This must be an awfully special person!"

He lowered his shy gaze and nodded.

A combination of great respect for him and jealousy fought inside her. *I know it's a sin to be jealous, Lord. Please forgive me.*

Again, she tapped the pencil and considered other details she'd need to know. "What's the occasion?"

When he spoke, he offered a half smile. "How 'bout a summertime arrangement?"

She nodded. "Okay. Summertime it will be." She thought a moment. "Oh, one more thing. You prefer flowers, right? Not a plant?"

He nodded.

She laid down her pencil and quickly proceeded to the refrigerated area. He followed her, and they stepped inside. "Remember, make the selection based on your opinion." He softened his tone. "Like I said, I want it to be your best work."

She nodded and smiled. "Okay. Well, here goes. . ."

He looked on while she pulled her favorites: white gardenias, mini blue and pink carnations, and tulips.

She stepped over to her small work area and created the loveliest bouquet of flowers and greenery she could imagine. Gardenias were rarely in stock, and they were expensive, but she followed his instructions. Gardenias were her very favorite flower for beauty and aroma.

Because she put together the project as if doing it for herself, it didn't take long. Afterward she selected a large white box and carefully displayed the masterpiece in the center. Before carrying it to the cash register, she gave it final approval and smiled a little. Showing her arrangement, she pulled in a breath and met his pleased expression.

"What do you think?" She smiled and added, "I hope it meets your expectations."

His smile was warm, and his eyes emanated happiness as he pulled out his worn leather wallet.

"How much do I owe?"

She told him.

He paid.

"You're very generous, Stephen, and I hope the recipient appreciates your kind heart." Several moments later, she realized she'd forgotten to ask him what to write on the card and where to deliver it.

His voice was soft. "I almost forgot to add my personal touch."

She handed him a courtesy card and a black ink pen. While he printed, she held her breath, ordering herself to be grateful that this wonderful man obviously felt someone was so special, they deserved this extravagant bouquet.

He handed her the card, and his smile warmed. "I hope you enjoy it."

She didn't understand.

"It's for you."

Providence, Rhode Island

The more time Trini spent with her brother, the more she realized how much she'd missed him. It amused her how he and his wife, Stephanie, enjoyed takeout. At the dinner table, Trini watched while her brother's wife carefully opened the individual cardboard containers and emptied them onto different platters.

Stephanie smiled at Trini before going back to dishing out the meal. "I hope you like Chinese food."

Amos grinned at Trini, and for a moment they shared a look. He chuckled. "I doubt she's ever tried it." His gaze stuck on Trini.

Trini made sure to express her great appreciation. "Whatever it is, it smells delicious!"

Excitement edged Stephanie's voice. "It is! And it's full of healthy veggies too."

Trini doubted that anything that smelled so delicious could be healthy, but maybe it was. Immediately, her thoughts turned to Serenity and the numerous health foods she'd asked Trini and Abby to sample. From the smell, Trini guessed that these dishes were nothing at all like Serenity's fresh herbal dishes.

After saying grace, Amos dished Trini something she'd never seen before. "It's called an egg roll, and you can put hot mustard on it." Stephanie cut in. "I prefer sweet-and-sour sauce."

"They're both good," Amos added. "I'm sure you'll love them."

Trini squeezed sweet-and-sour sauce onto her egg roll and took a bite. She nodded in approval. "This is delicious!"

Amos grinned. "You'd never find these at an Amish lunch."

Stephanie took a drink of tea and then directed her attention to Trini. "Catch us up! How's your new job?"

Trini smiled a little. "Good. I really like the shop. And the clientele seem to really love to sew and quilt."

Amos turned to his wife and nodded.

Stephanie nodded. "I figured. I hope you're comfortable here, Trini. It's wonderful to have you." Between bites, she went on. "I regret not having known you better." She swallowed. "By the way, any news on the house sale?"

Trini shook her head. "Not yet. Hopefully soon! I'm looking forward to buying my own place here." Trini added, "Not that I'm any less grateful for your warm hospitality. But I miss Honey. And it will be nice to eventually have her here with me."

Amos glanced at Stephanie. "That's her horse. Our Trini's an animal lover."

"After my home sells, and my business, I should be able to afford something close to Providence, maybe Foster, where there's pasture."

Stephanie's eyes lit up. "Now is a good time to purchase. And we'll help in every way we can."

"Thanks. I appreciate that."

Stephanie edged her voice with concern. "Don't you miss your place?" Before Trini responded, Stephanie went on. "It's so beautiful and spacious." She drew her hands to her chest. "I don't know—there's just something about the open countryside. When we came to get you, I just had this feeling."

The comment surprised Trini. She wouldn't have guessed that her sister-in-law liked her farm.

Trini considered an answer. Finally, she offered a slow nod. "Yes. I really love my house. And especially my peach orchard. And. . ." A knot formed in her throat, and she paused a moment to swallow. "Like I mentioned, Honey."

Stephanie and Amos glanced at each other before their attention returned to Trini.

"Right now my friend is keeping him, so Honey's in good care." She looked down at the floor.

Trini neglected to mention Jacob. She felt it best not to bring him up. The last thing she wanted was her brother and his wife speculating about her love life. Besides, the amazing relationship she'd had with Jacob was over. She intended to write him. He'd asked her to. But their day-to-day interaction was a thing of the past.

"Oh!" Stephanie snapped her fingers. "I forgot to tell you. A letter came for you today. After dinner make sure to remind me to give it to you."

"I will."

As they ate, Trini's pulse picked up. She couldn't help it. Instinctively, she guessed that the mail was from Jacob. At the same time, she hoped that nothing was wrong with her family or friends.

Excitement welled inside her as she contemplated looking for a new place to live. She'd enjoy things she'd never experienced. Electric heat. And eventually a car. She'd learned how to use Uber. And she loved having a cell phone.

Usually her brother or Stephanie dropped her off at work, but she'd used Uber to visit clothing stores in the city. She extended her arms to admire the colorful balloon-type sleeves on her new blouse. She felt at ease with her hair down. And she absolutely loved wearing jeans and tennis shoes. But as she rejoiced about her new life, her mamm, her sisters, and especially Jacob hovered in the back of her mind. "I hope everyone's okay."

Amos glanced at her. "Meaning Mom and our sisters?"

"Uh-huh."

Amos' voice took on a more serious note. "I wish I could visit them."

Trini didn't respond because she couldn't recall her family ever having mentioned him since he'd left the Amish church. He'd been a member, and breaking membership had garnered much criticism from the tight-knit community in Arthur.

"Maybe when I return to sign the paperwork for my house, you and Stephanie can drive me back."

His eyes lit up. So did his wife's. "Of course, we'll take you."

After dinner, Trini helped Stephanie clean the kitchen, which didn't take much time because they used paper plates. And also because they merely loaded the glasses and silverware into their dishwasher.

Trini reminded Stephanie of the letter.

"Oh!" Her sister-in-law stepped to the mail pile and retrieved the top envelope. She handed it to Trini. "Here."

Trini thanked her and quickly headed to her room. She propped her head on two pillows, unsealed the envelope, and anxiously read out loud:

My dearest Trini,
I hope you're safe and that you're enjoying your freedoms. Know

that even though I miss you, I'm praying that your new world is everything you've hoped for.

I paid Honey a visit and fed him sugar cubes. He's lost weight. As he scarfed down my treats, I told him they were from you. Far be it from me to read a horse's thoughts, but I sensed that he understood. He misses you. I miss you. Please let me know how you're doing.

Love always,
Jacob

──────── ⚓ ────────

Arthur

At the mailbox, Jacob flipped through the pile of bills. He'd written Trini two weeks ago. He'd assumed she'd respond. Frowning, he looked down at the ground before closing the small door and ensuring the flag was down.

Thunder rumbled. Dark gray clouds floated ominously. A storm wasn't forecast, but nature's signs told him that one was coming. Soon.

Again, he flipped through his mail. He wasn't sure why. Because he was fully aware that what he wanted more than anything wasn't there. Heaving a sigh, he returned to the house.

As he approached the front porch, his most recent conversation with Stephen floated through his mind as the cool August breeze caressed his face. *"It's not gonna happen. She's gone. For good. Jake, the sooner you accept that, the sooner you can move on with your life."*

Surprisingly, even Gabe seemed less optimistic than a month ago. Recently he'd said, "Jacob, I love you. And I hate seeing you like this. She doesn't even respond to your letters. How many hints do you need?"

I knew better. Jacob shook his head in sadness as the gusty wind picked up speed. When the sky darkened another notch, rain began falling. The grim surroundings and precipitation warned him to get inside.

Metal pans at the end of the garden rows clanked lightly against the posts to which they were tied. The old wooden porch swing moved with the wind while the old, rusty chains that suspended it groaned. The wind forced oak limbs to the ground. Leaves danced in the air. Cattle distress moans throughout the vast, open countryside morphed into one grim chorus.

Before stepping back into the house, Jacob did a quick check of the yard to ensure that everything had been secured. The air was thick. Thunder clapped. He thought of Trini's mamm and sisters and hoped they would be okay. Surely they were aware that the best place during these high winds was their basement.

He pulled the mail close to his chest to protect the unopened envelopes from getting wet. With his other hand, he removed his hat, which nearly blew off his head. Stephen's low voice alerted him as his younger brother quickly rushed down the path that led to the barn.

With a big wave of his hand, he hollered, "Jacob! Hurry up! Help us get the horses inside and secure the barn door. This is gonna be a big one!"

Inside the kitchen, Jacob laid the mail on the table before rushing out the back door to join Stephen and Gabe. Together the three headed toward the barn where their horses joined them from the pasture. Without wasting time, Jacob filled the food trough with oats while Stephen added water to the other trough.

They quickly stepped back outside, closed the large, heavy doors, barred them shut, and rushed back to the house. As they approached the home, more thunder cracked.

He knew the path to the house by heart. Lightning flashed. Above them, limbs on the old, large oak trees moved with the wind. Leaves floated chaotically in the air. The damp air smelled of rain.

The moment they were inside, the downpour began. Although it was only three in the afternoon, the darkness made it seem as though it were nine o'clock at night. The roots of the garden vegetables were hopefully strong and deep enough to stay intact. A series of lightning bolts brightened the sky, which was now a pool of dark, misty clouds. Rain came in through the screen door, and Jacob quickly shut the wooden door behind them.

Stephen headed toward the towel drawer and pulled it open. "I'll clean up the water."

Gabriel removed his shoes, placed them on the mat near the door, and hung his hat on the hook. "The weatherman sure missed the boat on this one."

Stephen chuckled. "So much for the sunny afternoon he predicted."

Moments passed while they changed to dry clothes. Back in the kitchen, Stephen let out a low whistle. "This is some storm, huh?"

Gabriel chuckled. "Our crops begged for water. Now they're getting it. I don't know about you two, but I'm ready for something to eat. Anyone care for a hamburger?" Before either brother answered, Gabe removed a pound of hamburger from the refrigerator, threw three patties in a skillet, and started the gas burner.

"Sounds good." Stephen separated the blue curtains in order to see out the kitchen window above the sink.

"In the barn, I called to check the weather. Four inches of rain are coming with hail. The storm's from the northwest." After Jacob spoke, his thoughts quickly went to the woman he loved with all his heart and the house for sale up the road.

He stood in front of the large window next to the main entrance while the conversation between his brothers eventually faded. From where he stood, Jacob took in Trini's backyard. The wind wreaked havoc with her peach trees. He smiled a little as he remembered helping her off the ground when she'd fallen from the ladder.

At that time, he'd been so full of hope. Excited to have a second chance with Trini. His lips automatically curved into an amused smile. Of course, the first chance with Trini didn't count, since they'd been children.

His gaze drifted to the old swing some distance away and traveled up the long, sturdy rope to the tall, strong branch that held the tire. He closed his eyes a moment while visions of pushing her in that very swing consumed his thoughts.

He found it ironic that the current storm paralleled the mental storm he now endured. Unlike the weather, his private storm wouldn't end. He considered it a blessing that bad weather never lasted long. Now if only his sadness and disappointment would evaporate.

The only way to recover from losing Trini is to move on. But how do I go forward when she consumes me?

While he stared at the house she'd lived in, an indelible sadness filled him. He swallowed an uncomfortable knot in his throat. Another knot quickly replaced it.

While he imagined the work that would most likely need to be done to his aunt's place after the storm, he considered Trini's dwelling and lifted a doubtful brow. He knew that her structure didn't go below the ground. *At least she won't have basement water. But by the sounds of debris blowing, after this storm there could be damage to her roof. Tomorrow I'll check her place to make sure everything's okay. Because I love her. Because it's the Christian thing to do. Despite the circumstances, it's nothing less than my beloved late aunt would have expected of me.*

To my knowledge, the only people keeping an eye on Trini's place are her two best friends. I wonder if they've heard from her. I'm disappointed she hasn't written me.

As thunder rocked the sky, Jacob frowned and shoved his hands deep into the pockets of his trousers. *How could I have been so wrong? While I hoped to marry her, she was planning an out-of-state move.* He shook his head.

Stephen joined him with a cup of coffee. "Want a cup?"

Jacob waved a dismissive hand. "No thanks. It's too late in the day."

An understanding silence ensued while they stood side by side in silence, watching the lightning and listening to the wind howl. "Jacob, don't worry. Her house has been around for many years, and it will survive this storm." Stephen cleared his throat after taking another sip. "You have to survive it too."

For long moments, Jacob took in the real meaning of his brother's words. He knew Stephen so well.

"How did you know what I was thinking?"

Stephen chuckled and rested his free hand on Jacob's shoulder. "You're easy to read. Besides, I've lived with you for years. And all this time, you've never changed."

"I know the kind of life I want and need. And who I want in it. Is that so wrong?"

After a slight pause, Stephen released a deep sigh. "No. I hate to be the bearer of bad news, Jake, but you've got to realize that your wants don't synchronize with hers."

"Jah. I'm in a bit of a dilemma. After Trini left, I learned something very important." He offered a small shrug of his shoulders.

"What?"

Jacob let out a sigh of defeat. "I've never considered what to do with my life if my plans with her didn't materialize. I understand that what I'm going through is my own doing. I've asked Trini to marry me twice. Both times she gave me no answer. Now I understand that my plan is exactly that."

"What?"

"It's *my* plan." He lifted his shoulders in a quick shrug. "Not hers. A plan is never guaranteed to play out. I'd love for Trini's goals and needs to align with mine, but they don't. And it's no one's fault but my own for believing she yearned for the same things I do."

Stephen looked into his brother's eyes. "Jacob, it's common knowledge that most Amish women are satisfied with a simple life." When Jacob turned to face him, Stephen raised his voice and lifted his palms in the air as if to emphasize his point. "They are. I mean, how could you have known that the woman you've loved for years had her heart set on leaving the Plain faith?"

"I couldn't have."

"Exactly. But the problem is, you love a woman who doesn't fit the typical Amish mold."

Several seconds later, Jacob nodded in agreement. "You're right. What I liked about her, oddly enough, was her independence. And that she's a free thinker, Stephen. The very things that caused her to leave." He clenched his jaw and jerked his head in the direction of Trini's vacant home. "Now she's gone."

Jacob looked away.

Stephen took him by both shoulders so that Jacob was forced to meet the intense gaze of his brother's serious brown eyes. Today they conveyed turbulence. Just like Jacob's emotions.

Stephen lowered his pitch so it was barely more than a whisper. "Jacob, she's gone. But you've got your whole life ahead of you." He released his hands from Jacob's shoulders and spread his hands wide apart. "That's the gut news! Did you hear me?"

Jacob looked down.

With a swift motion, Stephen pushed Jacob's chin up so his brother had to look at him. "Jacob?"

Jacob nodded, and Stephen dropped his arms to his side. "I heard you. Trini's gone." Jacob lifted his palms in a helpless gesture before crossing his arms across his abdomen. "My whole life's ahead of me." He grimaced. "Now what?"

CHAPTER SIXTEEN

Providence, Rhode Island

Trini was finally settled in. *There's something so exciting about where I am in my life.* In the air-conditioned Sew Shop, she nearly forgot about the unusually hot and humid August evening outside. Cool air flowed constantly from side vents, gently lifting her long hair, which she'd curled at the ends with her new styling iron.

As students mingled and found their seats, quiet voices eventually morphed into one sound. Trini glanced at her watch and lifted her shoulders a notch. *Time to begin.*

After getting everyone's attention, she welcomed her quilt club and reviewed last week's lesson before picking up where she'd left off. Excitement prompted her heart to pick up speed to an enthusiastic, happy beat while she showed samples, pointing to the seams.

"This week I'll tell and show you some dos and don'ts to maintain your quilt's smooth, seamless look." She went on to explain ways to keep fabrics from bunching. To demonstrate she held a sample quilt in front of her and began to convey her tips. As she did so, strong memories of many quilts she'd designed and completed flitted back and forth in her mind. Emotions tugged at her heart. She wasn't able to shake the odd sensation. Still, she did her best to focus on this evening's class.

Afterward she answered questions before gathering her props and stashing them in the large bag she'd brought. After the last student left, a light knock on the door made her turn toward the entrance.

Trini glanced up and smiled. "Stephanie, I'm ready." She retrieved the store key, but at the door, Stephanie's hand stopped her. The solemn expression on her sister-in-law's face prompted a bad feeling.

"Trini, something has happened. I have bad news."

———————— ⚜ ————————

The following day, Amos drove Trini and Stephanie to Urbana, Illinois. Mary Sutter had suffered a nearly fatal heart issue and was currently undergoing a serious operation on her aorta.

Sad, frustrated emotions flitted through Trini's heart as they made their way toward the hospital. They'd left at 4 o'clock in the morning. At eight o'clock that night, Trini's heart pounded with fear and anticipation as they approached the hospital. She closed her eyes to calm herself and enjoyed the feel of the cool air that flowed from her back seat vent.

While Trini listened to her brother brief his wife about the agricultural industry, she felt sorry for those who were privy only to city life. Although Trini had decided to leave the area she'd been born into, she still loved the spacious countryside. That would never change.

She especially appreciated the vast amount of unclaimed space on the roads. There was no doubt about it. Rhode Island was a nice place to live. But she admitted that after returning to the spacious Midwest, her new home out east seemed a bit crowded.

"Does everyone around here farm?" Stephanie asked.

Amos stopped at a four-way intersection. "Those who have land do. With the Amish, that used to be the case." After Stephanie glanced at Amos, he continued. "About farming. In the old days, the Amish were mostly farmers. But these days. . ." He whistled. "Land is pricey. So members of the Plain faith who aren't beneficiaries of family land are forced to pursue other lines of work. Like welding. Making furniture. Building homes. But that's not all bad. Amish are known for their savvy business skills. They're honest. And they work hard at what they do."

After smiling at his wife, he went on. "The Amish thrive at furniture making. And of course, there are other businesses. Like Trini's quilt shop."

"Oh! Could we drive by it?"

Amos grinned at her and laid his free hand on her thigh. "Not today, honey. After we go to the hospital, we'll drive to Arthur. It's somewhat close to where Mom is having surgery. We'll be at Trini's by midnight or so." He blew his wife a kiss.

Trini watched the obvious gestures of love between the two. By now she was used to their displays of affection. The Amish tended to be less demonstrative with theirs. But Amos and Stephanie were the antithesis of what Trini had seen her entire life.

When Trini's daed had been alive, he and Mamm hadn't kissed or held hands, at least not in front of the kids. But surprisingly, Trini admired the way her brother and his wife showed their love for each other. While Trini had been living with them, she'd never heard an argument.

In Urbana, traffic picked up. The college campus was nearby. Amos followed the sign to the health care facility's large parking garage. As he stopped and rolled down his window to take a small white ticket, the seriousness of this drive reclaimed Trini's thoughts. However, she was grateful for the brief change in subject.

Amos' voice reflected grave concern. "I hope Mom's okay."

Trini echoed, "Me too."

Stephanie laid an affectionate hand on her husband's thigh.

Inside, Amos led the women, asking at the information booth for Mary's room number and location.

The volunteer made a call. As she talked, Trini took in the stark white walls, the gift shop, the restrooms, people stepping in and out of the elevators. She closed her eyes and prayed. Her stomach ached. When the woman hung up, her face showed concern. "She's in ICU." She wrote down the number on a small slip of paper. She frowned. "I'm afraid they don't allow visitors on that floor."

The statement didn't surprise Trini. It further confirmed the dire circumstances she faced. The lady kindly motioned and gave them simple directions to where it would be best to wait. "A nurse will update you on her progress."

In silence, Stephanie walked alongside Amos. Trini followed. The only sound was the light bell when the elevator stopped on the lounge floor.

At the entrance, they suddenly faced several of Amos and Trini's sisters. Trini's jaw dropped. For long moments, the two different groups seemed to study each other with a curious intensity.

Then Trini broke into tears as she tightly embraced Sarah, who appeared the most approachable. They held each other at arm's length. Trini choked as her words came out. "How is she?"

After a soft lift of her shoulders, Sarah explained. Esther joined them, telling how they'd been in Mamm's kitchen yesterday, making sponge cakes for a sick woman in their congregation, when their mother had suddenly struggled to breathe and had passed out.

A long silence ensued while the words sank in. Then something wonderful started happening. Amos began embracing his family members one by one, and they reciprocated. Trini's heart melted with joy as they reunited as a family.

For over an hour, they discussed what the surgeon and the nurses had told them. Trini lowered her voice, grimly acknowledging that her mother's chances of surviving weren't guaranteed.

But the feeling she experienced right now—there was something special and surprising about it—how Amos' sisters seemed to accept

Stephanie and how much love and forgiveness were apparent. Tears of joy stung Trini's eyes.

Others seemed to feel the same way, and emotions were evident. Tears and hugging evidenced a camaraderie that was unique and new to Trini. And she prayed a sincere thanks to Gott.

Then Amos brought the group together for prayer. In a large circle, they joined hands while Trini's brother prayed for the role model they all loved so dearly.

Trini's words came out with great concern as she opened up to her family. "She *will* make it through this."

After a short time of silence, Rachel stepped opposite Trini. Her voice hinted a potent dose of resentment. "She needs to know you care, Trini."

"That all of us care," Trini corrected.

Rachel shook her head. "Especially you, Trini. You're the one who broke her heart."

———————— ⚓ ————————

Trini had a potential buyer for her house. But all she could think about during the drive to Arthur, after the visitor's hours had ended that evening, in the back seat of Amos' car, was the hurtful statement that Rachel had made with such resentment in the waiting lounge.

As if reading her thoughts, Amos glanced back at her. "It's okay, Trini. Rachel was out of line to say what she said. You know that your leaving had nothing to do with Mom's heart issue. The doctor explained about the tests they ran, and the results were there. You had absolutely nothing to do with her leaky aorta valve."

Trini's voice shook. "It was a very hurtful statement, and if she intended to cause me pain, she succeeded."

Stephanie cut in with her soft, calming voice. "Maybe your sister just needed to lash out at someone and it was easy to place the blame on you."

Amos flipped on the turn signal.

Trini's tone was thoughtful. "I suppose I'm an easy target for blame. And of course, I forgive my sister for lashing out at me. But in some ways. . ." She shrugged and tried to force herself to stay strong. "I can't help but feel guilty."

Amos pulled into Arthur. "Let's face it. Life wasn't going to be perfect if you'd stayed or if you'd left. At the end of the day, Trini, you had to follow your heart."

"But Sarah said something strange on my way out."

"What?"

"She told me that I'd always been the favorite. I can't believe it's true, because if it is, Mamm had a funny way of showing it. I just couldn't do anything to please her, or rather, that's how it appeared to me."

For a time, they rode in silence down the country road. Trini narrowed her brows and leaned forward in her seat a bit. She knew the landscape like the back of her hand, despite the darkness preventing a good view.

But her mind was still on her mother. "It always seemed that I couldn't measure up to her expectations. And it was discouraging."

Amos shook his head. "I think she was that way with all of us, Trini." He shrugged. Then his voice cracked with emotion. "I want to see her again. I pray she'll make it through this." He wiped at his eyes.

Trini nodded. "Me too." In the distance, she glimpsed her house, thanks to the car lights. And Jacob's. She pressed her lips together in a straight line and considered what his reaction would be to seeing her again. She wouldn't intentionally see him. In fact, she would take great care not to lead him on.

But within the small community, it was unlikely they wouldn't run into each other during her time here. She wasn't sure of the duration. It depended on her mamm's recovery. Sadness welled in the pit of Trini's stomach.

She knew her return would garner criticism. She'd take it because she had to. Most likely, there would be uncomfortable moments because some considered her a traitor, and Amos too. But it wouldn't be all bad. In general, Amish people were forgiving.

Regardless, right now she needed to be here. *Sometimes you have to do things you don't want to do. That's just how life is. And definitely, this is one of those occasions.*

Amos lowered the pitch of his voice. "We can stop by The Quilt Room on our way to the hospital tomorrow."

Stephanie's voice lifted in sudden enthusiasm. "Oh, that would be fun!" Suddenly it dawned on Trini that Stephanie was oblivious to what she and Amos would most likely encounter upon their return. She wasn't sure how much her brother had really shared with his wife about the Plain faith and the repercussions of desertion. Her family's surprising behavior toward them, for the most part, had been a welcome surprise.

In her heart, Trini hoped that she and Amos would be mostly welcomed with love in their community. But considering that Amos had parted ways with the church after having joined, she doubted that everyone would open their arms to him. Although she had never actually joined their church, she was aware that most no longer considered her one of them. She sighed.

I will be kind to everyone, even those who don't reciprocate. That's what every Christian should do.

———————— ⚓ ————————

There was unfinished business. The following morning, Trini's first thought was of her mother. *Please, Gott, let her begin a full recovery. I realize now how very much I yearn for her love and approval.*

Having Amos and Stephanie at her home felt gut. Trini looked out her bedroom window and smiled a little when she glimpsed them walking from the barn. Inside her bedroom, she paused and glanced thoughtfully around the four corners.

Emotions nearly drowned her. Uncertainty about her mamm, uncertainty about her home now that an offer was in the works, and uncertainty about her strong feelings for Jacob.

For years this place had been her haven. She bit her bottom lip and took in the simple bed and the beautiful quilt of white, cream, and sky blue that neatly covered it. Mamm had worked months to make it. Just for Trini.

Trini had always loved the simple yet elegant-looking oak desk and chair on the opposite side of the room. She traveled back in time to the day her loving daed had gifted his most special work to her for her sixteenth birthday.

Her eyes stung with salty tears, and she blinked to rid the sting. Both joy and sadness overcame her as she took in the ornate details. *I miss Daed.* She clutched her hands over her chest, and her heart ached.

The curved wood around the main desk frame was smoothed to perfection. The flat writing area where she'd composed many letters, especially during the holidays, held a slightly darker stain. He'd spent extra effort rounding the corners and designing a ridge underneath the overlay.

Her favorite part of the set was the chair's back that opened on the sides with two single curved portions in the middle where her back met the wood. Memories of her daed overcame her until she nearly cried. When he was here on earth, things had been different. Better.

Why am I an emotional basket case? For years I've admired this special piece, yet now I'm observing it as if it's the final time I'll see it. But it won't be the last. I'll take it back east with me. I just need to wait for this home to sell so that I can purchase something near my brother and Stephanie.

Trini realized, of course, that the set would always be extremely special to her because, out of the hundreds of pieces her daed had created, this was his final work before he had joined Gott in heaven.

I know he's with our Creator. Still, I miss him terribly. His calm, reassuring, gentle touch always balanced out Mamm's harsher, stricter, unbending nature. But I still love her. Gott gave her to me for a reason.

Daed, if you were still here, I would have stayed. Because after I lost you, Mamm changed. It was like she did everything within her power to make my decisions. Now I realize that maybe she feared losing me too.

Trini drew in a deep breath before finally stepping over to her hope chest, which was hidden under a small knit blanket in her closet. With a slow, deliberate motion, she knelt and opened the latch. Her fingers shook slightly as they lingered on the metal.

She swallowed a knot in her throat as her thoughts flew in chaotic directions. Time seemed to stand still while she pressed her lips together and considered her life's purpose. To force her confidence, she squared her shoulders.

Her thoughts drifted to Jacob. She'd tried so hard to rid him from her mind. But forgetting him was impossible.

I look forward to talking with him. She breathed in a hopeful, frightened breath. *I understand if he doesn't want to see me. He has written. He's also had plenty of time to change how he once felt about me.*

She considered her purpose while relishing the light, woodsy scent of the chest. *If not for this emergency, I might not have seen him until a wedding or a funeral.* She grimaced.

Her hands froze on the chest as she surprisingly realized how terribly strong her love for him was and that she'd never realized its tremendous strength until she'd been away. She stiffened. *I can't bury my love for him. My need for him. I tried.*

But Jacob was only human. Despite his love for her, there was only so much he would tolerate. And she had definitely crossed the line.

It is totally within my rights as an individual to choose where I want to live and how I want to play out my earthly days. I never chose the Amish church. I was born into it.

Pain and joy filled her chest with pain, and she closed her eyes to ascertain which emotion won out. When she couldn't decide, she opened her eyes and continued her reflections.

Returning to her roots had sparked an unexpected awakening within her. She yearned to define what it was. She was unsure of herself. Her fingers shook. The corners of her lips dropped. To her disappointment, she wasn't certain she wanted to return to Rhode Island. *I don't believe this. What a mess I've made.*

Trini's heart developed an uncertain beat. Her mother's sudden, unexpected crisis, along with being away from her humble beginnings, had opened her mind to an entirely different viewpoint than she'd had before she'd left. Instead of bringing her joy and certainty, living Englisch had actually forced her to take a good look at the love and security she'd been privy to her entire life. She'd never really realized how much she loved her mamm and sisters, and now she acknowledged that their interferences in her life had been intended to help and guide her in the right direction, not to intrude.

Stop stalling. Open the chest.

The latch clicked, and she slowly pushed up the lid. The metal hinge that connected the wooden lid to the body of the beautiful oak piece creaked as she continued to push it all the way open. She'd never looked inside this old treasure that had been gifted to her by her daed. The scent of oak stain filled her nostrils, and she smiled.

Her heart did a joyful jump as she lifted a stack of old greeting cards and spotted Jacob's simple handmade card bearing a red heart. Her body flooded with warmth as she touched it and slowly pulled it from the chest.

Will you marry me? The very heart that Jacob had drawn just for her at five years old suddenly sparked emotion that was so strong it tugged relentlessly at her entire being until her eyes filled with tears. His words claimed her breath.

She blinked to rid the salty sting, but the burning sensation lingered. Her vision blurred with tears as she stared with great appreciation at the drawing, deeply valuing the young boy's unconditional love for her that had prompted him to make it. With great care, she opened the folded card and released a deep breath as she took in the blank page.

She'd never responded. Not long ago, he'd asked her again. Same thing. No reply. She laid the card back in the chest.

With full certainty, Trini knew what she wanted. *I love my mamm, and I have to tell her. And I love Jacob and yearn to marry him.*

Quick, certain steps took her to her master list, hidden in the closet under a soft blanket. She carefully took it in her fingers and glanced at the top line. *Become Englisch.*

She studied it for a long time. Finally, she took the list to her desk and crossed off her primary goal. Still thoughtful about what she was doing, she finally relaxed her shoulders. Then she proceeded to tear the paper in half and discard the two pieces in her small trash can.

Surely God doesn't expect us to be perfect. His twelve disciples weren't even close to perfection, and He loved them. Neither was Moses. Neither was Noah. Or David. Neither is Trini Sutter.

The Englisch world was a distant dream. But my Amish life is where I belong. I had to figure this out for myself.

As she glanced down at Jacob's card in the top of the hope chest, she lifted a curious brow. *What would it be like to marry Jacob? He proposed twice. Will he try again?*

———————— ⚓ ————————

There are two options. The following day, Jacob used his best logic while raking the dirty horse bedding. As usual, he started at the back of the stall, where the barn's wall separated the inside of the structure from the large, vast pasture. As he raked, the metal made a light, unpleasant sound as it moved across the floor. As he worked, the heap of straw grew. Animal smells filled Jacob's nostrils.

The old barn groaned and creaked in response to the gusty wind that was predicted to become even stronger by the end of the day. His thoughts were on Trini's return and the realization that he might never be able to stop loving her. *I can put Trini out of my mind. At least, try. Or I can risk my heart again and propose a final time. There are no guarantees. Especially with independent Trini. I'm glad she came for her mamm. And I'm relieved Mary's prognosis is good.* By now, church members had spread the word after Sarah had phoned the bishop's wife with a recent update.

As he moved his arms, his energy grew. He enjoyed working in this atmosphere. Always had. Something about this large, old structure where his late aunt had loved to spend time brightened his outlook on life.

Survivor's tail swished back and forth as the handsome beast stepped outside to join the other two standardbreds. Jacob smiled. The horse would, in a matter of time, rejoin him in hopes of more sugar cubes. Since Trini's move, he'd prayed to forget her. He'd initiated numerous conversations with his brothers, but each time he'd mentioned her, he'd glimpsed tired, concerned lines around their eyes. *Now, she has a buyer for her house.*

Logic had told him that he was fighting his battle alone. Repeatedly, he'd prayed about his situation. *Gott answers prayers. And He hears mine—I know He does.*

Eventually Jacob worked his way to the front of the stalls. Metal clattered and a hammer pounded nails into the wall. Stephen was creating additional space to hang extra tools and equipment they had purchased for the farm.

When Aunt Margaret had been alive, the only horse had been hers. Now three horses called this barn their home. And that meant three times the food and three times the bedding.

The rake's metal fingers made an ear-piercing scratching sound as they slid across the concrete floor. As Jacob tidied the small area where he worked, Survivor joined him and gave a loud, demanding whinny.

Just as I predicted. The horse gave a strong shake of its head, and straw particles flew off the large body and into Jacob's face. He propped his rake against the stall as tears began to rinse his eyes. He wiped the moisture away with the back of his hand. Focusing on the animal, Jacob curved his lips in amusement and gently stroked the sensitive place around Survivor's right ear.

"Ah, that feels gut, doesn't it?" He edged his voice apologetically. "I've been preoccupied. I'm sorry for neglecting to give you the attention you deserve. But you've got it now."

The horse clomped its hooves again, stirring another generous dose of straw dust into the air. Jacob closed his lids for long seconds until he guessed the particles had settled. When he opened his eyes, he deepened the massage.

"If you could talk, you'd ask for an apple, wouldn't you?" Jacob raised a curious brow. "Or even better, a sugar cube. Which one would you prefer?"

Not expecting a verbal response, Jacob stepped to the bar that separated the stall from the rest of the barn and proceeded to the wall shelf to pluck a red apple from the large handmade basket that his late aunt had designed solely for treats.

He bounced the fruit on his palm before holding it in front of him. As he returned to Survivor, Stephen joined him. With humor in his voice, he said, "Whatever you do, Jacob, make sure you spoil him. That's what our aunt would have wanted. Nothing less."

Together they chuckled. Stephen followed Jacob back to the stall where Jacob stood outside the entrance bar.

A gentle slap on Jacob's shoulder stopped him.

Stephen's tone was serious. "What's wrong?"

Jacob narrowed his brows and pretended innocence. "What

makes you think something's not right?"

Before Stephen replied, he proceeded to push the wheelbarrow. At the same time, Jacob's horse gratefully accepted both treats before migrating outside into the vast, open area of pasture. Stephen pulled a pair of work gloves from his pockets and used a wide, oversized shovel to load the old straw piles into the wheelbarrow.

He spoke without looking up. "You're not humming."

Jacob smiled at the astute observation and glanced down at his work boots. Without thinking, he tapped the toe of his right boot against the concrete floor, then stood very still before lifting his chin enough to meet his brother's serious gaze.

"Jacob, working in the barn is what you love more than anything. Whether it's this barn or the one in Lancaster County, you always hum your favorite hymns while you clean the horse stalls."

He shook his head and filled his voice with sympathy. "It's been a while since Gabe and I have heard you hum." After a slight pause, he shook his head. "Something's wrong."

Jacob gave him a weak smile. "Guess I can't fool anyone, can I?"

Stephen replied with a quick, firm shake of his head.

As Stephen continued loading the wheelbarrow, Jacob raked more used bedding and added it to his pile. He couldn't hide his discouragement. "I don't know what to do about Trini."

Stephen stopped what he was doing, propped his shovel against the gate, and laid both of his palms on the wheelbarrow handles. After a slight pause, he looked away, as if making a serious decision.

When he turned his attention back to Jacob, conviction filled his voice. "I don't like to involve myself in your personal business, but it's funny."

"What?"

Stephen chuckled. "You said that Trini doesn't know what to do if she can't complete something on her list."

Jacob nodded.

"You're not a list maker and never have been. At least not in writing."

Jacob waited for him to continue.

"But in a way, you're a lot like her."

Jacob grimaced. "I don't get it."

"She writes her goals. You have always known yours, even though you don't pen them. So the way I see it is that your Trini feels that she has to physically cross off things that she finishes. You, on the other hand, need to accomplish mental lists. And because you've had in mind marrying her for such a long time, you don't know what to do when you realize that your dream might not happen."

Jacob stood very still while he considered Stephen's point.

"Jacob, we can't have everything we want. Maybe you could look at an alternative."

Jacob frowned. "You mean another woman?"

Stephen offered a slow nod. "Remember what Aunt Margaret used to say?"

Jacob listened.

"Sometimes we have to create a different path to get things done." A long, thoughtful silence passed while Jacob considered the wisdom. Finally, he realized that his brother's intentions were good. They always were.

Jacob offered a firm nod. "I get your point."

"There are other women in our church who would love to become Mrs. Jacob Lantz. I'm sure of it."

Jacob looked down at his boots before lifting his chin to meet his brother's sincere, hopeful gaze. "Jah. I could find someone else to court and eventually marry. But right now, I want to be with Trini." He laid a hand on Stephen's shoulder. "I'm looking for more than someone to bear my children and help with chores." He lowered the pitch of his voice. "I want true love."

Stephen nodded, looking down at the floor. Then he peered into

Jacob's eyes as if trying to send a message and get it to stick. "But my brotherly instincts are coaching me to remind you that there's absolutely nothing you can do about Trini not seeking the same thing. That's why relationships are tricky. Both people have to want each other. It's a two-way street. In my opinion, Trini's making it very difficult for you to have her. And honestly. . ."

Jacob waited for the remainder of Stephen's thought to turn into words.

"Life is short. Jacob, she's made her choice. How long are you going to mourn your loss?" Before Jacob could answer, Stephen's voice was firm. "Please, brother. Move on."

With one swift motion, Stephen lifted the handles of the wheelbarrow and pushed it toward the large doors. Outside, he turned back and raised his voice so Jacob could hear him. "After I dump this, I'm going into town with Gabe."

While Jacob finished his cleanup, he considered his brother's well-intended, straight-to-the-point advice. Sometime later he exited the stall, closed the gate behind him, locked the latch, and proceeded to the rustic-looking wood ladder leading up to the loft that housed bales of straw and hay.

At the top, he pushed out a breath and moved his hands to his hips while he pressed his palms against them. Jacob looked over the farming tools and the neatly organized items in various parts of the barn, and he seriously contemplated Stephen's dismal but realistic outlook on Jacob's future with Trini.

Jacob frowned. *He's written us off. So has Gabe. Am I unrealistic?* The more he rethought Stephen's terse statement, the more he reluctantly admitted that his brother might be right.

But Jacob had never been one to give up. *When Daed left us, Mamm insisted that love was a two-way street. That a never-ending love which endured throughout eternity was worth every compromise in the world.*

I need to move on. And I will. Aunt Margaret always had answers. I wish I could ask her what to do.

He closed his eyes and asked Gott to guide him. When he opened his eyes, he recalled an old Amish proverb that his aunt had often recited about regrets over yesterday and fears of tomorrow robbing us of today.

He considered the significance of that wise advice and how it played into his relationship with Trini. As the summer breeze moved the branches against the barn, he folded his arms over his chest and pressed his lips together in a straight, thoughtful line.

Several moments later, he let out a deep breath of relief and relaxed his shoulders. "Thank you, Lord, and thank you, Aunt Margaret. I understand what you meant. I'm going to live again and not waste another precious moment. Why did I wait so long to ask?"

CHAPTER SEVENTEEN

Mamm was making a strong recovery. Trini yearned to stay in Arthur where she belonged. Where her roots were. She needed to be here for Mamm and her sisters. They'd always been here for her.

Without a doubt, Amish life was her very being. That didn't mean it was perfect, but it did mean that it was her choice to be a loyal member of the Plain faith. Daed had often made it clear that the grass was never greener on the other side. Trini had needed to find that out for herself. She'd longed to leave. Now her heart told her to come home.

Most of all, she wanted to marry Jacob. Yearned for it so strongly her heart ached. She pressed her lips together in a thoughtful line that sank into a frown.

I can make things right with my family. And I can fix relationships in my church, for the most part. But Jacob—I'm not sure. I've turned down his two sincere proposals. I may have crossed the line, but I pray that I can win back his heart. I don't deserve him. But I see and understand things that I never could when I lived here.

I've avoided Jacob since I've been home, but not for the reasons he might think. I have steered clear of him because I'm so undeserving of his love. And I can't believe that I'm actually guilty of the very thing I disapprove of most within our church. I've shunned the best person in

my life. I'm ashamed of myself.
   I want to marry him. But is it too late?

———————— ⚓ ————————

An hour after Jacob mucked the horse stalls, the dark sky released heavy rain. The ground was still saturated from the last storm. Gott was gut to the farmers. Jacob didn't mind working inside the barn all day. In fact, he relished it. He loved the way the rain sounded when it hit the roof.

Today his dear aunt's personal touches in the barn created an eerie yet tighter-than-usual bond with her. A light sensation trickled up his spine, and he shook his shoulders to rid the odd feeling when it eventually landed uncomfortably at the back of his neck.

Aunt Margaret. He breathed in and stood very still with his hands on his hips. He knew it was impossible for her to be here, but he was sure Gott worked in mysterious ways. Despite the years of his pastors' schooling, Jacob was sure that there was at least as much that they didn't know as they did.

After his terse yet sympathetic conversation with Stephen, Jacob was certain that he would move on with his life for good. *There's no indication that Trini misses me. In fact, she avoids me. I get the hint. Finally.* He had no control over her reaction. But he could write off their strained relationship and move on. Thunder cracked. Tree branches scratched the outside of the barn as the wind blew limbs. Again, a peculiar sensation swept up his back and landed between his shoulders. This time he didn't try to rid it.

Today is not a normal day. I'm sure of it, but I don't know how I know it. He looked up at the loft and rubbed his palms together before returning his hands to his hips. *Rain is forecast the rest of the day and into the night. There's nothing I can do outside. I need to organize the bales in the loft. After that, I'll rebuild the ladder. The wood is rotting.*

He smiled a little and stepped up to the loft. At the top, he lifted each straw bale by the thick, strong twine that held it together. After he moved them to one side of the small area and stacked them, he repeated his actions with the hay.

The bit-by-bit organization created considerably more room. And with three standardbreds, he and his brothers would need as much bedding and food as this loft would hold. With one swift motion, he pulled a folded paper from his shirt pocket and carefully unfolded the paper with the ladder design and dimensions he'd worked on.

The point of rebuilding the ladder isn't merely to make it safer and easier to climb. It has much to do with adding to the already-homey ambience my loving aunt created over many years. The new project will provide larger, wider steps and railings on both sides. It will be a dressier version of the old rustic stairs.

On the ground floor, he whistled while pulling out his generously sized workbench, a saw, and a tape measure. He spent long, thoughtful moments deciding where to start.

He glanced down at his detailed drawing on the far side of the oak bench. Before he tore down what was here, he'd construct the new steps to ensure a quick, easy replacement.

I'm humming again. For some strange reason, positive vibes are with me now. I can't explain why. Perhaps because I've thanked Gott for my life and have decided not to waste more precious time. He has always been here for me in my time of need. He will never fail me, and I'll accept whatever plans He has for me.

Two hours later, he stopped and laid his saw in the center of the bench. One rule he'd learned from Margaret, many years ago, was to ensure a safe work environment. That meant always placing sharp objects where they were clearly visible and out of the way of causing an accident.

After taking a swig of water, he returned the remainder of the liquid to the far end of the bench and hummed while he studied his carefully measured design. He tapped the toe of his boot against the concrete floor while he glanced up at the loft.

He narrowed his brows. Finally, the corners of his lips dropped into a doubtful frown. He stopped his whistling of "Near the Cross," and chewed his lip.

These numbers just don't seem right. His aunt had often told him that doing a project right the first time was much less time consuming than rushing a job that would need to be redone.

He shoved his tape measure into his deep left trouser pocket, smiled with optimism, and proceeded toward the old ladder. At the top, he brushed his palms together to rid straw dust from his hands.

As he measured, an unusual, unexplainable sensation filled his chest. To his surprise, his written numbers were right on. He remeasured. *Same result.* He nodded in satisfaction.

He slipped the tape measure back into his pocket, stood, and pressed his palms against his hips as he imagined his finished project. He smiled a little and hummed as he bent to start down the old ladder that lacked a rail.

He looked forward to completing his new stairway. The carefully thought-out design would provide an incline.

With careful steps, Jacob started down.

"Jacob." A familiar-sounding female voice startled him. At that very moment, the step he clutched gave way in the middle. Before he could react, he fell and landed on his back.

Her scream was loud. To his surprise, he wasn't on the barn's hard concrete floor. Beneath him, Trini let out a moan that, without a doubt, conveyed excruciating pain.

As quickly as he could recover from his shock, he forced his aching body off hers. They lay side by side on the hard concrete, and their gazes met. Trini burst into laughter. He took in the expression on her face. She was not okay.

"Trini. . ."

Tears filled her eyes.

"What have I done?" He paused. "Trini, don't move." He was aware that she could have a spinal injury.

She closed her eyes, and her expression conveyed serious pain. Her voice cracked with apparent agony. "I can't move."

He got up and started toward the wall phone. "I'm calling for help."

After he hung up, he tended to her, checking her hands and feet to make sure she had feeling in her limbs. As he did so, he recalled her words after the fall. His fall. He softened his voice to the most gentle, most loving tone he'd ever used. "You saved me." He couldn't stop his eyes from filling with tears. His body ached, but he bent over her.

"Jacob. . ."

Paramedics rushed into the barn. He looked on as they did their job. Strangely, she laughed, seemingly unaware of her predicament.

Then reality hit him, and a fear like he'd never felt swept through him. *She's in shock. Please, Gott. Let her be okay.*

———————— ⚘ ————————

Trini had broken her right arm. She also had suffered a severe concussion and broken ribs. That evening she sat very still on her couch. Her sisters had just left. Mary Sutter was still in the hospital recovering in a regular patient room, and Amos and Stephanie had returned to Rhode Island.

Jacob was still here. Trini watched him with interest as he brought her the hospital's ice packs.

"Here."

With his usual gentleness, he propped her injured wrist on some towels that he had rolled up for support. As he bent next to her, he adjusted the ice pack in the towel that she rested her head on. Their gazes met. "I've had plenty of practice," he said with a twinkle in his eye. "Are you comfortable?"

She offered a nod and then winced from the concussion. But the piercing agony inside her had nothing to do with her broken arm, her broken ribs, or the crushing pain inside her head. It had everything to do with the man taking care of her and her strong feelings for him.

I don't deserve him. Does he still love me?

He smiled. As he did, she sensed something very different about him but couldn't pinpoint what it was. Everything was becoming painfully clear to her. *He doesn't feel about me like he did. He's here taking care of me only because he has a guilty conscience about my condition. But now I'm deeply and eternally in love with him.*

He softened his voice, and his eyes seemed to penetrate all the way to her soul as he whispered, "What am I going to do with you, Trini Sutter?"

His eyes didn't leave hers. She cleared the knot that suddenly blocked her throat. "There is something I need you to do." Uncertainty caused her to pause. "That is, if you don't mind."

His brows narrowed in a blend of concern and interest. "What?"

She swallowed again before blinking away the salty sting of tears that burned her eyes. "My hope chest—it's in my closet." She parted her lips a moment. "It's a mini hope chest." After another slight hesitation, her words came out in what was barely more than a whisper. "Would you bring it to me?"

He seemed to study her with a curious intensity. "Jah."

She added, "It's the first room on the right."

With one swift motion, he stood and stepped toward her room. As she watched him walk away, her fingers trembled. She closed her eyes in anticipation and breathed in while the sound of his boots clicking lightly against the floorboards eventually faded. She could hear the door hinges creak. She opened her eyes. Through the open space, she easily glimpsed the dining room table. She blinked back the sting of salty tears.

At that very table, they'd enjoyed the grilled cheese sandwiches Jacob had made. It was where he'd indicated how truly special she was to him. From where she'd sat on the straight-backed oak chair, she'd glimpsed such an honest, open, and sincere expression. As she pressed her lips together in a thoughtful, straight line, she automatically looked down at her removable cast and the evenly spaced, tightly fastened Velcro straps.

Her vision blurred while she blissfully drifted back in time to her fall from the ladder and Jacob's attentiveness to her. His gentle voice echoed through her. The concerned lines around his mouth and eyes were imprinted permanently in her mind. And her astonishment at his marriage proposal right outside her kitchen porch now claimed her heart, yanking at it until it nearly broke with sadness at what he'd offered her and what she'd refused. He'd wanted to give her his name. His life. His everything. And she'd thrown it away without fully realizing it was all she'd ever dreamed of.

I could have had my dream. It was in the palm of my hand. Only, at the time, I didn't realize that Jacob was and is my dream. I wasn't aware that I would come to appreciate and miss the people in my Amish community, the very ones who loved and nurtured me since my birth. Nor could I see how much my mother needed me and that in time I would realize we needed each other.

It took a drastic move outside the state where I was born and raised to realize that I voluntarily gave up everything I loved and needed. Everything and nothing less that would have made my tormented life complete. I'm going to be completely honest with him even though it might be too late for us. How could I have missed that everything I could ever have wanted was right in front of me?

As Jacob approached with her hope chest, Trini forced composure. It was difficult not to shake inside. She breathed in and closed her eyes a moment. *Dear Gott, please work a miracle for me.*

His eyes reflected uncertainty. Slowly and with great care, he placed the chest on the couch next to her. With one swift but careful motion, he joined her on the other side of the wooden chest.

She thanked him. Before she turned, she noticed his face held a confused expression. Soon she would explain everything. And he would understand. With one slow motion, she opened the lid, and time seemed to stand still while she reached inside. He watched her with great interest. When she spoke, her voice cracked with emotion. "A long time ago, a sweet young boy asked me to marry him. He was very serious. Mature for his age."

A short silence passed as they looked intensely into each other's eyes. She swallowed, knowing that this was her one chance to try to win him back. This was the only opportunity she would have, she was sure, to try to make him understand that she was the same person he'd loved since an early part of her life.

Tell him. Now. He'll understand. But will he still want me as his wife? Her voice shook, and her bottom lip quivered as she tried a smile. "I didn't want to hurt his feelings, so to be tactful, I told him I'd consider his proposal when we were older."

With great urgency and uncertainty, she handed him the card he'd given her years ago. His face was austere. Unreadable. In silence he took it between his fingers and looked at the hand-drawn heart. Seconds passed while he appeared to study it.

Finally, his eyes met hers and he smiled. Emotion filled his voice as he inched closer to her. His voice wavered. "I can't believe you kept it."

After a slight pause, her response was soft and sincere. "I'm surprised too." She hesitated, trying for the right words, knowing that she would never again take what he'd offered her for granted. She cleared the lump from her throat and went on. "But deep down inside my young heart, I must've known that I would fall deeply in love with the boy who gave it to me." She fought back tears and bit her bottom lip until it hurt. "And I have."

"Trini. . ." He leaned closer to her. The only sound was her own heart beating. She thought it would burst right out of her body. She tried to stymie the fast rate of her chest's nervous, anxious breathing.

"What if the man is Amish?"

Her smile widened in hopefulness. "That's the only way I would have it."

Uncertain flecks danced hopefully in his eyes as he continued to study the simple card. *What are you thinking? Please say something, Jacob. Tell me that you still love me and that it's not too late for us.*

"Trini, I've cared for you since you pushed me on the swing at my aunt's. But at that time, I loved you as a boy. Now I love you as a man loves a woman."

She released a huge sigh of relief, trying to hold back tears of joy.

"Jacob, I will join the Amish church." She looked away before meeting his gaze. "Not only to marry you but because it's where I belong. It is the very core of my existence. Obviously I've got some fences to mend. But the main thing is that I've finally found my true being. And who I belong with." She lifted her shoulders in a helpless shrug. "Unfortunately, I had to give up my wonderful life to know that I want it."

The expression on Jacob's face was of pure happiness. He caressed her fingertips that stuck out below the removable cast. "You've changed. I never thought I could love you more, but I do." Several heartbeats later, he smiled a little. "Gott works in mysterious ways."

"Jah, He does. And learning who I am couldn't have happened without me giving up everything." She softened her voice with emotion. "Jacob, you're all I've ever wanted."

For long moments, his expression was unreadable while he seemed to consider her words.

Finally, the corners of his lips lifted into a slight curve. "I'll help you take good care of your mamm." He nodded in gratefulness. "Thank goodness, she's going to be okay."

"I always thought she wanted to run my life."

He shook his head. "I knew that wasn't the case."

She lifted a brow for him to go on. "How?"

"After you left, she came to me with her fears." He shook his head and let out a low whistle. "Trini, she was scared to death of losing you. And I believe that her desperation to win your love caused her to be misunderstood."

Trini nodded. "Like I said—I have a lot of relationships to repair. I'll reassure her that I'm there for her just as she's been here for me. That I'll never leave her again. And I'm indebted to Amos too. My mission is to convince my family to keep in touch with him. And because of their reaction to seeing us at the hospital. . ." She smiled with great emotion. "I'm sure I'll be able to bring him back to us."

Jacob cleared his throat and gave the card a long, serious glance. "You've had a lot of time to think about that young boy's proposal." He looked down a moment before carefully placing the small hope chest on the floor and moving so close to her she could see the mischievous light that danced hopefully above his irises. Their arms touched.

His voice came out barely more than a whisper and cracked with emotion. "Trini?"

Her heart felt as if it would burst with happiness. She could sense his nervousness.

The house was so quiet, she could have heard a pin drop. "Open the card."

He breathed in and slowly did as he was told. He read out loud the hand-printed word. "Yes!"

Jacob didn't budge as he stared at her response. Suddenly, he looked at her with such an endearing expression, she wanted to kiss him. But she would wait till they were married. More than ever, she intended to follow the Ordnung.

"Trini Sutter, I will take care of you the rest of my life."

"Jacob, I want that more than anything. I can't believe that I had to leave to find out what I really wanted."

After a few moments of serene silence, Jacob's soft voice broke the quiet. "Looking back, I thank Gott that Mrs. Bontranger overheard your secret to put a rush on the sequence of events that have taken you from me and brought you back."

Trini's jaw dropped. "*She's* the one?"

Jacob offered a slow nod before readjusting her ice pack. "You know what?"

"What?"

"Looking back, my aunt helped to groom me for winning your heart."

"She did?"

He nodded. "She always told me that the most precious things in life are sometimes hard to come by, but in the end, they're worth the wait. I'm glad you did leave. Because of that, I have what I've wanted most out of life."

They both glanced at the card. Then, his eyes conveying his love for Trini as he rested his hand on her new cast, Jacob said, "And you, Trini Sutter, were definitely worth the wait."

Lisa Jones Baker writes Amish inspirational fiction. She grew up near Arthur, Illinois, and became acquainted with the Plain faith at an early age when Amish craftsmen custom-made and installed her family's kitchen cabinets. On weekends, she and her parents frequented the quaint Amish town, often the setting of her stories, where they purchased meat, cheese, and baking spices. Now, decades later, she still loves visiting; the town and the people yet intrigue her, and she appreciates the talent of quilt making almost as much as she loves buggy rides. But there is much more to this perplexing group than meets the eye; they are extremely disciplined, hardworking, and honest—and they don't all think alike. For these reasons, writing about the Amish is her passion.

Lisa was fortunate to have been raised in a loving, Christian home by two wonderful parents: a reading specialist mother who plays the piano, and a retired junior high principal father who is also an avid fox hunter. She has a BA in French education and is a former schoolteacher who loves gardening, cooking, reading, positive thinkers, and every dog she meets. Although she loves being home, loves spending time with her parents, and considers herself a homebody, travel has played a large part in her life. Over three decades of working with the airline industry landed her on five out of seven continents.

ACKNOWLEDGMENTS

First and foremost, credit for *The Quilt Room Secret* belongs to my Creator. He gifted me with tenacity, patience, and great privilege to write books that inspire and encourage a life with Jesus Christ.

Thanks also to:

My loving parents, John and Marcia Baker, who encouraged me from childhood to never give up on my dreams, to do my best, and to accept failure with grace.

To Pastor Ted Max, who helped me to nurture my belief and faith in God and instilled in me that He is all that matters.

To Margaret Schrock and her family, who have been so warm and kind to me. You inspire me with your goodness, and I'm blessed to know you.

I'm indebted to Dr. Jerome Oakey, MD, and his team at McLean County Orthopedics, for teaching me firsthand how to recover from a broken radius and ulna, as fictitious Trini Sutter does in this story.

Dr. Krauss at Johns Hopkins will always have my deep appreciation for saving my life and for treating me for the very illness that fictitious Serenity Miller once experienced.

To Dr. Robert Rosman, M.D., Chicago, Illinois, for simply being the best.

Tons of thanks to authors Patricia Johns and Mindy Steele for their wonderful endorsements, and most especially, to the late New York Times bestselling author Joan W. Anderson, for playing an enormous role in launching my writing career.

Huge gratitude to author Lisa Norato for her critiques and continued support over the past three decades.

Love and thanks to sister extraordinaire Beth Zehr for aiding my computer issues at all times of the day and night.

Thanks to the diligent Amish woman who prefers to remain

anonymous, for reviewing my past nine books to ensure that they conform to the Ordnung in Arthur, Illinois.

I can't forget fabulous agent Tamela Hancock Murray, who worked endlessly with me for years, when publication was no guarantee.

Thanks to everyone at Barbour Publishing. It's a dream come true to write for you.

To my best friend in heaven, Buddy, who was lovingly at my side while I typed this story and many others. You were the epitome of unconditional love, and my heart belongs to you.

THE HEART OF THE AMISH

Full of faith, hope, and romance, this new series
takes you into the Heart of Amish country.

The Flower Quilter
By Mindy Steele

Barbara Schwartz was born into a family of quilters, but she would rather eat dirt than partake in another quilting frolic or sew on another binding. When her parents send her to Indiana to help her grandmother in her quilting shop, she finds herself among a very different community where she is able to help landscaper Melvin Bontrager with a special project that leads to a romantic friendship. Could gardening also lead to an expression of artistry Barbara never knew she possessed?

Paperback / 978-1-63609-642-1

Ruth's Ginger Snap Surprise
By Anne Blackburne

Childless Amish widow Ruth Helmuth never dreamed her bishop would suggest she sell her family farm, let alone propose marriage! Now she must find a way to keep her home, avoid upsetting the bishop, and try to figure out what happens to her heart every time she catches a glimpse of Jonas Hershberger's adorable dimples. A spunky orange kitten and a feisty little girl help Ruth's heart navigate new paths as she learns it's not too late for her dreams to come true.

Paperback / 978-1-63609-689-6

JOIN US ONLINE!

Christian Fiction for Women

Christian Fiction for Women is your online home for the latest in Christian fiction.

Check us out online for:

- Giveaways
- Recipes
- Info about Upcoming Releases
- Book Trailers
- News and More!

Find Christian Fiction for Women at Your Favorite Social Media Site:

 Search "Christian Fiction for Women"

 @fictionforwomen